WITH FRIENDS LIKE THESE

KERI BEEVIS

BLOODHOUND
— BOOKS —

www.bloodhoundbooks.com

Print ISBN 978-1-914614-85-9

ALSO BY KERI BEEVIS

To Shell
Best friend extraordinaire
Thank you for always being you

1

BILLY

It was an unfortunate irony that The Primitives' song, 'Crash', was playing on the radio the night Billy Maguire had his accident. He wouldn't register that until much later, at which time his initial sniggering would turn into hysterical laughter then eventually to sobs, as it finally sunk in that he had actually killed a man.

Wind back to Friday night, though, and Billy was pumped. After a crappy eighteen months both professionally and personally he was excited to catch up with the old gang. It had been far too long since they had all been together.

It was Griffin who had suggested the meet-up. It was his birthday and after celebrating the last two in lockdown he had proposed a break away. Being Griffin he had to go the extra mile, which was how Billy found himself heading up to Scotland on a busy Friday night in April.

Maybe he should have flown like the others, but money was really tight at the moment and the only kind of high he liked didn't involve planes. He would drive he had decided, confident that his old VW Golf was up to the job. A solo road trip. It would be fun.

And it had been... well, maybe for the first hour or two, as he sang along with the radio, excited about meeting up with his friends, but he was also tired, and yes, okay, shoot him, but he might have had a few drinks when he had stopped for a break in the pub of the last village he had passed through.

It was medicinal. It had been a long day and he needed the alcohol to relax. Besides, he was almost there. Just a few quiet country roads to negotiate and he very much doubted there were many coppers out here in the arse end of nowhere. So what if he was swerving a bit? He hadn't seen a car in miles and had the road to himself.

Christ, he couldn't wait to get to the house and crack open another beer.

Billy had googled the place Griffin had booked. An Airbnb off the beaten track. He wasn't a big nature lover, but even he could appreciate the pretty woodland setting and the house itself was huge – typical Griff, equipped with all the mod cons, including a hot tub. For the next few days it would be party central as he caught up with his oldest and dearest pals.

Lockdown had kept them apart for too long and, although he had seen most of them on Zoom, they hadn't been together in person in over two years.

They had a lot of catching up to do.

The urgency to start that catching up had his foot pressing down on the accelerator. Less than fifteen miles to go.

Griffin had already called him twice, wondering where the hell he was. The others were hungry he had told Billy. They wanted to eat.

Billy had been halfway through his fourth pint at the time. Of course, he hadn't told his friend that, instead he had quickly downed his drink and staggered back to the car that he had been forced to leave a couple of streets away, due to the shitty parking situation at the pub.

2

He was staying locally with a friend. That was what he had told the landlord who had voiced concerns when he had ordered his last pint, worried about him getting behind the wheel.

He was fine to drive, and his little white lie wouldn't hurt anyone.

Griffin's last call had come just before eight thirty, the already inky sky growing darker by the minute. It was pitch black now and the car headlights offered the only visibility, as they cut a path ahead on the winding forest road.

Billy rubbed a hand over his eyes. He was really tired, having been driving for most of the day. Thoughts of dropping into bed were now taking precedence over catching up with his friends, that and feeding his growling belly.

A good night's sleep and he would be ready to invest in the weekend, put behind him his recent break-up and have fun with the people he knew would get the smile back on his face.

The road ahead curved sharply, and he stamped his foot on the brake, heart thudding and jolting himself fully awake as the car skidded, threatening to leave the road, before stuttering to a halt.

Fuck me!

He sucked in a breath, ordered himself to relax. It was all good, no harm done.

You've got this, Maguire. Almost there.

The tension eased out of his shoulders, the bravado of alcohol urging his foot to increase speed on the accelerator again. Another bend, but this time not so sharp, plus he was paying attention this time and negotiated it easily.

The local radio station he had tuned into was blasting out tunes from the eighties and the latest one from The Primitives had him turning up the volume. The track was as old as he was, but Billy was a sucker for eighties and nineties Brit pop.

3

He hadn't heard this song in years.

Singing loudly, and badly out of tune (not all drummers can hold a note) he was caught up in the music and didn't even register the man walking down the centre of the road as the headlights illuminated him. In fact he didn't register anything at all until the thud hit his car and for the second time that night he lost control.

Remarkably, despite spinning and swerving the width of the road, the car skidded to a halt facing the wrong way, but without hitting anything else, and Billy might have considered himself lucky if there wasn't a shape up ahead lying motionless on the road, caught up in the glare of the headlights.

Fuck, fuck, fuck!

He tugged at his hair, panic threatening to overwhelm him. *Maybe it's a stray sheep.* Though he already knew that it wasn't.

He tried to tell himself he hadn't seen him, but that was a lie. There had been that split second when he had realised, had caught the look of shock and horror on the man's face.

And now he was dead.

No, no, no. Not dead. Billy was certain he had seen twitching. This was good. He would get him into the car, drive him to the nearest hospital... No, that wouldn't work. He had been drinking.

If the police found out, there would be consequences.

Okay, so fine. He would get him to a hospital. He had to do that at the very least. But maybe he could leave the man anonymously outside the door.

Yes, that was better. He wasn't a complete arsehole. He wasn't going to hit and run.

He eased off his seatbelt with trembling fingers and pushed open the door, the cool breeze hitting him. It was so dark and aside from his car and the man lying on the road, it was deserted.

What the hell was the bloke doing out here? It had been fields and forest for miles and Billy didn't think there were any properties nearby.

The man was apparently out here all alone with no vehicle, which occurred to him was typical horror movie territory. Maybe it was some kind of ruse. Cause an accident and then ambush the innocent motorist when he stops.

He considered closing the door again, leaving the scene, but knew he couldn't do that. If the man was found, if he was somehow traced back to Billy... No, it wasn't worth it.

Besides, he was being ridiculous. This wasn't a film, and he was in the middle of nowhere. There was no getting away from the fact that Billy had knocked him down.

It had been an accident and somehow he had to fix this.

Still, he left the headlights on and the engine running (just in case he had to make a speedy getaway) before approaching the body, aware as he stumbled along the road just how much the beer had gone to his head.

It's probably the shock too.

Billy tried to convince himself of that, but knew he was well over the limit and that the alcohol had slowed his reactions.

The man was on his side, blood trickling from his mouth and his leg bent at an unnatural angle. He wasn't moving at all now.

Was he dead?

No, no, no. Come on, man.

Billy glanced around, as he ran worried fingers through his hair again.

No one knew this had happened. If the guy was dead there was nothing he could do for him. Calling the police and owning up to what had happened wouldn't help him and all it would result in was him going to jail. Two lives would be destroyed.

As the Devil and angel on his shoulders pulled him in

opposing directions, and he contemplated leaving, a rattly groan had him jumping back, and his eyes widened as the man rolled onto his back and started gurgling.

No, no, Jesus.

He dropped to his knees, tried to awkwardly cradle the man's head as he pushed him back onto his side.

'It's going to be okay. I'm going to get you to the hospital.'

His voice was high-pitched, sounded scared, which might be why the dude's eyes suddenly shot open. 'Help me.'

At least that's what Billy thought he had said. The second word was lost as the man's eyes rolled back then his head slumped to the side, and he started choking up blood.

Fuck, fuck, fuck.

Billy thought he was going to retch.

Hold it together, man.

He let go of the man's head, wincing when it cracked against the tarmac, and clumsily got to his feet.

'Wait here. I'll be right back.'

Stupid. He cursed his poor choice of words as he ran back to the car. The guy was hardly going to get up and leave.

Get in the car, turn around, and get the hell out of here.

No. He couldn't do that. The man had looked right at him, and Billy had promised he would help. He couldn't drive off and leave him.

Make a call then. You can do it anonymously. Give them the location, then hang up.

Did he even know where the hell he was? Besides, he had promised that he would come back, that he was going to get the man to the hospital.

He reached the car, his legs shaky, his brain more sober than it had been for the last hour, and collapsed inside, fighting the urge to panic. This was his mess. He had done this. It was up to him to clear it up.

Think, Billy. Come up with a plan.

Move the car closer, get the dude in the car, drive him to the nearest hospital.

He could do this.

His phone started ringing and he nearly fell out of the car.

Griffin.

No. No. He couldn't deal with Griff right now. His old friend was going to have to wait.

He let the call go to voicemail, released a shaky breath, fighting the urge to burst into tears.

It's cool, Billy. You can do this.

Move the car, get the guy inside. Take him to the hospital.

He drew another breath, managed steps one and two, wincing as he dragged the man towards the car (the dude was too heavy to carry) and dumped him on the back seat, before returning to retrieve the rucksack. That was bloody heavy too.

He screwed his face up into a grimace at the crimson puddle on the road, not needing a reminder of how bad this whole situation was.

Now behind the wheel, the rucksack on the seat beside his passenger and Billy went to rub his hands over his face, pausing when he realised his palms were red with blood.

Think. For fuck's sake, think.

Hospitals. He needed to find the nearest one.

He grabbed his phone, saw there were two more missed calls from Griffin and ignored the stab of guilt as he dismissed them, instead clicking onto Google.

From the back seat came another groan and again he fought the urge to panic. How the fuck had he got into this mess?

Because you couldn't stop at one pint, Billy. Quit trying to pass the blame for your own failings.

He located the nearest hospital, glanced at the rear-view mirror to reassure his passenger.

'I'll get you help as quickly as possible.'

The man was no longer moving. His face was pale, his eyes non-responsive.

Fuck.

'Hey, you hang in there. Okay? Hey, are you okay?'

There was nothing. No groaning, no heavy breathing, no choking.

Billy stared into the mirror.

Come on, pal.

He twisted in his seat, looked at the man, waiting for a sign that he was alive. Just a twitch. Anything to show he was still present. His eyes were staring, and Billy watched them waiting for the blink.

As the minutes ticked by and there was still no movement, no reaction at all, that was when he understood that he was really in trouble.

2

AMELIA

She shouldn't have come.

Amelia Abery topped up her wine glass and glanced round the room at the friends she hadn't seen in what felt like forever. She had made a mistake, but it was too late to back out. She was here now and would just have to make the most of it. It was only four days, after all.

Griffin caught her eye, raising his beer bottle in a silent toast. It felt more than that, though, as if it was a shared secret, one that only the two of them knew, which cranked up her unease at this whole charade. Flashing him what she hoped was an easy smile, she took a generous sip of her wine. Perhaps it would help loosen the tightening band of tension across her shoulders. Maybe that was the way forward, drinking her way through the long weekend. Though that was dangerous. Too much alcohol would lower her guard, leading to reckless decisions. God knows, she had made enough of those in the past.

She had expected Griffin's fiancée, Chantelle, to be here, and had been surprised to find it was just the six of them. Well, currently five. Billy had yet to arrive. It was more like a university reunion than a birthday bash. Wind the clock back fourteen years it was easy to remember them all as fun-loving and carefree students.

And that would have been okay, but fourteen years was a long time and there had been a lot of history between then and now. A lot of it hadn't been good.

'Can we please eat now? I'm starving.' That was from Nancy, who was already over a third of the way through a bottle of gin and had been the most vocal complainer about waiting for Billy.

'I'll call him again.' Griffin earned himself a sulky pout as he put his phone to his ear.

'He ignored you the last twenty times you called. I don't know why you think he'll answer this time.' Nancy rolled her eyes dramatically at his back, as Griffin turned away from her to pace. 'This is Billy we're waiting for. He probably hasn't even left London yet.'

Harsh, but perhaps true. Love Billy as she might, Amelia knew he was the least reliable of her old friends.

'It's going to voicemail.' Griffin slipped his phone back in his pocket, his irritation at being ignored evident in the tightening of his jaw.

'I could have told you it would.'

'We'll give him another half an hour,' he told Amelia and Ross, ignoring Nancy's comment.

Ross sighed and glanced at his watch and Griffin looked to Amelia, brows raised, dark eyes waiting for a response to the question they both knew he hadn't asked. Griffin didn't make joint decisions or take notice of other people's opinions. She remembered that well enough.

'Fine with me.' She kept her tone light, really not liking the way he kept looking at her, part challenging, part mocking. Picking up her wine glass, she took it over to the sofa where Nancy was sprawled on her back, bare feet dangling over the end showing off her freshly applied blood-red toenails.

'Budge up.'

Nancy gave a dramatic sigh but shifted to a sitting position to make room.

It was safer here. Although what had happened with Griffin had been years ago and they had since cleared the air, Amelia couldn't help but suspect he wasn't quite as cool with things as he made out.

Probably her imagination and guilty conscience. What she had done to him had been really shitty. It had been the right thing to do, but yeah, it had still been shitty.

At the time she had suspected they wouldn't be able to get past it – how exactly did you stay friends with the man who you had dumped just two weeks before you were supposed to marry him – and for a long while they hadn't spoken. But bumping into each other before the pandemic had given them a chance to clear the air.

Griffin was engaged to Chantelle now, and Amelia was single, so there hadn't been any animosity. He had seemed genuinely pleased to see her and it had felt like a fresh start.

That's why when he had proposed the get-together for his birthday, she had honestly believed it would be like old times.

She should have known better.

It had been awkward from the moment she agreed, from worrying about who else might be there to wondering what she should do about a birthday gift. She was conscious she couldn't turn up empty-handed, but what exactly did you get your ex-fiancé? Perhaps she should have suggested a group gift, but it was too late for that.

Nancy had gone for a personalised gift. She made papier-mâché sculptures as a sideline, mostly of people's pets, though in the last couple of years she had branched out into people. When Amelia had met her at the airport, she had a large box with her, which Amelia soon found out contained a sculpture of Griffin's head. It was done in a caricature style and was quite simply brilliant, with Griff's roman nose exaggerated and his bottom lip pouty, as it often was. While Nancy had caught him perfectly, Amelia did wonder how he was going to react. Griffin King was the vainest man she knew, and he often lacked a sense of humour. On the one hand, it made her generic bottle of whisky seem a bit lame, but she was also in awe of Nancy's boldness. Her friend must be aware that this could completely backfire.

'You could have picked him up.' Griffin had turned his attention on Ross, clearly needing someone to blame for Billy's absence. Billy was a screw-up, but for whatever reason, Griffin always chose to overlook his failings, and, as had always been the case, Ross was his go-to when apportioning blame.

'He was nearly 200 miles out of my way.'

'It's not that far. He's probably got lost or something. If you had travelled up together he'd be here by now.'

'I didn't know I was going to be driving until late last night.' Ross kept his tone even, but Amelia could hear the tension behind it. He glanced at his watch again, seeming just as annoyed that Billy was late.

He was no longer the smart but shy kid Griffin had taken advantage of all the way through university; but it seemed Griff still knew how to push his buttons.

'It's not Ross's fault that Billy is late,' she pointed out, feeling the need to stick up for him. 'Billy's thirty-three years old. No one should have to babysit him.'

Griffin scowled at her, but said nothing, instead reaching in the fridge for another beer, while Ross shot her a tight smile. One that she wasn't sure how to interpret. Was he grateful that she had sided with him or annoyed that she thought he couldn't fight his own battles? He had always been the one in the gang who had been the most difficult to read. Maybe because he was more of a loner. Amelia and Nancy had been best friends, while Griffin, Billy and Jonah had shared a house together. Ross had always been on the periphery looking in.

He had been booked on the same flight, but unexpected work commitments had held him back (of the six of them, he had been the most successful and had his own software company). Last to arrive, he had got to the house about an hour after the others.

It really was a gorgeous place. Despite her reservations about spending the weekend with Griffin, Amelia couldn't fault the location or the house. Maybe, if he would stop it with the vibes and she could get over her guilty conscience, they might actually have a nice time.

As she contemplated that, Jonah walked into the large open-plan kitchen-living room, yawning and stretching, his movements graceful like a lazy cat, and her guilty conscience cranked up another level.

Was it her imagination or did Ross, spotting her looking, smirk? Her face heated and she glanced at Griffin, hoping he wasn't paying attention.

Was she really that obvious?

For God's sake, stop being paranoid. You're allowed to look at someone when they walk in the room. No one knows anything.

Nancy chose that moment to lean forward and whisper in Amelia's ear. 'Meant to say to you earlier, lockdown worked for Jonah. I mean, really worked. He's always been kind of cute, but he's definitely improved this last couple of years.' She waggled her dark eyebrows suggestively. 'I know I would.'

Her throaty laugh had three sets of eyes looking their way.

It had been Amelia, Nancy and Jonah on the flight together, the others making their way separately, and much as she loved her old roommate, Amelia wished Nancy hadn't been there.

Not that anything was going on between her and Jonah. No, their timing had never been right on that front. It didn't stop him from being the one in her life she could never get past, but he was also her oldest friend, knew her better than anyone, and although they had loosely kept in touch over the last few years, it had only been via WhatsApp and Zoom. They hadn't had any real time together. She sorely missed that, just as she had sorely missed him.

Nancy had monopolised the conversation on the journey up, Amelia learning through her questioning that Jonah's long-term relationship with his girlfriend Nicole had been a casualty of lockdown. For the first time since they had met, both of them were single, but she couldn't focus on that because she knew nothing would ever happen.

Jonah was Griffin's best friend; Amelia, Griffin's ex-fiancée. If Griff ever found out about the kiss... if he ever knew that Jonah had been the reason why Amelia had backed out of marrying him, there would be hell to pay.

She had to keep her distance, had to survive this weekend without Griffin discovering her secret, the one she was convinced was written all over her face. She looked at him now, her ex-fiancé. He was oblivious to everyone else as he tried Billy again. Then her gaze drifted to Jonah, and she found him watching her. Earthy olive-coloured eyes and inky black hair curling around his lean face. Yeah, Nancy was right. Lockdown had worked for him and being around him this weekend was going to be tough.

The sound of tyres crunching against gravel broke the moment.

Billy?

Everyone was glancing towards the front window now, Jonah included, and Amelia reminded herself that she couldn't get sucked into the past, that while she was here her feelings for Jonah, for what had happened before, needed to stay secret.

'At fucking last.' Nancy was getting up from the sofa, heading towards the front door, no doubt to give Billy a piece of her mind. Griffin, Ross and Jonah weren't far behind her. The welcome party to check their basket case of a friend had actually made it. Amelia followed, keen to see Billy, knowing he would slice through the tension in this room and make everything a little more relaxed.

As she joined the others in piling out of the door, Billy almost fell out of the car.

'Where the fuck have you been?' Griffin didn't sound happy, but Billy was ignoring him. At first glance he looked drunk, but then as he staggered towards them Amelia saw the blank look of horror on his pale face. She registered that his T-shirt was stained and was already frowning, wondering what the dubious deep-red mark was, when he lurched forward and threw up all over the doorstep.

'Ugh!' Nancy, the closest, stepped back sharply, more interested in whether there was any vomit on her bare feet than whether Billy was okay.

Griffin was quick to lay into him. 'Nice. I pay a fortune to put you up in this luxury house and the first thing you do is empty your guts all over the place. You're a fucking liability, Maguire.'

'Griffin!'

'Don't start sticking up for him, Amelia. You've been

drinking, haven't you, Billy. I can fucking smell the fumes from here.'

'Is that blood?' That was from Ross, who sounded more curious than concerned.

'Mate, are you okay?'

Billy glanced up, wild-eyed and sweaty-faced, as Jonah pushed through the others.

'I think he's hurt.' Amelia stepped forward to join him. 'Billy, what happened?'

'Let's get him inside. Billy, can you stand?'

When Billy nodded, Jonah helped him to his feet. 'Move,' he snapped at Griffin, Ross and Nancy who stood gawping and blocking the doorway.

They quickly parted, Griffin still scowling, and followed Jonah and Billy through into the main room of the house.

'Sit him down on the sofa,' Amelia told Jonah. 'I'll get him a glass of water.'

As she returned with the glass, the rest of her old friends were all gathered around Billy, and she noticed the stain on his top had transferred onto Jonah's grey T-shirt.

It was definitely blood and the others, Griffin included, were at last showing more concern.

'Are you bleeding?'

'Did you have an accident?'

'Should we call an ambulance?'

Billy's eyes widened at that suggestion. 'No, no ambulance. I'll be okay.'

'You're covered in blood. I think a doctor should look you over,' Nancy pointed out.

Billy shook his head. 'It's not my blood.'

'Then who... or what the hell's blood is it?'

That was a very valid question, but one Billy didn't seem in a rush to answer.

Amelia handed him the glass of water and although he accepted it, he only took a couple of sips before handing it back again.

He looked up and met her eyes, and for a moment she saw a flash of the old Billy. He twisted his lips into something resembling a smile, but there was no humour in it. 'I think I'm going to need something a lot stronger than that.'

3

GRIFFIN

This weekend had been a long time coming and it had taken a lot of organising. Griffin King would be the first to admit he liked to be in control of every situation, and he had spent months working out every little detail for the get-together. Billy showing up with a dead body on the back seat of his car hadn't factored into his plans.

'Is he definitely dead? Maybe he's just unconscious.'

That had been from Amelia, his ex-fiancée and once the light of his life, but bless her, at times she could be gormless as fuck. It had taken every ounce of his willpower not to roll his eyes at her.

'He's dead.'

Griffin was no doctor, but he wasn't stupid either. He knew how to check for a pulse and the squelched-up body on the back seat (perhaps mercifully, because let's face it, Billy had done a number on him with his car and the best surgeons in the world would struggle to repair the damage) no longer had one.

And of course, that was his problem now because Billy hadn't done the right thing and called the police. Instead, he had done the exact opposite of the right thing, bundling the man into the back of his car and delivering him to Griffin's doorstep, just like a cat bringing home a present. Seriously, what had he been thinking? He was supposed to be an adult with responsibilities, yet he had screwed up everything. How in his messed-up head had he possibly thought this was okay?

The answer to that was already obvious. The reason Billy had ignored most of Griffin's calls was because he had been getting pissed in the pub. And that was why he had decided it would be a sensible idea to get back behind the wheel of his car, believing that he wouldn't run into anyone on the remaining leg of the journey. And in his defence, it had been shitty luck that he had.

Griffin had booked the Airbnb wanting a quiet location and privacy, and there weren't any other houses around for miles. This begged the question, who was the man and what the hell was he doing out here in the middle of nowhere?

'We need to call the police.' Jonah already had his phone in his hand and appeared to be making that decision on behalf of all of them.

'Wait. Not yet.'

'Are you serious?'

'We need to think about this.'

'You're kidding me, right?' Jonah's tone was incredulous, his expression bemused as he paced back and forth alongside the car. 'The guy is dead. Billy killed him. Yes it was an accident, but the police have to be informed.'

'Wind back a bit. You just said it yourself. The guy is dead. Billy killed him. But this is Billy, your friend, remember? What do you think is going to happen to him if we turn him over to the police?'

'What is going to happen if we don't call them?' Jonah countered, ignoring the question. 'What's your plan, Griff? What exactly is it you want to do? Are you going to hide the body? That man will have a family who are looking for him. You really want that on your conscience?'

Griffin ground his jaw. As usual, Jonah was the only one to challenge him, which was irritating him more than usual. He looked at Amelia, Nancy and Ross. None of them had said much, while Billy had maintained a distance, waiting by the front door as the others circled his car in disbelief. He had been reluctant to approach the vehicle and having seen the carnage inside, Griffin could understand why.

Nancy appeared disgusted that this was ruining her weekend, while Amelia was pale-faced and wide-eyed, her little brain no doubt ticking over as it tried to process everything. And Ross was unusually quiet. Not that he ever had that much to say for himself, but even so, this was a new level of quiet, even for him.

'I'm not saying we shouldn't call the police,' he said eventually in response to Jonah, 'but I do think we should go back inside first and talk things through.'

'We can't sit on this. The longer we delay calling, the worse the situation gets.'

'Look, just give me a second to think, okay?'

When Jonah huffed in exasperation, Griffin turned back to the others. 'I think we should have a vote to decide how to handle this. We're all in this together now, so we all need to have a say.'

Amelia and Nancy exchanged a look, while Ross stared off into the distance, distracted.

'I agree with Jonah,' Amelia said eventually. 'We have to call the police.'

Griffin bit down on the inside of his cheek. No surprise there. 'Okay, so the way I see it we have two options. We can call the police on our oldest and dearest friend, Billy, knowing he is over the limit and will likely go to jail or we can go inside and think this through.'

'We're not trying to get him in trouble.' Amelia had a pained expression as she glanced over at Billy. 'I just don't see where we have a choice.'

'There is always a choice, Mils.'

She flinched at his use of the pet name he had called her through their relationship and Griffin ignored the uncomfortable kick to his gut.

'Okay, so those in favour of calling the police, raise your hand.'

Jonah's hand shot up, while Amelia wavered. She looked at Billy again who still seemed to be in shock. Griffin wasn't sure how much of this he was even taking in.

'I'm sorry,' she whispered to him before holding up her hand.

Just the two of them, Griffin noted, pleased. Nancy was looking uncomfortable, paying particular attention to her toenails and Ross still appeared preoccupied. Had they even registered the question? He moved on quickly.

'Those in favour of going inside to talk this through?'

He raised his own hand, stared at Nancy and Ross, willing them both to look up. 'Ross?' he snapped when there was no reaction.

The other man turned to blink at him with bug eyes, and Griffin thought he was going to have to repeat himself, but then Ross lifted his hand. He was the most nervous of them all and he was also the one with the most to lose. If word got out that he had been involved with a drink-drive incident where a man had died, it wouldn't reflect well on his company.

From the doorstep, Billy recovered from his shock enough to raise his hand. 'I say we go inside to talk.'

It was the most coherent he had been, though Griffin noticed, with irritation, that he was still slurring his words. 'Your vote doesn't count,' he pointed out, turning his attention away. 'Nancy?'

His American friend glanced up, shiftily looking between Jonah, Amelia and Billy, before raising her hand.

'Nancy!'

'He's our friend, Amelia.'

'Don't you think I know that? But there's a dead man in his car.'

'It was an accident.'

'Which is why we have to call the police and let them handle this.'

'And we will. Once we have talked this through. You don't want to see Billy in jail, do you?'

Amelia shot another guilty glance at Billy. 'Of course not, but...'

'But the vote has been decided,' Griffin told her decisively, earning himself a scowl from Jonah. 'So why don't we all go back inside, try and sober Billy up, and decide how we're going to handle this.'

'So we're just going to leave him here?'

'Yes, Amelia. The dead man can stay in the car. I paid a lot of money for this place and I'm not having blood trailed through the house.'

Ignoring Griffin's order, Jonah reached for the car door, pulling it open.

'Hey, I said he's staying out here.'

Jonah glanced up at Griffin, green eyes heated. 'Relax. I'm just getting his bag. It probably has his ID. We should at least know who the poor bloke is.'

He had a point and Griffin nodded, though still waited after ushering the others back inside. To his annoyance Amelia hung about too. He had just about had enough of her tonight.

'Whatever he is carting about in here is heavy,' Jonah commented, hoisting the rucksack over his shoulder.

'Maybe he was homeless. Could be his belongings.'

Wishful thinking, but Griffin could hope. If the guy was a vagrant it would be easier to make the problem go away. Of course, he didn't tell Jonah or Amelia that, heading back into the house after making sure they were following him. It wasn't that he had anything against the dead guy, but he was gone, and it would be crazy to ruin more lives than was necessary.

Nancy, Ross and Billy were waiting for them inside and Griffin noted that Billy had helped himself to a beer, which wasn't particularly helpful if they did end up having to call the police.

Ross's eyes darted to the rucksack Jonah dumped on the rug in front of the sofa. 'Where did you get that?'

'It belonged to the guy Billy hit.'

'Do you have to keep reminding me I hit someone,' Billy protested, the fresh beer seeming to dilute his shock. 'I already feel bad enough.'

'Probably not as bad as the dead guy though,' Jonah muttered sarcastically as he sat down beside the pack and unbuckled the flap.

'Wait, should you be doing that?'

Jonah didn't bother to glance up at Ross. 'Do what?' he asked impatiently.

'As you said, the guy is dead. I'm not sure I'm comfortable with rooting through a dead man's possessions.'

'Yet you were comfortable enough to not call the police.'

When Ross didn't respond, Jonah did look up. 'We need to know who he is.'

Did they? Griffin wasn't so sure about that. At the moment the man was a bloody broken mess, and it was easier to dehumanise him. He didn't particularly want to see photos or learn his name. It was too late for that and if they were going to help Billy, it was better to remain as detached as possible. Still, he stayed silent, as did Ross, as Jonah pushed back the flap and glanced inside the bag, letting out a low whistle.

'What is it?' Nancy asked, suddenly showing an interest.

Jonah upended the rucksack, letting the contents spill out. Thick wads of fifty-pound notes fell to the floor shocking them all into silence.

'What the fuck?' Griffin was the first to find his voice. Of all the things he had expected, this wasn't on the list. There had to be at least fifty grand here, if not more.

'Wait. There's something else,' Jonah told them, tapping a side compartment. He unzipped it, reaching inside, pulling out first a creepy white mask. Griffin recognised it. Michael Myers of the *Halloween* movies. Then something else. A large knife with a sharp vicious blade.

The mask was fancy dress, and it was comforting to pretend the knife was too, but Griffin didn't need Jonah to tell him it was real. He looked at the blade, the mask and all of the cash, then over at Billy. 'Who the fuck did you hit?'

4

JONAH

'Where did you say you were when you hit him?'

Griffin had been firing questions at Billy, who was struggling to answer every single one of them. 'I don't know. All of the roads look the same around here. It was a country lane, lots of bends, and there were trees on either side.' Billy's voice was becoming whiny, and Jonah could tell he was bored of the situation now, just wanting Griffin to fix things and make it go away.

'So that could be pretty much any of the roads around here then,' Ross muttered under his breath. He had gone from being shocked to annoyed and Jonah suspected he was wishing he had never come on the trip. He knew the man prided himself on his professional reputation, which was why it had been a surprise when Ross voted to discuss things further before they called the police.

Billy had done a reckless thing. No, scrub that, Billy had royally fucked up. But would the damage to Ross's company really be that severe? Yes, he and Billy were friends, but Ross hadn't been behind the wheel. He hadn't been the one drink driving. No, this, what they were doing now, this was so much worse.

The contents of the rucksack had changed things slightly. Jonah couldn't see any way the man who owned it had been up to any good. The mask alone might have been a joke, but the knife was real and who the hell carried that amount of cash around with them?

If anything, it gave another reason why they should be calling the police. Had the bloke just robbed a place? Though if so, where? They were in the middle of nowhere.

Jonah had gone through the rest of the pockets in the rucksack, checking them all thoroughly, hoping to find something, anything, to tell him who the man was. There wasn't a wallet though, or even a phone.

'How many miles away were you?' Griffin was now pressing.

'I don't know.' Billy took a large swig of his beer.

'Will you put the fucking can down please and focus?'

'Calm down, Griff. I'm doing the best I can here. I don't remember.' Billy went to take another drink and Griffin snatched the beer away from him, went over to the sink and emptied the can.

'Hey, I hadn't finished with that!'

'I think we need to sober you up.' Griffin glanced at Amelia then appeared to think better of it, turning his attention to Nancy. 'Can you make Billy a coffee?'

Nancy rolled her eyes, not at his blatant sexist assumption that women were there to do his chores, but out of laziness. She had never been one for exerting herself. To Jonah's surprise though, she got to her feet, skulking over to the kettle without complaint.

'Who do you think he was?'

Jonah glanced at Amelia, who had moved to sit on the other

side of the rucksack, her voice quiet enough that the question was directed at him alone. She was close enough that he could smell her familiar vanilla scent, and when he looked at her, her amber eyes were questioning.

They hadn't seen each other in four years, other than on the group Zoom thing that Nancy had set up during lockdown. The last time had been Griffin's birthday, just before he and Amelia were supposed to marry.

He had done something foolish that night, had been shocked by the repercussions when Amelia had called off the wedding, but though he felt guilty, he couldn't bring himself to regret what had happened. The one action, though, had made everything feel sordid. Amelia was one of his oldest friends, and now, even sitting near her made him feel guilty.

They hadn't had any opportunity to talk at the airport or on the plane ride up, thanks to Nancy, and now they were here under the watchful eye of Griffin and the others.

It was good to see his old friends, but Jonah wished he could make them disappear for just a few minutes, wanting that precious time to talk to Amelia. To find out how she really was and how things stood between them.

'I honestly don't know,' he admitted. 'But whoever he was, it looks like he was up to no good.'

Ross was staring at the contents of the rucksack and Jonah noticed how stressed out he really was. He was the smartest of the six, but had always had a nervous disposition, and his face was pale, his fingers fidgeting. He had quit smoking during lockdown and looked like he was regretting it.

'You okay, mate?' For a moment Jonah didn't think he had heard the question, but then Ross blinked, his focus shifting.

'Do I look okay?' he snapped. 'This whole mess could destroy my company.' He shook his head, as though still trying

27

to register what had happened. 'Billy has really screwed up this time.'

Jonah didn't disagree with him there, but still. 'Which is why we should have called the police straight away,' he pointed out. 'Billy messed up, not us. At least we didn't until we made the decision to come inside.' He added the last words sarcastically, wanting to drive home the point that Ross had made a stupid choice.

Ross stared at him for a moment but didn't bite, his lips drawn in a tight line. As Nancy brought a mug of coffee over for Billy he turned his attention to her. 'Can I bum a cigarette, Nance?' Although he had asked the question quietly, the others were close enough to overhear.

'No, don't give in now,' Amelia urged. 'You've been doing so well.'

Ross shot her a dismissive look before turning his attention back to Nancy.

'You sure you want one?'

'I'm sure,' he told her stiffly.

'Okay.' Nancy shrugged at Amelia and Jonah. 'If you're going out for a smoke, I'll join you. I just want to go upstairs and get my boots first. I'm not going out there again with bare feet. It's freezing.'

'What's it been, six, seven months nicotine free?' Jonah asked as she left the room. When Ross simply looked at him, not answering the question, he continued. 'Don't quit now. You know you'll regret it if you do.'

Ross's gaze flicked from Jonah to Amelia and back again. 'Well, I guess we all have our regrets, don't we? Just as we all have our vices.' He smirked at what appeared to be his own private little joke and got to his feet.

'What was that supposed to mean?' Amelia whispered as he left the room.

Jonah shrugged. 'No idea.'

It had sounded like a dig, one at him and Amelia. There was no way Ross knew what had happened though. It was ridiculous to even consider he might.

Amelia's gaze lingered on Jonah, her eyes filled with silent questions, and he forced himself to break away, aware it was just four of them in the room now, and that Griffin and Billy had both fallen quiet. He didn't think either of them had been paying attention to Ross's comment. Billy was too busy feeling sorry for himself, while Griffin's mind appeared elsewhere.

'We need to call the police,' he reminded them, bringing their predicament back to the forefront. Ironically it felt like a safer topic. 'Every minute we don't we're just implicating ourselves further.'

'You know if we do call them, Billy is going to be in a whole heap of trouble.'

Billy nodded vigorously in agreement with Griffin. Jonah noticed he had barely touched his coffee. 'And it was an accident,' he pointed out. 'It's not as if I meant to hit him.'

'It might have been an accident, but you had still been drinking.'

'I only had a few pints.'

'Define a few,' Jonah pushed.

'Maybe three... ish.'

'So four or five then.' Griffin sounded exasperated. 'For fuck's sake, Billy. What the hell were you thinking?'

'I was excited about the weekend! I was looking forward to seeing you guys and I guess I just wanted to switch off and relax. I've had such a shitty year, man.'

'Why did you put his body in the car?' Amelia asked. 'You must have been thinking about going to the police. If not you'd have left him on the road.'

'He wasn't dead. At least, not at first. I didn't want to get into trouble, but I also didn't want to leave him there. I was going to drop him off outside the hospital.'

As they all absorbed that, Billy's eyes widened as if a brilliant thought had just struck him. 'See, that proves it. That proves it's an accident and I'm not a bad person. I was going to take him to the hospital.'

Jonah smiled sardonically. 'It doesn't change the fact you were drink-driving, mate.'

'So what are we going to do?' Amelia questioned, looking between Jonah and Griffin and avoiding eye contact with Billy. 'We came inside and talked a bit, but so far no one has come up with a realistic solution, so can we please call the police?'

'I want to know why he was carrying a rucksack full of cash and had a knife and a mask with him,' Griffin said instead of answering her question.

'I'm sure the police will soon find out.'

'But who is he and what was he up to? If he was up to no good, Billy might have done everyone a favour.'

'Are you serious?'

'Yes, Amelia. I'm serious. No one carries around this amount of cash just for fun, and the knife and mask suggest he was bad news. Maybe he had just robbed somewhere.'

'You guys could keep the money. Split it between you,' Billy suggested, a note of hope in his voice.

Jonah gave a harsh laugh. 'Don't be ridiculous.'

'Why not? I don't mean I'll take any. There has to be about fifty grand here. That's ten K each if you share it between the five of you. Don't tell me you couldn't use that money, Jonah. You too, Amelia. And I know you could, Griff.'

Griffin definitely could. His dad kept threatening to stop with the handouts and his job didn't pay well enough to fund the lifestyle he liked to lead. Jonah could see his eyes were flashing with interest at the suggestion and he was getting the distinct impression Griffin was seriously considering the idea.

'I don't want the money. I want to call the police.'

'Oh don't be such a martyr, Mils.'

'I'm not being a martyr. I'm just not happy being forced to break the law, because that's what we are doing. You know that, right?'

A flash of anger passed between Amelia and Griffin. Despite Griffin insisting he was no longer angry with Amelia for calling off the wedding, Jonah wasn't so sure he believed him. Although he agreed with Amelia, he didn't want to antagonise his best friend any further, so he changed the subject.

'I guess it would help if we knew who he was.'

'Exactly!' Griffin agreed.

'I don't see how that's relevant,' Amelia argued. 'The police will be able to identify him. Besides, if there's no ID in the bag, I don't see how you can find out.'

'He might have a phone or something in his pocket.'

'You're right.' Griffin was getting to his feet. 'We should go and check.'

'But regardless of whether he does or not, we still call the police after we've checked,' Jonah warned, also getting up. 'Agreed?'

'Of course.' Griffin looked at Billy. 'Stay here and drink that coffee. We need to sober you up.' He glanced fleetingly at Amelia. 'And you keep an eye on him,' he ordered, his tone disdainful.

Yeah, he was still holding a grudge and luckily he had already turned away, so didn't see her salute at his back.

That had always been Griffin's problem, Jonah mused, as he followed his friend out into the hallway. For all of his bluster and controlling nature, he had a fragile ego. He had never been able to handle being dumped, but to have it happen when he

31

had a wedding planned, and for the dumping to have been so public, well, that had been the ultimate insult.

Griffin had told him that he and Amelia were back on good terms, but Jonah had still been surprised when he had invited her along for his birthday weekend. And even more surprised that she had agreed to come.

They found Ross and Nancy just outside the front door, Nancy now huddled in a fur-lined coat while Ross shivered in just his shirt. The temperature had dropped considerably since they had arrived, and even further since they had gone outside to meet Billy, and Jonah's skin was goose-bumping under his T-shirt.

'What are you two doing out here?' Nancy eyed them curiously as she tapped ash from her cigarette, grinding it into the ground with her sleek black-heeled boot. Neither Griffin nor Jonah were smokers.

'We're going to see if our friend in the car has any ID or a phone on him.'

'Want some help?' It was the first constructive offer they'd had from Ross.

'We've got it,' Griffin told him. 'You finish puffing on your cancer sticks.'

Jonah pulled open the back door of the car, wrinkling his nose in disgust at the metallic odour. When he had earlier checked for a pulse he had been in shock and hadn't really registered much, but now, with the interior light on, he took a good look at the guy.

Billy had definitely done a number on him, and the only distinguishable features were his bald head, muscly build, and a stud in his left ear. It was impossible to gauge his age or much else about him, thanks to the crusted blood caking his broken face.

Griffin looked at him across the seat through the opposite

WITH FRIENDS LIKE THESE

open door. 'Handsome chap, huh?' he commented, his tone dry.

He shouldn't have laughed. Jonah knew that, but he couldn't help it. It was the craziness of the situation they were in, and he meant no disrespect to the dead man on the back seat of Billy's car.

Though he changed his tune on that shortly after they found the man's wallet. It was in his back pocket and Griffin had to pull the guy forward, complaining bitterly, first about the stench then about having 'a dead person' cradled against his chest, while Jonah searched the back pockets of his jeans.

'You'd better find something,' he had grumbled, releasing the man the moment Jonah held up the black leather wallet with the initials DAM embossed on it in tacky gold lettering, seeming more concerned with the bloodstain on his shirt than the fact he had let the dead guy almost fall out of the car.

Back inside, after Griffin had changed his shirt, they had gone through the wallet, learning Billy's victim was one Douglas Alasdair McCool then a Google search had revealed him to be a known criminal who had been in and out of jail for much of his adult life for robbery, criminal damage, breaking and entering, grievous bodily harm and most worrying, manslaughter.

'He sounds like he was a delightful individual,' Griffin said, his focus shifting between Jonah and Amelia. 'Seems like Billy did everyone a favour.'

Amelia scowled, though said nothing, and Jonah wasn't sure if she was annoyed with Griffin's attitude or the fact he had a fair point.

While he didn't agree with what Billy had done, Griffin was right, the world was perhaps better off without Douglas McCool (or Dougie as it seemed he was more commonly known) in it. He had burgled and terrorised families, had once bitten a man's ear off, and it was hard to believe he had any redeeming qualities.

It also seemed that he came from a family of hardened criminals. If they handed Billy into the police, would Dougie's family ever forgive him?

Jonah found himself swaying. He wanted to do the right thing, but equally, he couldn't see anything positive coming from calling the police. But what was the alternative?

'I suggest we bury his body and split the cash,' Griffin proposed. He had been skating around the issue for much of the night, but now he was laying his cards down, and Jonah was running out of objections.

When Griffin proposed another vote, he raised his hand with the others, trying to ignore Amelia, who he knew was looking at him in horror.

'Really, Jonah?'

The weight of her stare eventually had him trying to justify himself. He was all for trying to do the right thing and if Dougie McCool had been an innocent pedestrian he would have insisted they call the police. The man wasn't though, and the way Jonah saw it, they might actually be doing the public a favour.

As he went to the fridge for a beer, aware they still had to deal with the problem of what to do with Dougie's body, but wanting a drink, needing that brief respite first, he considered again what Dougie might have been doing out in the middle of the countryside.

Griffin had insisted that there were no properties for miles and Dougie's driver's licence showed that he lived in Greenock, which was three hours away.

That was the other thing. He had a driver's licence, but Billy had said there had been no car, that Dougie had been walking down the country lane alone.

Just what exactly had he been up to?

5

NANCY

Nancy Perez had been surrounded by money for much of her adult life, but unfortunately none of it was hers.

Something of a problem considering she was a girl with expensive tastes.

Her parents did their best. Her father had always worked hard, though he wasn't well paid, and her mother had taken on several cleaning jobs over the years to supplement his income. They had moved to the UK when Nancy was in high school and had saved to put her through university, had even found money to help her with the deposit for a flat, and Nancy's marketing job paid a modest salary, but her bills were high, and she had accumulated a lot of debt on credit cards and loans. The thought of the unopened demands for overdue bills made her feel sick.

Clothes were her biggest downfall. (Well, a girl has got to look nice, right?) She had a wardrobe filled with expensive dresses, designer shoes and gorgeous handbags that were to die for, but the flipside was she had often struggled to pay her mortgage and had to skimp on her food shopping.

Meeting Amelia Abery and her rich friends at university

had been both a blessing and a challenge. Nancy liked hanging out with wealthy people, pretending that she had no financial worries, and Amelia could be very generous, allowing her to borrow her things, and paying for both of them when she knew Nancy was struggling.

But of course Nancy never let on quite how badly she struggled. It was a pride thing, and she couldn't bear the thought of Amelia with her pretty heart-shaped face, her perfect shampoo-commercial copper hair, and her bottomless purse, finding out the truth.

Over the years things had evened out. Amelia's accountant dad had been caught stealing from his clients and Amelia's funds had been abruptly cut off. Like Nancy, she now had to be careful with money.

Still Nancy often felt that Amelia had been given a free pass through life. Despite her family's downturn in fortune, she never seemed to struggle, with everything falling in her lap.

Even Griffin, who was normally so judgemental of people, had stood by her after her father was arrested. Nancy often wondered how much he regretted that after Amelia had jilted him.

There was definitely tension between them, and she was surprised Griffin had wanted his ex-girlfriend here to help celebrate his birthday instead of his fiancée. Were things rocky with Chantelle? It all seemed very odd.

Of course, the whole Billy and the dead guy thing hadn't helped. They were all on edge, but Nancy's eyes had widened when Jonah opened the rucksack, tipping the wads of notes onto the floor. And while the others had questioned who the hell the man was, all she could think of was how the money could pay off all her debts and she would have enough left over to give her a fresh start.

She desperately wanted to start up her own business. Her

sculptures were good enough. Unfortunately she simply couldn't finance it and the bank refused to help her with a loan until she was back on her feet. She had come here hoping that her birthday sculpture of Griffin would convince her friends of her talent and that maybe Ross or Griffin himself might offer a private loan. She didn't want to beg though. If she could get her hands on at least some of the money, her problems would be solved.

That thought had arisen as she had gone upstairs to get her boots and her mind worked overtime trying to figure out a way. If they called the police they would seize the lot, but was it possible she could take a couple of the wads without the others seeing? The police weren't going to know how much had been there and she very much doubted that anyone had counted it.

Hearing the front door close below, she moved to look out of the window and saw Ross had gone outside to wait for her. He stood shivering in his thin shirt, reminding her again how cold it was. She reached for her coat, slipping it on, and as she buttoned up the front she studied Billy's car.

Where had the money come from? Had the man stolen it?

No one would keep that kind of cash at home, and certainly not separated into wads. Perhaps he had robbed a bank. That meant Nancy wouldn't have to feel guilty if she took some of the money. Banks were rich anyway.

As she looked out of the window again, another idea came to her. There was a way to earn money that wouldn't involve any kind of theft. Musing it over, she zipped up her boots and went downstairs to join Ross.

Later, when Griffin had proposed keeping the money, relief and disappointment swirled in her gut.

If they agreed to do as he proposed then she didn't need to find a way to sneak any of it behind their backs. Selfishly though, she didn't want to split it.

Her share would definitely help clear her debts, but she needed more if she was going to have a completely fresh start. Besides, the others didn't need it as badly as she did. Okay, Amelia could probably use it, though she had learnt to cut her cloth and was strict with her budget these days; and Jonah had turned his back on his high-flying law career, so no longer commanded a high salary. But that had been his choice. No one had forced him to start up his own landscaping business.

Griffin had a wealthy family though and Ross had more money than he knew what to do with. The idea of them taking a share seemed greedy and unfair. They simply didn't need it.

Of course she couldn't say that though, not without appearing ungrateful, so she sipped at her gin, chipping in when necessary, but mostly listening as Griffin commanded the conversation in that way he often did.

Amelia looked irritated, her pretty face screwed up in a frown as Griffin talked, while Billy had helped himself to another beer and was well on the way to being pissed. Billy being Billy was bored of this now. Only Jonah and Ross were taking an active interest in the discussion about what they should do with the dead dude's body.

'We should bury him,' Jonah proposed.

Griffin nodded his agreement. 'That's what I was thinking. But it can't be here.'

'We can take him out in the woods where no one is likely to find him.'

'No, it's too messy,' Ross argued. 'Messy and time consuming. Someone will discover the fresh earth and if the body is found they can link it back to us.'

'Acid then. We can destroy the body.'

'Are you crazy?'

Griffin scowled at Amelia. 'Do you have anything helpful to contribute to this conversation? If not, then please shut up.'

'You can't use acid. You sound like a serial killer.'

'In case you hadn't noticed, Mils, he's already fucking dead.'

'She's right though,' Ross interjected. 'For starters we don't have any acid. And if we go buy some it will be suspicious as fuck.'

'A fire then.'

'Wouldn't be hot enough to get rid of the body,' Jonah said, pouring cold water on that idea.

'Okay, so no burial, no acid, no fire. You're all telling me what we can't do. Could one of you please come up with another idea.'

Griffin was getting annoyed, pacing the room now, and Nancy watched him, indulging in the secret little crush she'd had on him for years. She wasn't his type, she knew that, which is why she had never let on about how she felt. She was too loud, too brash, and physically wrong for him. Plus of course he was engaged to Chantelle. Another Amelia clone with her pretty face and her vacant expression. He was completely off the table, but it didn't stop her wanting him.

She hadn't lied earlier when she had said to Amelia that Jonah had improved with age. Out of a suit, the manual labour had toned and hardened his lean physique, and true, she wouldn't kick him out of bed. But Griffin was still the one who caught her attention. He was bigger, muscular, and had an altogether more dominating presence. To Nancy he was the perfect specimen of an alpha male.

'There's a lake near here, right?'

Griffin paused and looked at her, dark eyes interested. 'There's a loch close by. What are you thinking?'

'Is it deep?'

'I don't know. I imagine so.'

'Do we have access to a boat?'

He nodded. 'We get use of a boat with the house, yes.'

Nancy could see his lips curving, knew he understood what she was suggesting, and a flush of satisfaction warmed her inside. He was annoyed with the others for being unhelpful and obstructive, but she had pleased him. Still, she was careful to keep her tone neutral, dismissive even, when she spoke. It was easier that way.

'Well there you go then. It's obvious, isn't it? That's where you take him. Weigh the body down and let the fish take care of the rest.'

She watched as everyone considered her suggestion, her confidence soaring when her idea wasn't completely dismissed. Maybe it was because no one had anything else to offer or because they didn't want to face Griffin's wrath, but there were no objections.

'So that's our plan then,' Griffin confirmed after they had discussed things further and voted once again. He looked around the group, seeming pleased that they were making progress. Only Amelia was unhappy, a sulky expression on her face. She was now the only one who still wanted to call the police and she looked fed up with being overruled.

Nancy intended to keep a close eye on her, conscious that her former roommate was now the one weak link in their chain. Griffin was being careful to ensure they were voting on every decision and Nancy agreed with him that it was the fairest way. Amelia may not like the way the vote was going, but she was going to have to accept it. They couldn't afford for her to go blabbing about what had happened after they had left here. They were all guilty now and too much was riding on Amelia staying silent.

'Are we doing this tonight?' Jonah asked.

Ross nodded. 'We need to.'

'Well it's pitch black out there. Do we have torches?'

Jonah had a point. Griffin had already told them it was a ten-minute walk to the loch. Maybe they would be better waiting until daylight. Nancy suggested that, and was shocked when Ross turned on her. 'Are you stupid? We can't take a body out in the middle of the loch during the day. What if someone sees us?'

Nancy had always been the most accepting of Ross. The others; Amelia, Griffin, Jonah and Billy; they belonged to the rich and pretty set. Ross came from money, but was unattractive and socially awkward, while Nancy could walk the walk and talk the talk but didn't have the cash to back it up. They had been drawn together through their inadequacies in a kind of them-versus-us scenario that the others were oblivious to.

In all the years she had known him, Ross had never spoken down to her like this, and her hackles rose, furious that he should dare. 'So you're proposing that we traipse through a dark wood to an unfamiliar lake and take a rowing boat out to dump the body without being able to see what we're doing? Seriously, Ross? Think this through. We have one shot at getting this right and we can't afford to get caught.'

He scowled at her, face reddening and lips pursed, but didn't respond.

'She has a point,' Jonah agreed.

Griffin nodded slowly, considering. 'Yes, she does,' he said eventually. 'We can't leave the body in Billy's car though. We'll need to move it.'

'To where? Every place we move him to becomes a crime scene.'

'Are there any spare sheets?' Nancy asked. 'We need something to wrap him up in. We can then leave him in the garage overnight and go down to the loch first thing in the morning.'

Griffin was studying her again, looked pleased with her thinking. Although the six of them had been friends for years, he had never seemed to take that much notice of her on an individual basis. She didn't ever hang out with him one-on-one away from the group, not like the others, and could barely think of a time when they had been alone together. He was seeing her now though and she liked how it made her feel.

'You have it all figured out, don't you?' He sounded impressed.

Nancy rolled her eyes dramatically. 'Well, someone has got to take charge.'

'Sheets will leak. Plastic would be better,' Jonah pointed out.

'You're right,' Griffin agreed. 'I think I saw some in the garage. There was some rope in there too. We can secure the body, leave it in the garage overnight, then take it down to the loch in the morning. As long as we go first thing then no one should see us.'

'I really think we should do it tonight,' Ross grumbled. 'The longer we have the body, the more we're incriminating ourselves.'

Griffin shook his head. 'If we do it tonight, we might fuck up. We go first thing.' He glanced over at Amelia, who had remained quiet through the whole discussion. 'Are you coming with us or are you going to stay here?'

She stared at him as she drained her wine glass, her amber eyes heated. 'I don't want any part of this,' she told him, getting to her feet and carrying the glass over to the sink. 'In fact, I wish I had never come. Who the hell are you people?'

'He's scum, Mils. The world will be a better place if he just disappears.'

'That's not your decision to make.' She glanced around the group, giving each of them a challenging look, goading them to justify what they were about to do. Griffin and Nancy were the only two who met her stare. Jonah looked away guiltily, while Ross and Billy refused to make eye contact in the first place.

'I'm going to bed,' she muttered, shaking her head in disgust.

Amelia had always been a do-gooder, which was quite ironic given her parentage. Unfortunately that also made her a liability. Could they trust her to keep their secret?

It was something they were going to have to consider before the weekend was over, because if she told anyone about what had happened, it wouldn't just be Billy who would be in trouble. All of their lives would be ruined.

Nancy decided she would have a word with Griffin about that. She would wait until the deed was done then talk to him away from the others. Before they left here on Monday, they needed to know they had Amelia's silence.

And they would have to get it by any means necessary.

6

ROSS

Waiting until morning was a really bad idea. They needed to be rid of the body now, but Ross didn't seem to be able to get that through to Griffin.

And of course, Griffin's word is always final, he thought bitterly.

It had always been that way, right back to when they had been at university together. Ask the others and they would say it was because he was a natural-born leader but ask Ross privately and he would admit that Griffin King was a bully.

Griffin used people and it had only been because he was using Ross that the pair of them had met and struck up a friendship.

Ross was smart and Griff had needed his brain. Too many late nights, drugs and parties had meant he had fallen behind in his studies. Ross was his golden ticket to catching up again.

It was a win-win situation. Ross would help Griff with his grades and in return, Ross was integrated into the group, invited to the best parties and, despite still being the stooge for most of Griffin's pranks, he was no longer a nobody.

He wasn't fool enough to be under the illusion that it meant anything. He was useful and had that usefulness dried up, Griffin would have dropped him and moved on. Ross learnt quickly that it paid to continue being useful.

Of course, things had shifted in recent years. Ross had built his tech company from scratch and was now far more successful than Griffin. Okay, he didn't have Griff's looks or charisma, or the ability to hold command over a room, but money could buy a lot. It had bought him laser eye surgery and new teeth, and a wardrobe full of designer label suits. It had also proven persuasive when he decided he wanted to settle down and start a family.

As far as the others were concerned, Ross and Maya enjoyed a fairy-tale life together and had been blessed with the perfect family. They didn't know that the marriage was a sham, that Maya had her own bedroom in their extensive country house or that he had agreed to a financial arrangement with her where she would provide him with two children and accompany him on social engagements, in exchange for a lavish lifestyle and a healthy monthly allowance.

They were two strangers living under the same roof and that suited both of them fine. He knew that Maya took lovers and he belonged to a discreet hook-up service that provided company if he was ever in the mood, which to be fair wasn't often these days. The guilt about Tim's death, even though it had happened years ago, was gradually consuming him.

His younger brother had always been the more outgoing of the two and Ross had struggled to fill the void that had been left by his death, the unresolved guilt that he hadn't been there when Tim had taken his last breath still festering away.

He went through the motions of living a comfortable, but vacuous life, but even that was now under threat, thanks to Billy fucking Maguire.

Seriously, what were the chances? The roads around here

were deserted, yet Billy the screw-up had managed to run over the only pedestrian in miles.

There was no way Ross wanted the police involved. He didn't want a whiff of this getting back to any of the shareholders. Tomorrow morning, first thing, he would go with the others, take Dougie McCool's body out to the middle of the loch, weigh him with rocks, and watch him sink, then he would return to the house, pack up his stuff and get the hell out of here.

Griffin still planned to stay for the full weekend (he was tight as hell and liked to get his money's worth) and Nancy, Amelia and Jonah's flight didn't leave until Monday. Of course, they could take Billy's car, but given it was currently bloodbath central, that wasn't going to happen.

They were effectively trapped here but Ross wasn't. He had his car and intended to leave as soon as McCool was in the loch. He would do it discreetly, as he didn't plan on taking any passengers. After what had happened this evening it was better if he put some distance between himself and the rest of the group, at least for a while.

He had never been as close as the rest of them were, had at times felt like the outsider, and he had a sneaking suspicion that if things went wrong and they turned on each other, he would be the first one thrown to the wolves.

That wasn't going to happen.

The only one he felt slightly bad for was Nancy. She was a little kooky and blunt, and lacked morals, and he wasn't sure if he admired or was repelled by the fact she had slept her way through uni, but at least she had always been cool with him, never looking down her nose like Griffin sometimes did or ignoring him as Amelia had mostly done. Nancy had even given him a pity fuck once. A drunken fumbling encounter that could have easily ruined their friendship if she hadn't been off her face on drink and drugs. He sometimes wondered just how much of that night she remembered.

No, when it came down to it, Nancy was the only one he gave a toss about. It wouldn't actually bother him if he didn't see the others again.

He realised that more than ever as they went outside to move the body. It was just four of them. Amelia had gone to bed; and Billy got a free pass because he was pissed as a fart, having moved from beer on to vodka.

Yes, that was how fucked up Griffin's logic and sense of loyalty was. Billy, who had caused this shitshow, got to sit it out while the rest of them cleared up his mess.

Nancy was given the job of spreading out the plastic sheeting that they had found in the garage, while Ross, Jonah and Griffin dragged the body out of the car. Actually scrub that, Ross and Jonah did most of the lifting as Griff moved himself to a supervisory role, barking orders like a drill sergeant.

Despite the cold, Ross was sweating buckets and his back was fucking killing him – the TV shows weren't lying when they talked about dead weight – by the time they dropped the body on the ground.

Ross winced as McCool's head smacked against the concrete and he had to remind himself the man was dead and couldn't feel a thing.

As he tried to catch his breath, rubbing at the bloodstains on his shirt, Griffin snapped at him. 'Don't just stand there, you idiot. We need to get him wrapped up.'

Ross looked up slowly, struggling to keep his expression neutral when he saw Griffin's sneer and wished, not for the first time, that he was bigger, stronger, and could take a swing at the man. Instead he bit into his bottom lip hard enough to taste blood.

Jonah was already on the ground, rolling McCool so Nancy

47

could wrap the plastic and Griffin tossed a coil of rope at Ross, nodding towards the body.

'Here. Use this to keep the plastic in place.'

Ross looked at the rope, thinking about how he would like to wrap it around Griffin's neck. Nodding, he dropped to his knees and helped the others secure the body.

'Hey, Mr Supervisor. Think you could trouble yourself to open the garage door?' Jonah's tone was sarcastic. He hadn't missed that Griffin had left them to do all the work either.

'As you ask so nicely.'

'You really are a lazy fucker, Griff.'

If Ross had said it, Griffin would have bitten his head off, but of course Jonah was the chosen best friend, so he got away with it, Griffin simply laughing off the insult.

'Come on. Let's get him in the garage.'

Jonah and Ross lifted the now mummified body, Griffin having the good grace to get his precious arse out of the way, and Nancy gathered up the unused sheeting. They were heading towards the garage when the purr of a car engine sounded in the distance.

All four of them froze, looking at each other as the noise grew louder and the vehicle neared, and Ross fought to stop himself shaking as a tremor of fear travelled down his spine.

'I thought you said this place was in the middle of nowhere?' he snapped at Griffin, his fear manifesting itself in anger.

'It is. The nearest neighbour is over three miles away.'

'Then who the fuck is it?'

Griffin stared into the darkness of the driveway, seeming as shocked as Ross. 'I don't know,' he finally answered, his tone uncharacteristically soft.

'Whoever it is, they're coming here,' Jonah urged. 'We need to get this body in the garage now.'

When Ross's legs refused to work, Nancy pushed him out of the way, picking up the slack of Dougie McCool's body. Ross watched as they dragged him into the garage, his heart thumping.

The noise from Jonah backing into something – it sounded like a spade or similar – sending it crashing to the floor, seemed to pull Griffin out of his shock. He rushed forward, hissing at Jonah and Nancy to be quiet.

As the three of them exchanged angry words, Ross saw headlights illuminating the driveway. 'Griffin.'

He was still arguing with Jonah.

'GRIFFIN!'

'What?' Griffin stepped out of the garage, realised how close the car was and that it was almost to the house. 'Get inside,' he demanded, shoving Ross towards the front door, before going back to the garage. As Ross's legs finally started working, he heard Griffin talking in angry whispers to Jonah and Nancy before pulling the garage door down and shutting them inside.

Then he was hurrying after Ross, pushing him through the front door and closing it behind them.

'You panicked and froze out there. You can't afford to fucking freeze,' Griff stormed as the headlights were full on now, lighting up the front of the house as the car pulled to a halt. He grabbed Ross by the arm, dragging him through the central living room. 'Stay here!'

Ross had no problem doing that, as Griffin skulked back into the hallway. He didn't miss the man sucking in his breath though, and realised he was preparing himself. Griffin, who was usually unflappable in most situations was having a bout of nerves.

There was the slam of a car door then the crunch of gravel, and moments later someone knocked on the door.

Who the hell was it, this late at night?

Griffin took a moment before stepping forward and throwing the door wide to greet the newcomer, and Ross peered around the corner of the hallway, a fresh wave of anxiety hitting him when he recognised the police uniform.

If Griffin was freaked though, he wasn't showing it and had somehow got himself under control. 'Good evening, officer? Can I help you?'

'Sorry to trouble you, Mr...?'

'King. Is there a problem?'

'No, Mr King. No problem, and like I say, I'm sorry to disturb you. I'm PC Murray and I'm on the trail of this chap.' Ross couldn't see the photo that was being held up. 'I don't suppose you've seen him, have you? He's been missing since earlier this evening.'

Seriously? Billy had hit Dougie McCool in the middle of nowhere; how could he already be missing? Perspiration was beading on Ross's forehead and pooling under his arms. He wanted to see the photo, but his shirt was covered in bloodstains, so he didn't dare make his presence known.

'No, I'm sorry, I haven't seen him.'

'Little bugger. This is the second time this month. We need to find him before he gets himself into any trouble. Got into Enid Stewart's house and stole a whole cooked chicken last time.'

'Well I'm sorry I can't help.' Griffin started to close the door.

'Wait. Can I ask you to keep an eye out for him for me? Answers to the name of Ralph. Give me a call if you see him?'

Ralph? Not Dougie then. Ross's heartbeat slowed slightly.

'Sure thing. I'm now off to bed, but if I see him tomorrow I'll let you know.'

'I'd appreciate that, though hoping we will find him tonight.'

'Does he live nearby then? Mrs Campbell said there were no close neighbours.'

'Aye, he lives a few miles back towards the village.' Ross waited as the officer gave Griffin his details.

From the garage to the side of the house came a clatter. It sounded like something had crashed to the floor.

Fuck! Jonah and Nancy.

PC Murray's eyes shot to the adjoining wall. 'Sounds like we have company. Ralph? Is that you?'

Ross saw him step back, ready to go check it out.

'No!' Griffin's tone was sharp enough to stop Officer Murray in his tracks. 'It's not Ralph.'

'It's not? Are you sure?'

'I'm sure.'

'But–'

'Look, this is a little embarrassing.' Griffin leaned in, conspiratorially and dropped his voice to not much more than a loud whisper. 'A couple of my friends went in the garage a short while ago. I think they've liked each other for a while.'

'Are they...?' The PC took a moment to process what he meant. 'Oh, I see.'

Even from his hidden position, Ross could see his cheeks colour. Griffin had definitely wrong-footed him.

'So, you're holidaying up here, are you, Mr King?' he asked, swiftly changing the subject.

'Just up for a long weekend.'

'Well I hope you enjoy yourselves. Weather is supposed to dry tomorrow. You should try and get out on the loch.'

'We actually thought we might do that.'

Ross could hear the smile in Griffin's words. The bastard was actually enjoying this.

'You have my number, so let me know if you see Ralph or if you need anything.'

'I will do. Thank you, officer.'

Hearing the door close, Ross stepped out into the hall. 'There's a chicken-stealing neighbour called Ralph?' he hissed.

Griffin turned, rolling his eyes. 'Relax. Ralph is about two foot tall and covered in black-and-white fur.'

'What?'

'He's a dog, Ross.'

'He's hunting down a dog? Seriously?'

'Not many people up in this neck of the woods, so I guess there's a low crime rate.'

'We're the exception to the rule then.'

Griffin's lips twisted. 'Apparently so.'

As soon as PC Murray's car had disappeared from sight, Griffin stepped back outside, Ross on his heels, and went round to the garage, opening the overhead door.

McCool was a mummified swathe of plastic being propped up by Jonah, while Nancy stood just behind him, arms folded, and a pissed-off look on her face.

'What the hell was all that noise? I warned you both to stay quiet.'

'There was a fucking rat.' That was from Nancy.

'It was not a rat!'

'I felt it brush up against my leg,' she snarled at Jonah. 'I know what a rat feels like.'

'Really? You've touched a lot of them then, have you? Anyway, you're wearing boots. How did you feel it?'

'Enough!' Griffin's bellow had them both looking back at him. 'Honestly, all you had to do was wait in here and be quiet.'

'And prop up a dead body,' Jonah grumbled sarcastically.

'In the dark, with rats,' Nancy added.

'There was no bloody rat.'

'Stop! Please!'

Griffin looked on the verge of losing his shit and Ross stepped back into the shadows, aware that even though it was Jonah and Nancy who were antagonising him, things could quickly twist to make him the victim of Griffin's wrath. He had been caught up in this scenario too many times before.

'Who was at the door?' Jonah asked.

'The police.'

'What? You're joking, right?'

'What the hell did they want?' Nancy was wide-eyed, clearly believing Griffin more than Jonah did.

'Lost dog.'

'Seriously?'

'We're going to have to be careful moving the body tomorrow. If they haven't found him they will still be out looking.'

Griffin had a good point and it only added to this whole nightmare situation.

If the police were still looking for the stupid dog, it heightened the risk of them getting caught.

'Maybe we should do it tomorrow night, just before dark,' Nancy suggested.

'No!' They all looked at Ross and he fumbled to explain himself. 'The longer we have the body, the more we will be implicating ourselves. We need to get rid of it as soon as possible.'

It was actually the truth. He had watched enough true crime documentaries to know they were putting themselves more at risk by waiting. If the police discovered that McCool was missing, if they came back and asked to search the house...

No, he couldn't even think about that.

The others didn't understand. They didn't have as much to lose as Ross did.

Again he cursed Billy for putting them in this terrible position.

Billy had caused this and the rest of them now had to clear up his mess. Then Ross wanted to get the hell away from Scotland. By Saturday night he wanted to have put as much distance between himself and this place as possible.

7

BILLY

There were three things Billy loved most in life. Sex, alcohol and his drums. He hated exercise (well, except for swimming) and nature bored him.

Music festivals, hot tubs and barbecues were probably the closest he got to being outdoorsy, and when Griffin had invited them all to the house in Scotland, he hadn't considered it might involve hiking and boating, and lord knows what else.

Admittedly the reason he was up at shit-the-bed o'clock was because Griffin was forcing him to go with them down to the loch, which hadn't factored in any of their original plans and, yes, okay, it had been Billy's fault that they now had a dead body to deal with. But still, he was getting the impression Griffin's itinerary had already included some of this at-one-with-nature bullshit, and it seemed he had prepared himself for all of Billy's excuses.

'I don't have the right stuff to wear,' he had grumbled when Griffin had first woken him. His mouth was dry and his head pounding with the headache from hell, as he desperately tried to think of a way to get out of going.

'Jeans, T-shirt.' Griffin picked both items up from where

Billy had dumped them on the floor a few hours earlier. 'You're good to go.'

'It's cold outside though.'

'I have a spare jacket you can borrow.'

Billy sat up, scrubbing his palms over his face, and looked at the alarm clock. 'For fuck's sake, Griff. It's five bloody thirty. This isn't morning. It's still the middle of the night.'

'It's not long before sunrise. We need to move now.'

'I thought you said when you came in last night that we were going to wait until tonight?'

Griffin flared his nostrils, already looking bored with the conversation. 'We considered it briefly but decided against it. We need to get rid of the body as soon as possible.'

'But I don't have the right footwear for traipsing through the woods.'

'I brought my spare hiking boots for you.'

Fuck! Billy was running out of excuses. Griffin seemed to have an answer for everything. 'Look, Griff, mate. You'd be better off leaving me behind. You and I both know I'm a liability. I'll just be in the way. You can handle this much better without me.'

'Get dressed, Billy. This is your mess; you can help us deal with it.'

'If I stay here though I can keep an eye on Amelia.'

Griffin paused, staring at him. 'Why do you need to keep an eye on Amelia?'

It often surprised Billy that given how smart he was, Griffin sometimes had to have things spelt out for him. 'She's not on board with any of this, right? Still thinks we should go to the police? How do you know that while we are out she won't call them?'

The fear that Amelia might have already done just that had woken him up in the middle of the night in a cold sweat. She had been so insistent they call the police, furious with them all when she had stomped off to bed. Billy knew what she was like. When she made up her mind about something there was no changing it.

'Mils wouldn't do that.'

'Are you sure?'

'We voted. She will respect that.' Griffin spoke the words with conviction, though Billy didn't miss the twitch just under his eye and knew he had found his friend's weak spot. The others considered him to be a misfit and a pisshead, and true, he wasn't very good at the whole responsibility thing, but Billy was observant when he needed to be. Griffin might be engaged to Chantelle and telling anyone who would listen that he and Amelia were just friends, but Billy knew that he wasn't yet over her. Perhaps would never be.

'Okay, well, as long as you're sure, because we weren't voting which pub to go to or what movie to watch this time, and you know what she's like. Remember when she caught me smoking weed in her room and threatened to report me?' He chuckled, as if the memory amused him. Griffin had probably forgotten about it and Billy wanted it fresh in his mind. Seeing the cogs working, he resisted the urge to smile.

Billy had nothing against Amelia Abery, even if she did want to turn him in to the police. They had always been good friends, despite being polar opposites, and while he didn't exactly get her moral core, he mostly tried to respect it. He knew it had been hard for her finding out about her father and understood she felt she had to prove that she was nothing like him.

Yes, he did think they should keep an eye on her, but Amelia was most likely asleep and still would be when they returned. If she was going to call the police, it would have already happened. This, what he was doing right now, pushing Griffin's buttons and trying to manipulate the situation, was about nothing more than him getting to stay in bed for another few hours, while the others dealt with his mess. Because, truthfully, when it came to clearing up mess, there was no one better at it than Griffin King.

Unfortunately his grand plan wasn't working.

'Just get dressed, Billy, and leave me to worry about Amelia. If anyone is to stay behind, it won't be you. Given how badly you've already fucked things up, I've lost all trust in you.'

Griffin threw his jeans and T-shirt at him. 'I want to see you downstairs in fifteen minutes.'

Billy continued his protests, but knew Griffin had made up his mind, and he had little time to wallow about the early morning excursion. When he eventually went downstairs, purposely five minutes late, just to tick Griffin off, he found Jonah, Nancy and Ross sat round the table waiting for him.

Nancy grunted 'morning' to him, but the others were silent and he could tell from their expressions they were equally enthusiastic about the trip to the loch.

'Where's Griff?' he asked Nancy.

'Loo, I think.'

Billy nodded, going to the fridge and poking his head inside, needing food in his belly.

'You don't have time to eat,' Jonah told him.

'I'm hanging, man. I need to have something. My head's banging.'

'Here!' Nancy pulled something out of her bag and threw it at him. Billy caught it, realised it was a packet of painkillers. Not exactly what he had planned.

'Thanks.' As he fished a bottle of orange juice out of the door of the fridge, swigged straight from the bottle, washing down a couple of the pills, Griffin strode into the room.

He glared at Billy. 'Nice of you to finally join us.'

'Griffin! Get the hell back here!' Amelia's voice carried down the hallway and Billy glanced past Griffin in time to see her stomp into the room. Her copper hair was a tangled mess, and she was dressed in just an oversized navy T-shirt, her feet bare. From her expression she was struggling to contain her anger.

Ignoring her, Griffin opened the cupboard, grabbed the promised jacket and hiking boots for Billy and dumped them on the table.

'That's bad luck.'

'What?'

'Putting shoes on the table,' Nancy elaborated. 'It's bad luck.'

'Whatever.' Griffin shook his head in annoyance, turning to Amelia who was trying to grab hold of his arm.

'Give me my damn phone,' she snapped.

'You can have it when we get back.'

'I want it now.'

'Whoa, wait.' Jonah suddenly looked a whole lot more awake. 'Why have you taken her phone?'

'Insurance,' Griffin told him tightly. 'She's staying here alone while we go down to the loch. We can't take the risk she might call the police while we're gone.'

'What?' Amelia looked insulted by his suggestion. 'I wouldn't do that.'

'Wouldn't you, Mils? Remember when you were going to report Billy for smoking weed in your room?'

Seriously, that was the example he was going to go with?

Billy kept his head down, not wanting Amelia to realise he had caused this.

'Give her the phone back, Griff.' Jonah's tone was heated. 'You're being ridiculous.'

'Yes, give it back. You have no right to take it, just as you had no right to come into my room while I was sleeping.'

'She can have the phone back when we get back from the loch.'

'This is theft,' Amelia accused.

'There's a dead fucking body in the garage. Trust me, Mils. Theft is the least of my concerns right now.'

'Give me my damn phone back and stop calling me Mils. My name is Amelia.'

'I've always called you Mils.'

'And I've always bloody hated it.'

Billy watched the exchange from his position by the fridge, the bottle of orange juice still in his hand. He was hard pressed to tell who was the angriest.

Griffin was a dominating presence; his voice was raised and his jaw set. This was the side of him Billy knew better than to mess with, but Amelia, damn her, she looked like she might just rip Griff's heart out of his chest and stomp on it. He had never seen her so worked up, and guilt stabbed at him, knowing he had caused this.

You're a complete shit, Billy.

Ultimately Griffin won. He was always going to, being physically bigger and stronger, and when Amelia tried to attack him, he easily held her at arm's length.

When she looked at Jonah in frustration, he got up and went over to Griffin, Billy assumed to try and reason with him, but then he saw the look on Jonah's face and realised he was about to lose his shit.

Uh-oh. This isn't going to end well.

Griffin didn't cope well with being challenged and Jonah was the only one who ever had the balls to do it. Usually he was level-headed enough to talk Griffin down, but right now he looked like he wanted to rip his head off.

'Give her back the phone.'

'No.'

'Griffin. Don't be a dick.'

Griff's jaw tightened and he looked as though he was going to say something, but then changed his mind. Instead he went to push past Jonah, actually looked momentarily surprised when Jonah got in his face, shoving him back against the counter.

'Where is it?'

'Get your hands off me.'

'Where's the fucking phone?'

Then Griffin was shoving back, and Jonah looked ready to punch him in the face, and things were getting far too heated for this early in the morning.

'STOP!'

It wasn't so much the yell that had them complying, but the person it had come from. Mild-mannered Ross who hadn't said a word since Billy walked in the kitchen, slammed his fist down on the table, making them all jump.

'We don't have time for this shit,' he stormed. 'Griffin is right. If Amelia is going to stay here alone, we need to be careful; we have to take precautions. Yes, she's our friend, but she has also been completely opposed to all of this. We can't take the risk of her calling the police while we are gone.'

'I'm right here. Can you stop talking about me like I'm not in the room?'

Ross shot Amelia a quick smile, though it held no warmth. 'Right now, we have to protect ourselves. We have to stop every potential threat.' He glanced at her again. 'No offence meant, Amelia.'

'It's still taken,' she told him coldly.

'She's not a threat,' Jonah snapped.

'Then she won't mind Griffin hanging on to her phone for a couple of hours, will she?'

Amelia waved at Ross and Billy could tell she was getting annoyed at him constantly referring to her in the third person. 'Still here, still do.'

'You know this protects you too, right?' Ross said, finally addressing her directly.

'And how is that exactly?'

'If we do get caught you can tell the police that we took your phone to stop you trying to call them.'

'I'm not going to call the sodding police!'

'He's right, Amelia. It makes you an innocent party,' Nancy pointed out. 'You can't be implicated.'

'I am innocent!' Although she was still protesting, Billy could see Amelia was mulling that over. He knew she had wanted no part of this and had so far been forced to go along with the others.

'So that's three of us in agreement that we take the phone,' Griffin commented. He was still keeping a close eye on Jonah. Ready to react if the other man made a move. 'Billy, you get the deciding vote.'

Oh great.

Billy was feeling pretty shitty about stitching Amelia up. If she was going to call the police, she would have done it last night. He honestly didn't believe she would do it now. If he sided with her and Jonah, though, then it would be stalemate and this could go on for fucking hours. He didn't have the patience for that. Besides, it always helped to keep Griffin on side.

'We take the phone,' he agreed.

'Good man.'

Griffin eyed Jonah as he slowly pushed past him, and Billy could already tell it was going to be a fun walk in the woods with all this unresolved aggression bouncing between them both.

'Sun will be up soon. We should get going,' Ross muttered. 'Get this over and done with.'

'We should. Billy, get your boots on.'

Billy attempted one more half-arsed protest, but Griffin wasn't having any of it. Reluctantly he did as he was told and followed the others to the door.

For a moment Jonah hesitated and Billy wasn't sure if he was going to join them, but then he exchanged a brief unreadable look with Amelia and pulled on his jacket.

Griffin also glanced over at her. 'You can have your phone as soon as we get back. I promise.'

When she didn't respond, he muttered something to Ross, who walked back over to the table and snatched up his car keys. He winked at Amelia, slipping them in his pocket. 'Just to be on the safe side.'

Griffin opened the door and herded them all out. 'Right, let's go fix Billy's latest fuck-up,' he muttered, closing the door behind him and leaving Amelia alone in the house.

Billy wished he was still inside with her. The next couple of hours were going to be pure hell.

8

AMELIA

How fucking dare he?

Now dressed, Amelia had spent ten minutes pacing the length of the open-plan living room, muttering to herself, furious with Griffin for stealing her phone.

And it wasn't just that he had let himself into her room while she was asleep and taken it; no, it was his accusation that she would turn them in to the police that had left her reeling.

Yes, she was bitterly unhappy with current events, livid even that she had been forced to be a part of this, but the idea of going to the police behind her friends' backs hadn't even occurred to her, and it was that lack of trust that hurt more than anything.

Jonah had been the only one who had stuck up for her; Nancy, Billy and Ross had all sided with Griffin, and it had her wondering if perhaps her loyalty towards them all was misguided. She clearly thought more of their friendship than they did.

As for Griffin, he had reminded her exactly why they were no longer together. She had been a fool thinking he had changed, and she deeply regretted agreeing to this weekend away. He still knew how to press her buttons and although he was telling her he had moved on from their break-up, she was beginning to suspect he was lying.

And that bothered her. If he hadn't forgiven her for calling off their engagement, why had he invited her to come on this trip?

Right now though, she was angry he had taken her phone, and also more than a little worried. She had a security lock on it, but had used the same code for years, and Griffin, with his memory of an elephant, could easily bypass that.

He wouldn't seriously go through her phone, would he?

She wracked her brain trying to remember exactly what was on there, knew her text and WhatsApp conversations dated back years. If he went back through her conversation history with Jonah though... She couldn't even dare think about that.

It didn't matter that they had broken up years ago. Griffin held grudges. Amelia had been his fiancée and Jonah his best friend. It didn't bode well for either of them.

She couldn't afford to focus on the worry. If he did look there was nothing she could do to change it, so instead she channelled her anger.

Amelia wasn't usually one for petty acts of revenge, but Griffin was seriously pissing her off and she decided if he could wander into her room and go through her stuff then she could do the same.

Not that he had a huge amount of interesting stuff to go through. He had taken the master bedroom at the front of the house, a beautiful room with exposed wood beams and a four-poster bed that was tastefully decorated in forest greens and creams. As was typical Griffin, everything was neat and in its place: the duvet crease-free; his travel bag pushed under the

Queen Anne chair in the corner of the room; and his toiletries perfectly lined up on the shelf in the en-suite bathroom.

He was such a bloody neat freak.

She pulled out the bag, unzipped it and looked inside. It was all clothes. Black jeans, a couple of jumpers, socks and underwear. In the side compartment she found a paperback novel, *Over My Shoulder* by Patricia Dixon, and a packet of mints, then wedged inside another internal pocket was his wallet and a CD in a slim clear case.

She pulled out the CD first, curious. Griffin favoured digital music, so why did he have it? She twisted it over, saw in his neat writing *Compilation Mils*. Had he seriously made her a mix CD? Why the hell would he do that? Unless it was an old one he intended to play. Was there even a CD player in the house? If so, she could have a listen. Slipping it back in the bag for now, she turned her attention to his wallet, flipping through his credit cards and ID. He looked so stern on his driver's licence, like he was really angry at whoever, or whatever had taken the picture, that she found herself smirking.

The cash compartment: nothing to see there. Then the little purse for loose coins. Nothing to see there either, or so she thought. As she went to zip it back up, something glinted up at her and she reached inside, fishing between the pound coins, her heart beating a little quicker as she pulled out the ring.

It was the one he had given her for their first Christmas together. A simple silver twisted band with a tiny topaz stone.

She had loved that ring, but six months ago it had vanished. She didn't wear it all the time and was convinced she had left it in her jewellery box, but when she went to get it, it wasn't there, and she had wracked her brain for weeks after trying to figure out where she had put it.

Had Griffin had it this whole time? And if so, how the hell did he get it?

You're being paranoid. It probably isn't your ring.

She turned it over in her fingers. It wasn't a unique design and probably mass produced. It was quite plausible that Griffin might have bought Chantelle the same style ring he had given to Amelia.

Though why was it in his wallet?

She slipped it on her finger, twisted it around. It did feel like her ring and... was one of the clasps that held the stone in place slightly bent?

She swallowed hard and she realised it was.

It had to be her ring, but why did Griffin have it? And, more worryingly, how did he get it?

Had he been inside her house?

Although she had a dozen questions, how was she supposed to get answers?

If he learnt she had been snooping through his stuff, she would lose the moral high ground. And she couldn't just take the ring, as he would notice it was missing.

Reluctantly she slipped it off and put it back in the wallet before returning it to Griffin's bag. Pushing the bag back under the chair, Amelia then returned to the bathroom. She had to think of a way to get it back, but she couldn't see how she could do that without confronting him. She knew from history that she normally lost on those occasions.

Frustrated, she picked up his toothbrush, and was toying whether to dunk it in the toilet, when there was a loud bang on the front door. She jumped, almost dropping the brush and quickly replaced it in the beaker.

Were they back already? There was no way they could have reached the loch and come back again? Had something gone wrong?

What if Griffin came upstairs? He was so bloody organised. Would he realise she had been in here?

She glanced around the room, panicking. She had only touched the toothbrush and his travel bag. Both were back as she had found them, but wait, was the bag the right way round?

Another knock at the door had her flustered. It would have to do.

It wasn't until she was heading downstairs, relieved at her narrow escape, that she considered the fact that if her friends were back, they would have let themselves in the house.

That thought had her pausing on the bottom step. So who was at the door? Griffin had said they were in the middle of nowhere.

What if it's the police?

Was it possible the others had been caught with the body?

No, she was panicking. It wasn't going to be the police. Still, she was trembling as she crossed the room and headed into the hallway to the front door.

If it's the police, play innocent. You haven't done anything wrong.

Except she had. Her friend had killed a man and she hadn't reported him.

She could see shapes through the frosted glass panel. At least two of them. Two police officers? Or maybe it was the others. Had they forgotten to take their keys? If it was Griffin and snidey Ross, she was actually going to be happy to see them.

There wasn't a key in the lock and Amelia realised that Griffin hadn't left her one. Did that mean she was locked in the house? Part of her hoped so, as it meant she wouldn't have to face whoever was on the other side of the door. But as she pulled on the handle and it opened, she understood he probably hadn't felt the need to lock up. They were, after all, in the middle of nowhere.

Discomfort gnawed in her gut when she found herself face

to face with three unfamiliar men. They weren't her friends, they certainly weren't the police, and the way the one at the front of the group was looking at her, a sly smile on his face, had her guard going up.

Don't panic. It's all okay. Maybe they are hiking or something. Just pretend the others are here. Don't let on that you're home alone. 'Hi. Can I help you?'

'Is this your house?' the bald man at the front asked. She could tell from his stance that he was the dominant one of the three. The man with the sandy hair who was closest behind him wasn't being at all discreet in checking out her tits, while the younger guy standing by a dirty white van, a baseball cap twisted the wrong way on his head, looked like he had just stepped off the set of *Deliverance*.

Amelia kept one hand on the handle, afraid to let the door swing wide open. Her mouth was dry when she spoke. 'No. We're on holiday.'

We're. That's good. Keep reminding them that you're not home alone.

When baldie simply nodded, she asked again, 'Can I help you?'

'Yeah.' He reached inside his jacket, and she nearly lost it, fearful he was going to produce a knife or worse. This scenario was all too familiar. Gang of friends go into the woods, one of them gets separated...

He had shifty eyes that were too close together, a clear sign that she shouldn't trust him, and his bald head was pointy. Not that his head factored into anything, but still she didn't like it.

Why the hell hadn't she gone with the others?

Because you refused to help them hide the body. You were trying to be the responsible one, remember?

Fuck being responsible. Amelia made a pact with herself

right there and then that if she survived this encounter she would be fully on board with the whole bailing-out-Billy thing.

It took her a moment to register that he was holding up his phone, not a knife, and she tried to hide her relief by scrutinising the close-up picture of the man on the screen.

'My brother went missing last night. I was wondering if you had seen him.'

Amelia could see the family resemblance and baldie's brother hadn't fared much better in the looks department. He had that same shiny pointy head (must be a family thing) and a smile full of teeth that looked like they had never been introduced to a toothbrush.

She was relieved that it was an easy answer for her. 'No, sorry. I've never seen him before.'

'Are you sure?' Baldie was looking at her intently now, as if he didn't quite believe her. 'Because I'm pretty certain he was here last night.'

'What? No he wasn't.' Even as the words were leaving her mouth, Amelia clicked. The one person who had been here last night and who wasn't part of the gang.

Fuck!

'I'm sorry, there must have been a misunderstanding. I don't know your brother.' Icy fear stroked her spine and she tried to shut the door.

Baldie put his foot in the way, stopping it from closing. 'Not so fast. I have a few more questions.'

She swallowed hard, tried to hold eye contact.

'You said you're here on holiday?'

'We are.'

'When did you get here?'

'Yesterday. Look, I'm really sorry your brother is missing, but there's nothing I can do to help.' Her gaze flickered to the sandy-haired mate, irritation taking the edge off her fear. She wanted to call him out on staring at her chest, but equally didn't want to antagonise the men.

'You're here with family?' Baldie pushed.

'Friends.'

'Maybe they saw my brother.'

'They wouldn't have. They haven't been anywhere.'

'I would like you to ask them for me.'

'They're all still asleep.'

'Right.' A shadow of something, was it disbelief or realisation that she was home alone, passed over Baldie's face.

Shit, shit, shit.

'What's your name?'

'I'm sorry, but that's really none of your business.'

'Oh, I think it is.' He pushed on the door, a sudden movement that had her jerking back. 'Look, I'm trying to be a nice guy here and give you a choice. We can do this the easy way or the hard way. Your choice, so I'll ask you again. What's your name?'

This time she answered after a brief pause. 'Amelia.' She could have made something up, but there seemed little point in lying at this stage. She needed to be convincing if she was to get him to leave and not tell too many lies.

'Okay, well look, Amelia. I would appreciate it if you would ask your friends about my brother when they finally get up. My name is Kenny McCool and my brother's name is Dougie. Maybe that might jog their memories. I'll leave you with my number.'

When Amelia didn't react, he gave her a questioning look. 'Well do you have your phone?'

'Um, not to hand.' Kenny's eyes narrowed and she added quickly, 'But I do have paper and pen.' *Thank God for small mercies,* she thought, grabbing the pen and jotter from the hall table, grateful that the houseowners had thought of every eventuality.

Kenny reeled off his number and she wrote it down, her hand shaking.

'Read it back to me,' he instructed.

When she did, he nodded, seeming satisfied. 'You speak to your friends, Amelia, love, and you tell them to call me if they know anything about my brother, okay?'

Somehow she held eye contact, though everything was trembling inside. 'I will.'

'Good girl. I'm going to trust you to do that, because if you don't, I'll have to come back, and you really don't want me to come back.' He looked her up and down lasciviously and twinned emotions of anger and fear raged inside of her.

How fucking dare he threaten me like this? Part of her wanted to punch him in the face, while the other part was terrified he might try and force his way into the house.

Ultimately she just wanted him gone and she forced herself to smile at him, knowing she needed to appear confident. 'I said I will. But I don't like being threatened. So I'd appreciate it if you would take Shrek and Banjo Boy here and leave me in peace.'

Baldie stared at her for a moment, and she thought from his expression that he was going to change his mind and force his way into the house, but then he gave her a wide smile and a wink before turning back to his goons. 'Come on, boys.' He glanced back, waggling a finger at her. 'Speak to your friends.'

Then all three of them were back in the van and driving slowly away from the house.

Amelia closed the door and pushed her back up against it, wishing she could lock it. She didn't trust them not to come back, and that made her vulnerable.

The others would be gone for at least another hour, maybe

longer. Perhaps she should try to catch them up. It was a stupid idea. She knew that. She had no clue which direction they had headed in. No, she was trapped here. In the middle of nowhere, no phone, no locked doors.

If Kenny and his friends decided to come back, she was in big trouble.

9

GRIFFIN

A mug of black coffee in his hand and sat on the decking with a view of the woods; that was how Griffin King had envisioned spending his first morning in Scotland.

He certainly hadn't anticipated traipsing through those woods just before sunrise carrying a dead body.

Okay, so technically he wasn't carrying the body. Jonah and Billy were taking care of that, while Nancy and Ross were lugging the ancient stove that Griffin had found discarded behind the bar at the bottom of the garden. He only needed to worry about his water bottle and the life jacket he had insisted on bringing from the garage.

Although the body wasn't visible, being wrapped in a tarpaulin and a tangle of rope, it was obvious they were up to no good, which is why Griffin took the role of lookout, partly because he didn't trust the others to do it, partly because he knew a good manager took charge and let his employees do the legwork.

He didn't expect to find anyone out and about this early in the morning. Mrs Campbell, the woman he had rented the house off, had told him it was possible to go weeks without laying eyes on a soul. Typical then that a fucking dog had gone missing and that the local police had nothing more pressing to do than to look for it.

Still, PC Murray had to sleep and after driving around the Scottish countryside door-knocking late last night, Griffin hoped he was now tucked up in bed.

He could see the loch up ahead, through the clearing in the trees, and picked up the pace, ignoring the whining from Billy who had thrown a tantrum when he realised he would be helping to carry McCool's body.

'Your mess; you're helping to carry him,' Griffin had stormed, getting in Billy's face.

Billy knew better than to argue with him when he lost his temper, but although he had done as he was told and helped Jonah carry the body, it hadn't stopped his whining.

The loch wasn't even a ten-minute walk and so far he had struggled with the weight, complained they were walking too fast, that his head and then his leg hurt, that he was dizzy and now that he was dying of thirst.

It was honestly like dealing with a toddler.

As Billy stumbled through the clearing, letting go of his end of the body without giving any warning to Jonah so the slack weight thudded hard against the ground, Griffin tossed his water bottle at him.

'Shut the fuck up complaining and drink.'

While Billy gulped from the bottle in an exaggerated fashion, Jonah glanced towards the loch. 'Are those both our boats?'

'Just one of them. Why?'

'Well there are five of us... technically six, plus we have the stove. We're not all going to fit.'

Griffin looked at the boats, saw he had a point. 'So we'll

borrow the other one. No one will know. Two of us can take the body in one and two more can take the stove.'

'There are five of us,' Nancy reminded him.

'Someone needs to stay here and keep a lookout.' He glanced her up and down. Billy was unreliable, they needed Jonah's strength, and Ross, well, Griffin wasn't quite sure where his head was at the moment. 'I was thinking that could be you,' he suggested.

She appeared to consider the idea, not seeming appalled by it, then shrugged. 'I guess I can do that.'

With that sorted, the boats were untied, Griffin and Ross clambering into one with the stove, while Jonah and Billy were in charge of McCool in the other. As they rowed out towards the centre of the loch, Nancy watching from the shore, Griffin was struck by the serenity of the place. The expanse of water was bigger than he had realised, the only sound coming from the lapping water against the boats as they worked the oars, and the sun was slowly rising over the treetops in a sky of golds and pinks. It was beautiful and peaceful, and unspoilt, and it was hard to believe they were about to dump a body out here.

'Here looks a good enough place,' Jonah yelled eventually, drawing his oar into the boat.

Griffin wasn't so sure. Were they quite deep enough? 'I think we need to go another twenty yards or so. We're not quite centre.'

'Looking pretty central to me.'

His hackles rose. Why did Jonah insist on arguing with him?

'Well, it's not,' he snapped back.

'Yeah, it is, Griff.'

Griffin scowled at Ross, ignoring his comment. 'We need to go further out,' he told Jonah, as they pulled the boat up alongside him and Billy. He wondered how much Billy had been grumbling about the rowing on the way out here. A lot, he guessed from his sulky expression.

Perhaps it was for the best that Griffin hadn't gone in the boat with him, as he would have likely ended up pushing him overboard.

'The sun is already rising,' Jonah pointed out. 'At the moment it's early and we have this loch to ourselves. The sooner we get rid of the body, the safer we are.'

Annoyingly, he had a point.

'Okay, fine, we'll dump him here.' Griffin glanced over the side of the boat trying to gauge how deep it was, but it was impossible to tell. It had to be at least thirty or forty feet down to the bottom though, right?

They were going to have to guess, as he didn't do water, and he was fairly certain none of the others would volunteer to go check it out. Of course, he could force Billy to do it. This whole situation was his fault, but Billy being Billy, he would no doubt fuck it up and drown.

Grabbing a length of rope, he fed it through the handle of the stove, knotting it tightly and tossed the slack over to Jonah.

'Tie this through the eyelets on the tarpaulin and make sure it's secure.'

As Jonah did as instructed, Griffin glanced around the shoreline again. There was still no sign of anyone other than Nancy. From this distance he couldn't make out her features, could only tell that she was now sitting down. That was good. If anyone else saw them out on the boats, they hopefully wouldn't be able to tell what they were up to.

They were really doing this, hiding the body. He watched as Jonah finished tying a bowline knot. The mummified body of Dougie McCool was now attached to the stove by only a short slack of rope that kept the boats pulled together, and he worked to keep his breathing even as a bout of last-minute nerves skittered through him.

It was too late to back out now, he knew that. They hadn't called the police when Billy had shown up last night and the consequences of not doing so, started right there. Hiding the body, wrapping it up in plastic tarp and rope and taking it out into the middle of the loch, steadily made things worse. Once the body was in the water, it was over.

Well, other than cleaning up the mess in Billy's car. They would move it into the garage when they returned, just in case PC Murray came back again.

'Are we ready to do this?'

Griffin looked at Jonah again, not quite sure if he meant physically ready to push McCool overboard or if they were morally ready to go through with the task. If they were caught, the consequences were unthinkable. Still, beneath the nerves, a sliver of excitement heated his belly.

'I'm ready.'

He glanced across the stove at Ross, who had barely spoken since getting in the boat, waiting for his response.

'Let's get this over with,' he muttered eventually, clearly unimpressed with the whole situation.

Griffin didn't bother to ask Billy if he was ready. His friend had fallen quiet, his face pale and sweaty. He was hungover and sorry for himself and too shallow to consider the consequences of what they were about to do. He didn't get a say in any of this.

'We're going to have to drop the body and the stove at the same time,' Jonah warned. 'We don't want to tip the boats.'

Griffin nodded, well aware of that, and reached for the stove. It was too heavy to lift while he was sat down, so he attempted to stand, the boat rocking violently and scaring the shit out of him. He had the life jacket on, but there was no way he was going in the water.

'Jesus, Griff, be careful.' Ross's eyes were bug wide and his tone indignant, as water splashed him.

'A hand would actually be nice. This thing is bloody heavy.'

'I know. I helped carry it down here, remember?'

Griffin scowled at Ross, annoyed by the sniping comment. He was sure it wasn't his imagination that Ross, who had always been the meekest of the six, was becoming more antagonistic. Whether it was an ego thing, his confidence growing with the success of his business, or something else, Griffin wasn't sure, but it was definitely starting to annoy him.

'Then you should realise I'm going to struggle to throw it overboard by myself,' he snapped.

Jonah already had hold of McCool's body, not even bothering to get Billy to help, and he was waiting on Griffin and Ross. 'Whenever you two are ready,' he grumbled.

'We'll go on the count of three,' Griffin instructed as he and Ross managed to lift the stove.

It should have been so easy. Count to three, drop the body and the stove at the same time, watch them sink to the bottom. Job done.

Griffin hadn't counted on losing his balance, but as the body and stove dropped into the loch, the boat wobbled and, panicking, he reached out to Ross to steady himself, knocking the smaller man forward. One second Ross was in the boat, the next he was stumbling forward and head first into the water. When he disappeared beneath the surface, Griffin stared at Jonah, his mouth open.

'Oops. He can swim, right?'

As he asked the question, Ross's head broke through the surface and although he was splashing and spluttering, his focus was firmly on Griffin.

'This is your fault,' he huffed.

'What? No it isn't. You were the one who lost your balance. You should have been more careful.'

'You pushed me!'

'I did not.' It was an inappropriate moment given that they had just thrown a man's body into the loch, but Ross was so angry, his tiny head bobbing up and down on the surface of the water and his eyes bulging, and Griffin couldn't help but burst out laughing.

'Seriously? You think this is funny?' Ross stormed. 'I'm going to have to walk back to the house in soaking wet clothes.'

'You'll be fine. It's not far.'

'Stop laughing at me.'

'Sorry. You do look a bit of a tit though.'

'Thanks.'

'While you're in there, can you check the body has sunk okay?'

'No, I bloody well cannot.'

'We need to know for sure, right, Jonah?'

'We should check, mate. Sorry.'

'Well one of you two bloody go down and look.'

'You're already in the water,' Jonah pointed out. 'You're really going to make us get wet too?'

'What about Billy? This is his mess.'

'No! I can't. I'm not well.'

'You're hungover.' Griffin shook his head in disgust. 'That's not the same as being sick.'

'Don't make me do it, Griff. You know I'm a shit swimmer.'

It was a lie. Billy had told Griffin before that he loved swimming. He was unreliable though. 'Ross will check,' he said firmly.

'I bloody well will not.'

'It'll take a minute. You're already in the water. You just need to check it's not visible and has sunk far enough.'

Ignoring him, Ross started to swim towards the boat.

Griffin grabbed hold of the oar and started batting it at him when he tried to grab hold of the side.

'What are you doing? Are you fucking crazy? Let me on the boat.'

'Not until you've checked on the body.'

'Let him in the boat, Griffin. I'll go.'

'Shut up, Jonah. Ross is going to do it. Aren't you, Ross?'

'Griffin. Don't do this.' Ross looked like he was about to burst into tears. 'Please.' There he was, the kid who had been at university with them. This wasn't Ross Onion (pronounced Oh-nye-on. He was always very careful to point out the correct way to say it), tech genius and respected businessman. No, this was Ross Onion, pronounced as in the vegetable, who had been Griffin King's stooge all the way through university.

It was good to see him back.

'Stop pissing about, Onion. Get down there and check. We're all ready to go back.'

Griffin saw the moment Ross accepted defeat and he revelled in the power trip. He had missed this.

'I fucking hate you.' Ross spat the words at him, before drawing in a deep breath and disappearing beneath the surface.

'You're a dick, Griff.'

'He was already in the water.'

'You're still a dick.'

Griffin and Jonah glared at each other, as tension rippled between them.

They had been best friends for a long time, but in recent months, Griffin was beginning to question where Jonah's loyalties lie.

He glanced at Billy who was still milking his hangover for all it was worth. When they got back he would get a couple of cups of strong coffee inside him then make sure Billy helped with the clean-up job on his car. Griffin was also going to have to spend some time coaching him, making sure he knew what to say and what not to say once they left the house and returned to their regular lives on Monday. Of all of them, Billy was the one most likely to blurt out what had happened, not intentionally, but just because he was a fucking liability.

'Do you think he's okay?' Jonah dragged Griffin's attention back to the water. 'He's been down there over a minute.'

It wasn't that long, was it? Ross could swim. They didn't need to be worried, did they?

'I should go check.' Jonah was kicking off his boots and unzipping his jacket. 'Just in case.'

As he said the words, there was a splash and Ross broke through the water again, taking a gasp for air.

'Did you see him?' Griffin demanded.

Ross didn't answer. He was still taking a moment to catch his breath.

'Ross?'

'Give him a second,' Jonah ordered. 'Ross, you okay, mate?'

Ross nodded, turning to face Jonah's boat. 'Yeah. No one is going to find him.'

'Good. Job done.' It was irritating Griffin that Ross was ignoring him and had chosen to address Jonah instead. 'Get back on the boat and let's get the hell out of here.'

'It's deep. Bloody freezing too,' Ross continued, treading water as he ignored Griffin.

'Well, get back in the boat and stop complaining.' Griffin's voice was raised now.

'Yeah, can you get back in the boat, Ross,' Billy pleaded. He was looking rough as fuck, shivering and hugging himself. 'I don't feel well.'

Jonah scowled at him. 'Can't say I'm surprised. You had a lot to drink last night.'

'Mate.' Griffin leant over the edge of the boat and offered his hand. 'Come on. Get in and let's get back to the house.'

Finally, Ross cut him a glance, his look withering, before splashing his way to Jonah's boat instead.

'Seriously, you're going to be petty about it?'

'Can you give me a hand please, Jonah?'

Griffin shook his head, both angered and frustrated by Ross's behaviour. 'Suit yourself,' he snarled as Jonah helped him into the other boat. Picking up the oars, he started to push away. 'I'll see you back at the shore.'

Nancy was on her feet waiting for them when they returned, Griffin arriving only a few moments before the others. 'What the hell happened?' she asked, mouth falling open as a sodden and shivering Ross climbed out of the second boat.

'Griffin pushed me in.'

'I did not push you in. Stop saying that. You bloody well fell.'

'It was your fault and now look what you've done!' Ross had pulled his phone from his jeans pocket and was holding it up, the screen black. 'It's broken.'

'Chill out. We'll stick it in some rice or something. That's supposed to work, right?'

Griffin was looking at Nancy for confirmation, but she didn't comment. Instead she turned to Jonah. 'Is it done?'

'Yeah.' Jonah finished tying the boats to the mooring post. 'It's done. There's no going back now.'

He was right, Griffin realised. There was no going back. Dougie McCool was dead, and they had just disposed of his body. As he looked at Jonah's stony expression and listened to Ross bitch about his phone, the friendship between them all felt like it was fracturing. They couldn't let it completely crumble though, because the secret they now shared was one they were going to have to take to the grave.

10

JONAH

Jonah realised Amelia was upset the second he stepped back inside the house. Her tanned skin was unusually pale, and she was chewing away on her bottom lip, one of her clear giveaways that something was bothering her.

'What's wrong?' he demanded, first through the door.

Her amber eyes were troubled when they met his, but she didn't say anything, just giving a brief shake of her head as she glanced behind him, and he understood that she wanted to wait for the others.

Had something happened while they were down at the loch?

'Did you fall in?' she asked in surprise as Ross stormed past her, heading for the stairs. Although his clothes were starting to dry off, he was still a damp mess. He had been in a foul mood, stomping ahead, on the way back up to the house.

'Griffin pushed him in,' Billy commented, going straight to the fridge for a beer.

'Seriously?'

'I did not push him in. Billy, for fuck's sake, it's 9am, not pm.'

'It's 9pm somewhere.'

Griffin ran his fingers through his hair in frustration, turning back to the others with an exasperated shrug as Amelia held her hand out expectantly.

'What?' he questioned, bemused.

'Give me my phone.'

'Oh, yeah. Sure.'

He reached into his jeans pocket, paused, frowning, then checked his other pockets.

'Griffin, stop messing around.'

'I'm sure I put it in my back pocket,' he muttered, checking again.

'You're not funny. I want my phone and now.'

'I can't find it.'

Jonah had just about had enough of his attitude to Amelia. It was obvious Griffin still had some pent-up aggression towards her, so why the hell had he invited her on this weekend?

'Give her the damn phone, Griff.'

'I said I don't have it.'

'Liar!'

'I'm not lying, Mils. Here, you can check.' Griffin held his hands up.

'You want me to frisk you?' Amelia sounded disgusted.

'You're the one who doesn't believe me.'

'GIVE ME MY PHONE.'

'I DON'T HAVE IT.'

'Griffin!' Jonah snapped.

Nancy, who had been removing her boots, shook her head. 'Jesus, you lot are like a bunch of kids,' she muttered. 'Here, I'll check him.' As she patted Griffin down, his expression went from surprised to amused and, as he was distracted by Nancy, Jonah glanced over at Amelia. She met his eyes briefly, though her expression was unreadable. Something was bugging her other than the phone.

'He doesn't have it,' Nancy announced eventually.

'I told you I didn't.'

'So where the fuck is it, Griffin?' Amelia was in his face now, looking like she was about to punch him, and Jonah was torn between intervening and letting her roll with it. He decided on the latter. She looked like she could handle herself and Griffin was big enough to fight his own battles.

'Maybe down by the boats?' he guessed. 'Look, I'm sorry. It must have fallen out of my pocket.'

'How convenient,' Amelia snapped coldly.

'I can go with you to check?'

'No!'

'What the fuck is wrong with you, Mils?'

'I want my phone.'

Griffin went for humour. 'We've gathered that.'

Big mistake, as it set her off on a rant. 'You left me here alone! I had no phone, and all the bloody doors were unlocked!'

'You're overreacting, don't you think? We're in the middle of nowhere.'

'That's what you keep saying, so why the fuck did I have visitors just after you left?'

'What?' Jonah spoke in unison with Griffin, while Nancy's eyes widened.

'There were three men. One of them was Dougie McCool's brother. They wanted to know if I had seen him. This place is supposed to be off the beaten track, so how would they know about it? Why would they think to come here unless they know what we... no, correction, unless they know what *you* did?'

She had a point. How did they know about it? Was there something Billy wasn't telling them?

Jonah glanced over at him, his temper fraying as Billy drank his beer while checking his phone, completely oblivious to the trouble he had caused.

'Slow down, Mils,' Griffin ordered. 'You're saying our dead guy's brother was here at the house looking for him?'

Amelia rolled her eyes, exasperated. 'Yes. Didn't you just listen to a single word I said? He's not the kind of person you want to mess with either.'

Anger heated in Jonah's gut. 'Did he threaten you?'

Amelia shifted her focus to him, her tone softening. 'He wasn't pleasant, put it that way. And he did warn me he might come back. I got the impression he didn't believe me.'

'Why would he want to come back? Goddammit. What the hell did you say to him?' Griffin started pacing the room, his hands bunched into tight fists. 'For fuck's sake, Mils. You always had a big mouth.'

'I didn't say anything to him!'

'Well you must have said something for him to disbelieve you.'

Amelia went over the encounter and Jonah could tell she was struggling to keep her tone calm. Griffin had always known how to push her buttons and it seemed he had simply become better at it.

'We should leave,' Nancy proposed. 'Before they come back to the house.'

'No, what we should do is stay right here and enjoy the rest of my birthday weekend.'

'Are you nuts?'

'Not at all.' Griffin gave Nancy a measured look. 'If we leave suddenly then we might as well paint guilty signs on our heads. No one can prove we had anything to do with Dougie McCool's disappearance. We'll clean up Billy's car then we'll stay and carry on with our plans. It's less suspicious that way and if McCool's brother comes back, we'll just play dumb.'

Amelia didn't look convinced, but Jonah could see Nancy was mulling it over. He guessed Griffin had a point. If they left abruptly it would look suspicious.

'We need to hide the rucksack,' he pointed out. 'We don't want that lying around if they come back.' It was propped against the side of the sofa, out of sight of the front door, but visible if anyone came into the room, and he saw Amelia gulp when she realised that.

He didn't like the idea that she had been alone here when McCool's brother had shown up and wasn't at all happy that he had threatened her.

'Maybe in one of the wardrobes upstairs?' Nancy suggested.

'No.' Griffin shook his head. 'We need to put it where it can't be found.'

'We could bury it outside somewhere.'

Griffin nodded as he considered Jonah's idea. 'That's a possibility.'

'What about beneath the floorboards?' Ross suggested, coming back into the room wearing dry clothes and a calmer look. He must have heard them talking. 'There are a couple of loose panels in my room. We could hide the bag under them.'

'That would work better, I think. Good idea, mate.'

'Thanks Griff. Shall we go look now?' Ross beamed as Griffin patted him on the shoulder, nodding at the suggestion.

Jonah shook his head, part amused, part frustrated, at how quick their earlier fall-out was patched over. Ross seriously needed to stop being a pushover. He was indignant one moment at being the butt of Griff's jokes, but the second he was thrown a bone, he was crawling back up the man's arse. The charade was both frustrating and sickening, as it only encouraged Griffin's bad behaviour.

'Wait!' Amelia demanded, hands on hips as Griffin swung round to face her.

'What now?'

'My phone.'

'I told you I don't have it.'

'He really doesn't.' Nancy backed him up.

'So where the hell is it?'

'I honestly don't know, Mils. I told you it must have slipped out of my pocket.'

'Griffin. Please. I need my phone.'

'Probably not as badly as I need mine.'

'What?' Amelia scowled at Ross, her tone impatient and clearly not in the mood for him.

'His phone isn't working after he fell in the loch,' Jonah told her.

'Oh, right.' She didn't look too bothered by that and he guessed she was thinking it was probably karma after he had voted for Griffin to keep her phone. 'Jonah? Can you please call my number?'

Jonah did as she asked and there was silence as they all listened for her ringtone.

When it didn't come, Griffin gave a smug smile. 'I told you I didn't have it.'

'You are so full of shit.' Amelia stomped out into the hallway, coming back moments later with her coat and boots. She dumped the boots on the floor as she shrugged into her jacket.

'Where are you off to now?' Griffin sounded amused.

'To try and find it.'

'Sure you don't want me to come with you?'

'NO!'

'I'll go with her.'

Griffin's eyes darted between Jonah and Amelia, as if he didn't trust the two of them alone together. *Probably wise.* Jonah quashed the thought, tried to keep his expression neutral. He glanced at Amelia as she bent down to lace her boots, getting a full view of her shapely bum, and quickly averted his gaze.

'You think you may have dropped it by the boats, right?' he asked. Griffin had seen him looking and so he was keen to get his mind on to safer topics.

'Yes.' Griffin gave them both another look, this time his expression more curious, but he didn't say anything, instead grabbing the rucksack and following Ross from the room, much to Jonah's relief.

Fuck, am I really that transparent?

He followed Amelia out of the front door and down towards the wooded path that led through the trees to the loch, neither of them saying a word until they were out of sight of the house.

The sun had broken through the clouds and was illuminating the trail ahead. Along with the chirping of the birds in the trees and the scent of the forest pines, it conveyed a feeling of hope and of beginning. Suggesting everything was starting over, that it was going to be okay.

But of course it wasn't.

'He did this on purpose,' Amelia grumbled as he eventually fell in step beside her.

'Maybe.' Jonah wouldn't be surprised if Griffin had, but he was trying to stay neutral, not wanting to antagonise her further. Griff was being a dick, but it was easier for everyone if he and Amelia weren't at each other's throats the whole weekend. 'Let's give him the benefit of the doubt though until we check down by the loch.'

She huffed a little, but didn't argue, and as they walked along in companiable silence, Jonah studied her, feeling safe to do so for the first time since they'd arrived.

It was the paranoia and the guilt, he understood that. What had happened between them had been years ago, but Amelia had been Griffin's fiancée at the time and although it had been just one kiss, she had then broken off her engagement. He couldn't help but feel responsible for that, even if he didn't know for sure if he was the reason why she had ended things.

He had secretly been in love with Amelia Abery since meeting her on their first day of university. They had quickly become friends, and he remembered how he had been working up to making a move when Griff had swooped in. Ten years later, when Amelia was weeks away from marrying Griffin, Jonah had decided to finally tell Amelia how he felt, and just to make sure he was the shittiest friend possible; it had been at Griffin's birthday bash.

He hadn't expected her to dump Griffin; but she did, and then she had disappeared off the radar. Apart from the odd WhatsApp message, and the Zooms that Nancy had set up, Jonah hadn't had any contact with her since. But now they were here, at yet another birthday celebration for Griffin, and finally alone together.

'What are you doing here, Amelia?'

He had been taken aback when he heard she was coming. Although she was back in contact with Griffin, the whole called-off wedding thing was always going to be hanging between them. It had shocked Jonah that Griffin had wanted her here, but also that Amelia had agreed to come.

If she was surprised by his question she didn't look it, her golden gaze locking onto his as she answered.

'I almost didn't come. After I called off the wedding I didn't think Griffin and I would ever be at a point where we could be in the same room together again, which was shit because the six of us go way back. I accepted I had been the one to upend things and it was on me to step away. Then I bumped into him before the first lockdown, and I thought enough time had passed. He was with Chantelle, and he no longer seemed angry with me. We ended up having dinner, I met Chantelle, and he seemed different... happy. When he invited me I immediately said no. I thought it would be too weird, but he kept trying to persuade me to come and he said you guys were going to be here... and, well, I missed you.'

Jonah's heart hitched. By 'you' she probably meant the whole gang. The way she had said it though, the way she was holding his gaze, it felt like she had meant it only about him. He thought back to that night again and the mixed signals. She had told him it was too late, but then she had ended her engagement. Still though, she hadn't contacted him.

Truth was, perhaps he should have reached out again, but he had laid his heart on the line and been honest with her once. At the time he wasn't sure he could do that again and face a second rejection.

There were so many things he wanted to say to her now, but he still wasn't sure how she felt about everything, about him, so he decided to play it safe.

'We all missed you too,' he told her, keeping his tone light and breaking eye contact as he focused on the path ahead. 'It's not much further.'

He had told her how he had felt, but after dumping Griffin she hadn't come to find him. She had disappeared.

Probably because you already had a girlfriend.

'I'm sorry to hear things didn't work out with Nicole.'

Was she a fucking mind reader? 'Thanks. It had been on the cards for a while.'

He had tried to make the relationship work, but if he was brutally honest, deep down he had always known that Nicole wasn't a forever thing. He liked her a lot and they had enjoyed plenty of good times. He had cared for her, okay, maybe loved her, but no, he hadn't ever been in love with her, and it probably would have been a whole lot kinder if he had ended things a long time ago, instead of letting it limp on.

'Are you seeing anyone else at the moment?'

Is she fishing or just making conversation? 'Nope. You?'

She shook her head, a thoughtful look on her face, though she didn't say anything for a few moments. Was she thinking back to that night in the bar at Griffin's birthday? The night everything had changed?

'I thought Chantelle was going to be here,' she said eventually.

'Didn't Griff tell you it was just the six of us?'

'No, he didn't, and he never corrected me when I assumed she was coming.' She looked at Jonah again. 'I should have stayed away. I thought he had changed, but he's still the same old Griff. I'm really not sure why he invited me.'

Jonah wasn't either, but he didn't say that. Instead he said, 'Well, I'm glad you came. I really have missed you.'

Amelia's face softened, her lips curving, and she was about to say something when there was a noise up ahead. She glanced towards the loch, then back at Jonah.

'There's someone down there.'

'It's probably just people fishing,' he told her, unfazed. There had been two boats when they had come down earlier, so someone else obviously used the loch.

She seemed anxious though as they approached the clearing and without really thinking about it he caught hold of her hand, giving it a reassuring squeeze. Her eyes widened slightly, but when he went to let go, she surprised him by tightening her grip.

As they stepped out of the shadow of the trees, he spotted the men by the boats.

'Jonah?' Amelia's voice was barely a whisper. 'It's them.'

He didn't have to ask who she meant by 'them'. The place was remote enough for him to know it was the three men who had come to the house and threatened her, and he didn't like the

93

way they were looking towards the loch as they talked, as if they knew Dougie McCool was out there.

But that was probably just his guilty conscience. They didn't know that at all. As far as McCool's brother knew, he and Amelia were just two innocent holidaymakers out for a morning walk.

'Come on. Let's go check for your phone.' He tugged on Amelia's hand, pausing when she tugged right back.

'I don't want to go down there, not while they are about.'

'It'll be okay. They don't know what happened. We look more guilty if we try to avoid them.'

'I don't care. Please, Jonah.'

Reluctantly he let her pull him back into the shelter of the trees. 'I thought you wanted to find your phone?'

'I do, but maybe we can come back in a bit when they're gone.'

'Which might be sooner rather than later,' Jonah told her, glancing over her head and seeing the three men starting to make their way back towards the woods.

'What?'

'Come on.' He pulled on her hand, leading her off the main path and through the brush, positioning them so they were hidden behind the wide trunk of an old oak tree.

'Why are we–'

Jonah pressed a finger against her lips. 'Shh.'

She tensed against him when they heard the crunch of footsteps then voices.

'So what's the plan now?' A thick Scottish accent. 'He's not here.'

'You're sure you have the right house?'

'He never gave us the address, but it has to be.'

'She said she hadn't seen him.'

'So maybe she was lying. The tracker on his phone put him right there before it died.'

What?

Dougie McCool hadn't had a phone on him. They had checked.

Jonah kept his eyes on Amelia, willing her to stay quiet. It was so silent out here in the woods, just the slightest sound could alert the men to their presence.

'So why hasn't he made contact?'

'How the fuck would I know? But if he's in there I'm going to find out. I'm done playing games. He told me he had my money and I want it back.'

11

ROSS

When Ross had first arrived back from the loch, his early morning wet walk of shame had put him in a foul mood. He had been uncomfortable, couldn't stop shivering and his teeth were chattering, both with cold and the urge to punch Griffin in the face.

Of course, he never would. Griffin would swat him like a fly. So instead, the anger had continued to build and, ignoring the others, he had stomped up to his room as soon as they arrived back at the house, desperate to get out of his sodden clothes.

Standing under the hot shower spray, the temperature turned so high it was scalding his skin, he had winced against the pain, even as he welcomed it.

At least it was making him feel something other than the anger. Anger towards Griffin, anger towards the others for allowing Griff to ridicule him.

He told himself he had been an idiot to think he could make this weekend work. He never should have come. He wasn't the runty kid at university anymore. He was their equal. Better than their equal. His company was successful, he was respected and admired, and with his stature, his confidence had grown.

Why then, when the group got together, did he always revert to his role of the underdog, of the stooge to Griffin King's jokes?

It was time to get out of here. The body was in the loch and there was no need for him to stick around.

Yes, okay, they were supposed to be here for Griffin's birthday, but it hardly felt right having a celebration after everything that had happened.

But then he had walked back into the main living room where they were all arguing about what to do with the money and it had given him a blinder of an idea.

He had noticed the loose floorboards in his room last night. They had irritated the fuck out of him, and he couldn't help but wonder if Griffin had given him this shitty back bedroom on purpose.

The loose panels would be the perfect place to hide the rucksack full of cash though.

Suddenly it was worth sucking up to Griffin for just a little while longer.

'What about beneath the floorboards?' he had suggested. 'There are a couple of loose panels in my room. We could hide the bag under them.'

Griffin had nodded in approval, liking the idea. 'That would work better, I think. Good idea, mate.'

And just like that, they were back on good terms. Or so Griffin thought.

It was a pattern. One that Ross had repeated for far too long, and it had cost him dearly. There were things Griffin had done, that Ross had allowed him to do, that had been at too high a price. Things that couldn't be undone, that he could never get back. This had gone on for far too long and today, at long last, he was finally going to break the cycle.

The rucksack was now hidden in his room, so he had access

to the money. Because that was the thing. Griffin might treat him like a fool, but he still trusted Ross over the others to have his back.

Foolish. Because Ross was now going to betray him. He would sneak out quietly and he intended to take all of the cash with him.

He didn't need it. In fact, he was the only one who really didn't. But that wasn't the point.

Griffin might come from a wealthy family, and currently wanted for little, but his career choice of being a personal trainer didn't bring in a huge salary, and Ross knew his father was getting sick of giving him handouts to fund his extravagant lifestyle. Barnaby King had threatened more than once to cut him off and when that day eventually came, Griffin was going to be in trouble.

As for the others, they could certainly do with the cash. By taking the money, Ross would be getting his revenge. And once he was gone, they were going to be stranded here.

Although the plan was to clean Billy's car up, were they really going to be able to get all of the blood out of the seats? Ross couldn't see any of them wanting to drive it anywhere.

He would leave when none of them were paying attention and head south of the border. Check in at that little hotel he liked in the Lake District. He could enjoy a nice meal and a good bottle of red and put this ghastly mess of a weekend behind him, remind himself he was better than this. Better than the rest of them.

Being around Griffin and the others made him weak. It was a toxic atmosphere and one he couldn't wait to leave. He didn't intend to have contact with any of them for a very long time after this. And honestly, what could they do about it?

They could hardly report him to the police. At least not without implicating themselves.

They didn't deserve the money and okay, neither did Ross, but that wasn't a problem. Maybe, in time, he would reach out to Nancy, and offer to share some with her. She was the only one he was bothered about taking it from. As for the rest, well maybe he would give it to a charity or something. It might help ease his conscience, even though he wasn't quite sure what he should be feeling guilty about.

Yes, a man was dead and yes, they had hidden his body, but they hadn't killed him. Well, okay, Billy had killed him. It had been an accident though. And Ross might have now implicated himself, but he had hardly had a choice. Just being connected to Billy was bad enough. He simply couldn't afford to get caught up in this mess.

Dougie McCool was already dead. And it wasn't as if he had been a law-abiding citizen.

No, it was better that no one ever found out what happened to him. Especially not his brother and his friends. If they came back looking, as Amelia seemed to think they would, Ross didn't want to be here.

He took his opportunity a short while later. Nancy and Griffin were in the garage looking at the car and Amelia and Jonah weren't yet back from the loch. Griffin had insisted that Billy was going to help clean up the car, but it took just fifteen minutes of his whining for that plan to change, and Billy was now engrossed in daytime TV and already on his second (or was that his third) beer.

The man was a fucking liability.

After putting his phone in rice, Ross disappeared back into his room, relieved that Griffin hadn't dragged him into the garage on his clean-up mission. He was probably figuring he should cut Ross some slack after the morning dip. That would be typical Griff. Push Ross a little too far, but then reel him in again by doing something nice and convince him that he had overreacted. It was a familiar pattern.

He made sure he locked the door, not wanting to risk the others barging in, and dropped to his hands and knees, carefully removing the loose floorboards.

He emptied his briefcase first, putting his work documents on top of the socks and jumpers in his weekend bag, before transferring the bank notes from the rucksack into the case. As he did so, he kept licking his lips nervously. It was one thing wanting to do this, but another actually going through with it, and as he locked the briefcase, his bowels knotted uncomfortably.

There was no going back now.

And he had the most difficult bit to still do, which was get out of the house unnoticed.

In his head that had been easy, but now he worried about getting the case to his car. That Billy might see him and alert Griffin, or worse still, that Griffin might be back from the garage and see Ross himself.

If he caught him before he was in his car, Ross knew he would be in serious trouble.

And God help him if Griff found out he had taken the money. The consequences were unthinkable.

Ross couldn't delay leaving though. Amelia and Jonah were still out, and he really needed to go before they returned, aware it would be even more difficult to leave if there were more people in the house.

As he psyched himself up to unlock the bedroom door, he reached for his damp jacket, feeling inside the pocket for his keys.

They weren't there.

What the hell?

He checked his other pocket, just to be sure, and found it

empty, before mentally retracing his steps and remembering how he had picked them up from the kitchen table before they left for the loch, not trusting Amelia with them.

So where the hell were they?

He hadn't removed them, so had they fallen out his pocket? He hadn't heard them hit the ground.

He did a quick panicky check around the room, soon realising they weren't there, which meant they could be any-bloody-where on the trail between the house and the loch.

The loch.

Fuck.

For a moment Ross actually thought his heart had stopped beating, but then it started thumping crazy hard in his chest, his skin heating up and the simple act of breathing became a chore.

Griffin had pushed him in the water. Well, pushed, or he had fallen. Either way, it was still Griffin's fault.

Were his keys in the loch?

He had swum down to check on Dougie McCool's body after Griffin refused to let him back on the boat and hadn't even given the keys a thought.

Without them, he couldn't leave. The fob was on the key ring, and he needed it to get in the car and to start it. It was too far to walk. And his keys, if he had lost them in the loch where Dougie's body was, wouldn't that implicate him if the police ever found the man?

He broke out in a sweat now, realising that somehow he had to get his keys back. But how?

He couldn't use his phone to call for help. He was effectively trapped here.

If McCool's brother comes back...

No, Ross couldn't bear to even think about that.

He needed to come up with a new plan and fast.

12

NANCY

'He knows what you did. We need to get out of here.'

Amelia didn't waste any time getting to the point when she barged into the garage where Nancy and Griffin were still trying to scrub the stains out of the back seat of Billy's car, frustratingly with little success.

Jonah was hot on her tail, trying to hold her back. He clearly didn't want Amelia spilling whatever information they had, catching her by the arm and pulling her back, hissing her name, which had Nancy paying attention to what her friend was saying.

Secrets were dangerous and, while Amelia could be a drama queen, Jonah's reaction suggested that perhaps this was something they did need to know about.

'Slow down. Who knows what we did?'

'Kenny McCool,' Amelia snapped impatiently, as if Nancy was stupid. 'We saw him down by the loch.'

'You spoke to him?'

'God, no. He didn't realise that we were there, but we heard him talking.'

'About what?' Griffin asked. He was now paying attention

too.

'Dougie's phone. There's a tracker on it.'

'Dougie didn't have a phone on him, we checked.'

'Well clearly you didn't check thoroughly enough. Kenny said it had tracked him to this house.'

Nancy leaned against the bonnet of the car and glanced from Amelia to Jonah, who gave a brief nod, confirming Amelia wasn't making this up. This wasn't good. It wasn't good at all.

'It has to be in Billy's car somewhere,' Griffin announced, rummaging on the floor under the back seat.

'Or not.'

They all looked at Jonah, waiting for him to elaborate.

'McCool said the tracker had put his brother at the house right before the phone died.'

'Your point?' Griffin asked, looking annoyed as he climbed out of the car.

Jonah huffed impatiently. 'Did the phone really die as soon as Billy got here? Or did someone switch it off?'

Nancy saw the cogs turning as Griffin realised what Jonah meant. One of them had McCool's phone.

'But why?' he eventually asked. 'It makes no sense.'

'One of us has it.'

'Who?'

Griffin glanced at Nancy, and she was quick to hold her hands up. 'Don't look at me. I didn't take it.' No way was she taking the hit for this.

'There's more,' Amelia piped up before the finger of blame could be pointed anywhere else.

'I can't wait.'

'Shut up, Griffin. This is important. They know about the money.'

'What do you mean?'

'She means the money belongs to McCool's brother,' Jonah said. 'It's why he is trying to find Dougie.'

'Oh. Fuck.'

'Oh, fuck, indeed.'

'They know we took it?' Nancy demanded. Her heart was thumping. This wasn't good.

'I don't think so. They're trying to find McCool to get it back. And they think he is here.'

Fuck. This really wasn't good.

Nancy looked at Griffin, could see Jonah and Amelia were too. He had always been the leader of sorts. Not by election, but because it was in his nature to take over, and the rest of them seemed to let him. But right now he had a blank expression, seeming floored by the news.

'We need to throw him off the scent,' Jonah announced, stepping into the role.

'How are we going to do that?' Amelia asked.

'Well, for starters we need to put the money back in the rucksack, then I suggest we dump it somewhere, at least a mile or two away. We can't do anything about the tracker showing he was here, but if they find the bag, they will at least assume he left here alive.'

Nancy nodded. Frustrating as it was about the money, he was right. They had to get rid of it. Kenny McCool wasn't going to leave them alone until he had found it.

'We can use Ross's car, head a mile out and dump the rucksack on the side of the road. Somewhere where they are likely to spot it.'

'Do you think it will work?'

Jonah shrugged at Amelia. 'I can't say for sure, but it's better than any alternative plan we have.'

Griffin mulled over the idea, a flash of annoyance passing over his face. He seemed not to like that it had come from Jonah.

He clearly couldn't think of a better alternative though, because he slammed the back door of Billy's car shut. 'Come on, I think we need to have a group chat.'

He led the way back into the house, trying to re-establish control, yelling to Billy and Ross to join them, then once the six of them were gathered in the living room, he updated them on the situation with McCool's brother before laying out Jonah's plan, as if it had been his own idea.

Both men seemed panicked. Billy's eyes widening at what might happen if Kenny McCool found out Billy had killed his brother, while Ross had turned a deathly white. He looked the most nervous of them all, unable to keep still and looking like he might throw up and Nancy found herself watching him closely.

'Maybe we should just go,' Amelia suggested. 'Let's get the hell out of here before those thugs come back.'

'And leave Billy's car sitting in the garage, covered in bloodstains?' Griffin rolled his eyes at her.

'Can't we take it with us?'

'Not until we clean it up some more. There's still bits of the dead guy on the back seat.'

When Amelia screwed up her nose in disgust, Billy chipped in. 'I'm gonna need the car to get home, Griff. How much longer do you think it will be?'

'What am I? Your fucking valet?'

'That's not what I meant.'

Jonah shook his head, getting up from the sofa. 'Anyone want anything from the fridge?'

'I could use another beer.'

'You don't need any more beer, Billy. It's 11am. I'll get you a bottle of water.'

Billy scowled at Jonah before turning back to Griff. 'I just wondered what the timescale was. How long it was going to take to clean.'

'I guess it depends. It'd be quicker if you got off your arse and actually helped us.'

'But you know I'm not good at stuff like that.'

'How the hell did you get to be thirty-three years old, Billy? You need to start taking responsibility for your own cock-ups.'

'Enough!' Nancy held her hands up. She couldn't be doing with all this pointless arguing. 'We have another car, remember? Two people can go in Billy's car and the rest of us can ride with Ross.'

It made sense and she was certain the others would agree, but then the laugh started, low, mocking and filled with bitterness, and her attention swung to Ross.

'What?' she snapped sharply, not in the mood for his sarcasm.

'My car won't be going anywhere.'

'Why not?'

'Because I've lost the fob.'

'How?'

Ross glared at Griffin. 'I guess my keys must have fallen out of my pocket when arsehole here pushed me in the loch.'

They were all silent for a moment as they absorbed that information and Nancy began to understand why Ross was so edgy. His keys were gone and there was no way he was going to find them if they were in the loch.

'Firstly, I did not push you. You fell.' Griffin's tone was tight with anger. 'Secondly, you were a bit bloody stupid taking them out on the boat.'

'Can we start the car without the fob?' Amelia asked.

'This isn't a fucking movie.'

'I was just asking the question.'

Griffin huffed loudly. 'Well unless you have anything useful to contribute, which we all know you never do, perhaps you should keep your pointless little suggestions inside that empty head of yours.'

Ouch.

Nancy had her own gripes with Amelia, and she understood Griffin had his reasons for being bitter, but that was harsh.

Amelia's eyes flashed hot with temper. 'You are such an arsehole.'

'Maybe I am. But we both know I'm right. Just sit there quietly and look pretty, Mils. We all know that's what you do best.'

Jonah caught the comment as he rejoined the group. 'Don't talk to her like that!' he snapped; his tone heated. He tossed a bottle of water at Billy, who looked at it in disgust, before twisting the cap on his own bottle.

'Why not?' Griffin challenged. 'It's the truth. And why the hell do you have such a problem with it anyway? Do you think I haven't noticed you keep defending her? Just what is the deal with you two, Jonah? Is there something I should know?'

The room fell silent as Jonah exchanged a brief glance with Amelia.

Griffin was right to be suspicious. Nancy was too. She had travelled up to Scotland with the pair of them and had been aware of the tension between them. At the time she had assumed it was mostly from Amelia because it was the first time they were going to be together as a group since she had jilted Griffin, but the continual shared glances and how Jonah was quick to rush to Amelia's defence each time Griffin made a jibe had her now thinking maybe it was more.

Jonah took a long swig of his water, buying time, then scowled at Griffin. 'I'm her friend,' he said. 'It feels like you only invited her this weekend to tear her down.'

So he was going with denial. Nancy wasn't so sure.

'You have no idea why I invited her.' Griffin smiled tightly, his dark eyes still full of distrust, and for a moment Nancy thought he was going to push the issue, but then he turned to the rest of the group. 'Okay, so we need to dump the rucksack. We're going to have to do that on foot. But before we do, I'm going to need a show of faith from you all.'

Nancy narrowed her eyes as she wondered where the hell he was going with this. 'Meaning what exactly?'

'Your phones.'

He had already accused both Billy and Ross of having Dougie McCool's phone when they had first gathered around the sofas. Both men had, of course, vehemently denied it.

'What about our phones?' Jonah demanded.

'There is obviously a lot of distrust between us at the moment. Does one of us have McCool's phone? Is one of us going to call the police? Is one of us going to stab the others in the back?' Griffin made a point of looking at Jonah then Amelia when he added that.

To their credit, both kept their cool.

'So what are you proposing?' Jonah pushed.

'We all surrender our phones.'

'Are you stupid?'

'No, I am protecting us, as a group.'

'I think you're doing the exact opposite of protecting us,' Amelia pointed out. 'We need to sort transport and get the hell out of here.'

'Have you not listened to a word I've been saying?' Griffin slapped his palm against his head. 'Billy's car incriminates us. We can't just leave it.'

'So you drive it and the rest of us can get a taxi or a hire car.'

'Good luck with that, Mils. We're in the middle of nowhere.'

'It's 2022. If Amazon deliver here, and I'm pretty sure they do, I'm sure I can get a taxi.'

'We're not going anywhere until we've destroyed all evidence of McCool, have our story straight, and know that we can one hundred per cent trust each other, so stop bleating on about taxis and leaving, and accept we are all in this together.'

'I didn't do anything.'

'You didn't stop us either.'

Ooh, another low blow. Nancy winced for Amelia as Griffin smirked.

'You bastard.'

'You really think you'll get away without going to jail if we're caught?' He paused to let that sink in. 'Sorry, Mils. You're a part of this whether you like it or not.'

'What's the plan with the phones, Griffin?' Frustratingly he was right, and Nancy was keen to move forward.

He turned to face her. 'There's a safe. I say we put them all in there.' He glanced around the group, gauging their reactions. 'We have to trust each other. And without our phones we know that no one is going to make any calls or do anything stupid. Once we are in the clear then you all get them back.'

Ross was first to respond. 'Well, mine is in that bowl of rice over there,' he muttered, his tone sarcastic. 'Help yourself. It's no longer any good to me.'

Griffin nodded but didn't bite, instead looking to Billy.

'Really, Griff? You know you can trust me. You don't need my phone.'

'Hand it over, Billy.'

They all knew Billy was constantly looking at his phone and that taking it would be like removing a limb. He was also the biggest liability.

'I won't tell anyone what's going on. Please let me keep it.'

'You mean you haven't updated Twitterland yet?' Ross smirked.

It was Billy's favourite medium and he regularly tweeted his

18,000 followers, not just on updates of his band, but his personal life too.

'That's not fair. I'm not that irresponsible.'

Nancy sniggered at that and was aware of Jonah and Ross both laughing too.

'The phone, now, Billy.' Griffin held his hand out. 'You're the one who got us into this situation, so you need to lead by example.'

Billy pouted, for a moment looked like he was going to continue arguing, then let out a petulant huff, before reluctantly doing as he was told. As soon as the phone was out of his hand, he sat back, his shoulders slumped and a scowl on his face. His expression reminding Nancy of a kid who had just dropped his ice cream or burst his balloon.

She wasn't keen on giving up her phone either, but Griffin was right, this was to protect them all, so she passed her handset to him without any complaint.

That left Amelia and Jonah – and Griffin had already taken Amelia's phone from her and had lost it – as she was quick to remind him.

'You're really not going to let that drop, are you?'

'Do you blame me? First you steal my phone then you apparently lose it.'

'It was an accident.'

'I don't believe you!'

'And I really don't care what you believe. Jesus fucking Christ, Mils. I had forgotten what a pain in the arse you are.'

'Shame you didn't remember you felt that way before dragging me out here!'

Griffin opened his mouth to reply, seemed to reconsider whatever he was about to say, then closed it again.

'Why did you invite her, Griffin?' The question came from Jonah, his tone hushed. Nancy was pretty certain they all wanted to know the answer to this question. She had been shocked when she had found out Amelia was on the guest list for Griffin's birthday weekend, especially as his own fiancé hadn't been invited, and she had wondered more than once how Chantelle felt about that.

Or doesn't she know Amelia is here?

Jonah had asked the question on the spur of the moment, and she could tell from the regret on his face that he was wishing he had kept his mouth shut, that he could take it back.

Griffin didn't answer immediately, as his gaze flickered between Amelia and Jonah, his expression unreadable.

Were Nancy's suspicions right? Was something going on between the pair of them? Did Griffin know?

For a moment she thought he was going to confront them, but then he simply answered, 'I wanted it to be a reunion. The six of us back together again.'

Jonah's shoulders relaxed slightly, most probably with relief, though his olive eyes were still full of distrust, while Amelia was ashen.

Something was definitely going on there and Nancy's mind was racing. Pieces of a puzzle slowly slotting into place. There were secrets here and she didn't like them. Secrets could be dangerous. 'We need your phone, Jonah.' She held her hand out, softening her request with a half-smile. 'Yours is the last one.'

He looked up, his eyes locking on hers, and in that moment she knew, and she could see that he knew she knew too.

She thought he was going to protest about his phone, but that would only make the others more suspicious. Instead he silently handed it over, though she could tell he was seething.

'So what's your plan now, Griffin?' Amelia demanded. 'You've taken everyone's phone, which frankly I think is stupid, and you've effectively made us sitting ducks for when Kenny McCool returns.'

111

'What I have done, Mils, is put us all on a level playing field.'

'Really? Where's your phone then? Or do you get to keep it?'

A muscle twitched in Griffin's jaw as he stared at her, reaching into his pocket and placing his phone with the others on the table. 'Trust,' he said simply.

'And I suppose we are *trusting* you to safeguard the key to the safe too,' Jonah muttered.

'It's a number lock. We need to set the combination.'

'So who is going to do that? It's not going to be you; I can tell you right now.'

'Who do you suggest then, Jonah? It's not going to be you either.'

'How many digits?' Ross asked.

'Six I think.'

'So two people then. Three numbers each.'

Griffin and Jonah both pondered that idea and didn't seem unhappy with it.

'Who?' Griffin asked, casting his eyes over the group.

'I don't mind,' Billy volunteered, perking up.

'Not you.'

'The girls,' Jonah suggested. 'Three numbers each.'

Griffin considered and nodded. 'Okay.'

That suited Nancy. Knowing part of the combination would give her that little bit of control. Amelia seemed okay with it too.

'So we put the phones in the safe,' Amelia pushed. 'What next?'

'Next we get the rucksack and dump it as I suggested.'

Actually, it had been Jonah's suggestion, but it appeared Griffin had taken it as his own.

'Who goes?' Nancy asked, her heartbeat racing. 'I can do it.'

If she helped herself to a few wads of cash before ditching the rucksack, would it really matter?

When Griffin seemed to consider, she quickly added, 'I can go on foot. I used to run track. I'm small and I'm fast. I will be quickest.'

'There should be two of us,' he eventually answered, and her heart sank. 'You and Jonah can go.'

'You're volunteering me?'

'You're in best shape.'

'Says the personal trainer.' When Griffin smiled wryly at that, Jonah let out a sharp laugh. 'Yeah, okay, to hell with it. I'll go.'

Griffin nodded. 'Ross, go get the rucksack. Nancy, Mils, let's get these phones in the safe.'

Nancy and Amelia followed Griffin through to a room with a bureau and bookshelves. They had seen it only briefly when Griff had given them a quick tour of the place when they arrived.

After bundling the phones inside, Nancy waited for Amelia to set her three digits of the combination before stepping forward to do her own. Frustration burned at her gut that Griffin was making Jonah go with her to dump the money. It seemed such a waste to just leave it all sitting on the roadside. Maybe she could talk Jonah into splitting the cash. Either that or could she use blackmail? He had secrets that she knew he wouldn't want exposed.

The others had left the room while she set the combination and once the safe was securely locked, she went back through to the empty kitchen area, opening the fridge and pouring herself a glass of juice. As she sipped it she pondered.

Griffin, Amelia, Jonah, Ross and Billy. The five of them had been her friends for years, but that friendship was fracturing.

They all had their weaknesses and they all had their secrets, but whose secret was worth the most to them?

Her mind made up, she went in search of the person she felt was most valuable to her, deciding it was best they had the conversation now before the money was dumped. When Ross's eyebrows raised in question as to why she was there, she closed the door behind her to give them some privacy.

'We need to have a talk.'

13

ROSS

The scream pierced Ross's ears, and it was followed by a sickening thud. Racing down the stairs he saw Nancy lying face down on the hall floor, her body twisted at an awkward angle.

Fuck!

His heart thumped furiously as he dropped to his knees, sickness and fear slamming into him when he realised she wasn't moving.

'Oh Jesus, Nancy?'

Was she okay?

The trickle of blood on the floor suggested she wasn't, and he searched his panicked brain, trying to figure out how to deal with this whole mess. He had been angry with her, but he had never wanted this to happen.

He had his head in his hands, was struggling to keep it together, and didn't hear Griffin and Billy approaching from behind.

'Nancy?'

'Ross? What the fuck have you done?'

'What? I didn't do anything. I heard a scream and found her.'

'Did she fall?'

'I think that's pretty bloody obvious, Billy.'

'I was just asking the question, Griff.'

'Question is, was she pushed?' Griffin looked at Ross again and angry heat flushed into Ross's cheeks. Did they know he had been with Nancy?

'I already told you I found her like this! If she was pushed, how do we know it wasn't you?'

'Oh my God. Nancy?' Amelia was down on her knees, even as Jonah (who had conveniently appeared at the same time) tried to hold her back.

'What the hell happened?'

'We don't know,' Ross told her, his tone calmer than he felt. He might be harbouring secrets, but he wasn't the only one. He just had to stay calm. No one knew about the conversation he and Nancy had just had or that she had tried to blackmail him. 'We found her like this.'

'We need to roll her over. Jonah, go get some towels. Billy, get one of the sofa cushions.'

'Can we do this without wrecking the place, please?' Griffin grumbled. 'I have to pay for damages.'

No one responded to his unnecessary comment, other than Jonah, who rolled his eyes, shaking his head as he went to fetch the towels. Amelia was too preoccupied with Nancy, while Billy appeared to be in shock or stoned. Ross honestly couldn't tell.

Had they really all become so desensitised to Griffin's lack of tact?

'Cushion, Billy.'

'What? Oh, yeah. Right. On it.'

Amelia appeared to have taken charge though Ross wasn't

aware she had any first aid training. 'Do you actually know what you're doing?'

'She used to watch *Casualty*,' Griffin muttered sarcastically.

'I'm trying to check for her pulse,' Amelia answered, ignoring him.

'And?' Ross was aware his tone was impatient. He needed to know if Nancy was going to be okay.

His nerves were on a knife's edge, and it wasn't just because of the whole Nancy thing. He couldn't flee, as breaking his phone and losing his key fob had effectively made him a prisoner here, and of course there was the issue of the money. He was terrified that Griffin was going to find out it had gone.

At the moment Griff seemed preoccupied with Nancy, but for how long?

'I don't know. I can't find one,' Amelia told them.

'She's bleeding really badly for fuck's sake!' For the first time there was a hint of panic in Griffin's tone, and Ross looked at the puddle now oozing under Nancy's head.

Oh Jesus.

'Out of the way, Mils.' Griffin decided to take charge, pushing Amelia to one side and checking for a pulse himself.

'Anything?' Ross was aware his voice was far too high-pitched.

'I can feel a really faint one.'

Billy returned at that moment with the cushion. 'Is she going to be okay?'

'She's alive, but she's bleeding really badly.'

'We need to get her to a hospital,' Jonah pointed out, coming back with the towels.

'Shall I call for help?'

'How the fuck are you going to do that, Billy?' Ross snapped, the stress of the situation now getting too much. 'By using the Bat Signal?'

'I meant should I call an ambulance.'

'How?'

Billy's expression was so vacant that for a moment Ross thought he wasn't going to get what he meant, but then the realisation dawned. 'Oh. Our phones. Oh, fuck.'

Seriously, how could someone be so stupid?

Griffin and Jonah had been helping Amelia get the cushion under Nancy's head and they had moved her onto her side, checking her airways and pressing a towel against the wound. Nancy was too pale, too still and at this point, looked close to death.

Emotions churned in Ross's stomach and the threat of tears burned his eyes, as everyone glanced at Billy who had just voiced out loud that none of them had access to a phone unless Nancy woke up. This whole weekend was turning out to be such a bloody mess.

'It's three digits.' Jonah was trying to be optimistic. 'Did either of you see what numbers she used?'

Griffin and Amelia both shook their heads.

'Okay, so it was probably a date or something memorable to her. Amelia has three digits. We just have to figure out the rest.'

Which could take forever, as they discovered a short while later.

Nancy was still lying in the hallway with Ross and Billy keeping an eye on her, while Amelia, Griffin and Jonah went to try the safe. He could tell from the look on their faces when they returned ten minutes later that their attempt to get it open had been unsuccessful.

'What are we going to do?' Amelia was pale-faced and on the verge of tears as she looked down at Nancy. 'She's going to die if we don't get her help.'

Jonah reached out to touch her arm and she turned towards him, wrapping her arms around his waist and letting him hold her, not seeming to give a shit that Griffin was watching, his nostrils flaring.

Whatever Griff was thinking though, he didn't voice it. Instead he turned his focus back to Nancy. 'The nearest hospital is over twenty miles away.'

'So we take her there.'

Griffin glared at Jonah over Amelia's head. 'How? Ross lost his key fob, remember?'

'There's Billy's car.'

'Which is a bloody crime scene.'

'Mostly on the back seat. There's not much damage to the car itself.'

'If we get pulled over, what the fuck are the police going to say?'

'Firstly, as you keep reminding us, we're in the middle of nowhere. Secondly, we put Nancy on the back seat. If by some remote chance we get pulled over, they will think it's her blood.'

'He has a point,' Ross agreed. No one was going to stop to question whether the blood had come from someone else.

'There's a neighbour just over three miles away,' Griffin said, seeming determined not to like the hospital idea because it had come from Jonah. 'They will have a phone. It will be quicker to go there, ask them to send an ambulance.'

'Damn it, Griff. Let's just take her to the hospital.'

'One person goes,' Griffin continued, ignoring Jonah's outburst, 'gets the neighbour to call an ambulance. It will be safer than taking Billy's car to a hospital where there is going to be CCTV.'

'Who goes?' Ross asked. 'I'm not comfortable driving Billy's car. It's covered in blood.'

It was the truth. If there weren't traces of Dougie McCool all over the car, he would be tempted to offer to go. Get the neighbours to call an ambulance then get the hell out of there.

'And I've been drinking,' Billy added helpfully.

'We draw straws,' Griffin suggested, ignoring them both.

Jonah shook his head. 'No, screw that. We're just wasting time. I'll go.'

'You're sure about that?'

'I'm sure.'

'No, it's better if Griffin goes,' Amelia argued. She still had hold of Jonah, but looked at her ex-fiancé now, her chin raised in challenge. 'He knows the area better.'

The look of cold anger on Griffin's face might have brought a smirk to Ross's in different circumstances. 'She makes a good argument,' he agreed.

'It's not difficult,' Griffin said through gritted teeth. 'He just has to follow the road. He's not going to get lost.'

'It's fine. I'll go.' Jonah looked down at Amelia. 'It's ten minutes down the road. I'll be back before you know it.'

A ghost of a smile touched Amelia's lips, but she looked like she didn't believe it. She didn't argue the point further though, casting a worried look down at Nancy. 'Do you think we should move her?'

Griffin shook his head. 'I don't think you're supposed to after a fall.'

'She can't be comfortable though.'

'I very much doubt she can feel it.' There was a sarcastic edge to Griffin's tone, but Amelia didn't bite.

Jonah ran his hand up and down her arm. 'It's best to leave her where she is. I'll be as quick as I can, I promise.' He looked to Billy. 'Where are your keys?'

'Here.' As Billy gormlessly patted his pockets, Griffin produced them from his, tossing them to Jonah who caught them easily.

'I'll be back in a bit. Someone stay with Nancy and keep an eye on her.'

Ross didn't miss Griffin's eyes narrow in suspicion when Amelia followed Jonah as he headed through to the garage, and he couldn't help the smirk that crept onto his face.

It was short-lived though as he remembered the money. Nancy had proven a distraction, but sooner or later Griffin was going to remember the rucksack of cash that was supposed to be under the floorboards. Somehow Ross needed to find out where the hell the briefcase was and replace it.

Because, like it or not, he was stuck here with the others for now.

He needed for Jonah to hurry up and get the ambulance and when they arrived, he intended to be the one who rode with Nancy to the hospital.

Although he hated the places, dreading the memories they conjured up, he wanted to be away from here and in particular, away from Griffin. And the sooner that happened, the better.

14

JONAH

Billy's car wasn't quite as bad as Griffin was making out. Yes, the back seat was still covered in dubious stains, but there was no sign of blood or damage to the outside of the Golf.

'Maybe we should put the seats down,' Amelia suggested. 'It would hide the blood.'

It was a good idea, though it would look less suspicious if they were down for a reason and Jonah glanced around the garage, spotting the paddleboards up against the far wall.

Perfect.

While Amelia sorted the seats he brought one of the paddleboards over, lifting it into the boot.

Much better.

It was unlikely Jonah would be stopped, but if he was, there was no reason to question why the seats were down. No one would ever guess the car had been involved in a collision or that the seats were bloodstained.

'Do you want me to come with you?'

Tempting as it was to say yes – he was keen for them to spend more time alone together – they had already roused

Griffin's suspicions. Jonah hadn't missed the look Griffin had given them both in the hallway when he had been comforting Amelia.

'It will be quicker if I go alone. Besides, you should stay and keep an eye on Nancy.'

When she looked disappointed with his answer, he wrapped his arms around her, pressing a kiss against her forehead. The gesture could be read as friendly, but they both knew it was more than that. Neither of them had talked about what had happened four years ago or why Amelia had abruptly called off her wedding to Griffin. It still hung between them and they were going to have to address it sooner or later.

Jonah was reluctant to let go of her, but Nancy needed help and quickly. Running his palms up and down her bare arms, he stepped back, breaking the contact, and climbed into the driver's seat. 'I'll be back before you know it.'

Amelia nodded, though said nothing, and she stood watching as he started the engine, pulling the car out of the garage. Jonah glanced at her in the rear-view mirror just before the driveway twisted into a tunnel of green and she disappeared from sight.

Griffin had given him directions, instructing him that once he had followed the narrow dirt-track lane down the main road (well, he had called it a main road, but Jonah remembered the bumpy taxi ride from the airport to the house and knew it was no more than another, albeit slighter wider, country lane) he should turn right and keep heading straight. Apparently there was a neighbouring property about three miles along the road.

Hopefully they would have a phone he could use.

The driveway from the property was long and winding, reminding him just how secluded it was. If Dougie McCool's brother returned, they could be in a lot of trouble.

Almost as an afterthought, Jonah remembered the rucksack of money. They were going to dump it on the road and he could have brought it with him, dropping it off somewhere en route. They had all been so preoccupied with Nancy, they had completely forgotten about it.

There was no time to go back for it though. Nancy needed to be the priority now. Dealing with the money would have to wait until later.

He had nearly reached the end of the long driveway when there were two thumps in quick succession, the whole vehicle vibrating violently, and Jonah eased his foot off the accelerator as he fought with the steering wheel to steady the car.

After swerving across the driveway, he gained control, coming to a halt a few yards before the gates.

He took a moment and heaved out a breath, before killing the ignition and climbing from the car. He spotted the problem immediately.

The front tyre – no, both front tyres – were flat.

What the fuck?

He ran a frustrated hand through his hair, glancing back down the driveway towards the house, looking for the source. Because there had to be a source, right? Both front tyres didn't just burst at the same time.

He found what he was looking for maybe thirty yards back, the row of metal spikes that were sticking up across the driveway, glinting in the sunlight that was cutting through a gap in the overhead trees.

Someone had put this down intentionally and his mind went to Kenny McCool, quite simply because there was no one else out here in the arse-end of nowhere, and Kenny was the only one who would possibly do this.

So the plan had been to prevent any cars from arriving or leaving, but why? What else was he planning to do?

Jonah was torn. He could jog back to the house and warn the others, but that would take time. Nancy needed help and fast. Besides, if he could get to a phone he could also arrange transport and get the rest of the group out of the house, hopefully before Kenny showed up.

Deciding it was best to carry on, he walked to the end of the driveway, pausing briefly to take in his surroundings.

The lane was narrow, high hedgerows on one side and woods on the other. He spotted a path that ran through the trees, almost parallel with the road, wondering if it would be safer to follow. Although there was no traffic, the road was winding, which reduced visibility. Given that Billy had already caused a fatality, Jonah decided he would rather not take his chances.

He stepped down from the road and into the woods, picking up pace as he hit the trail. Although he wasn't wearing the right gear for running, he found it easy enough to maintain a decent speed, the rhythm of his heartbeat and his steady breathing intermingled with the forest sounds of chirping birds and twigs crunching underfoot.

This place might be isolated, but it was beautiful, the lush greenery and earthy scents of the cool spring day making him wish he had time to enjoy the location.

Of course he didn't. Billy had screwed that up from the start.

Just as he hadn't had more time with Amelia. But then he couldn't blame Billy so much for that one. This weekend was always going to be tricky with Griffin around.

If... no, when they got out of this mess, he was going to make the effort to go see her, have that long overdue conversation about how things stood between them.

Jonah was single, Amelia too. For the first time since they were teenagers, they were both on the same page. Griffin was the only thing standing in their way, an obstacle they had both put there out of the sake of friendship; but after everything that had happened, Jonah was no longer sure he had any loyalty to Griff.

They had already wasted too much time. Jonah had been in love with Amelia Abery for longer than he could remember. He wanted her in his life, and he was pretty certain she felt the same. They would have the chat and they would figure it out.

But first they had to help Nancy.

Of the group, she was one Jonah was least close to. She had always been Amelia's brash American roommate and because he had been infatuated with Amelia, he had accepted Nancy as part of the package.

They had bonded though over the years and he was fond of her. He certainly didn't want to see anything happen to her. That thought on his mind, he picked up pace, knowing at the moment he was Nancy's only hope.

He was about halfway to the neighbouring property when, over the sound of his breathing, over the noise of his heavy footfall, as the soles of his boots hit the dirt track, he heard what he thought was an engine.

Was someone really driving down this goddamn deserted stretch of road?

Whoever they were, they were bound to have a phone. If he got close to the road and flagged them down, an ambulance could be on its way to the house in minutes.

As he paused running, started to pick his way through the undergrowth towards the verge, the vehicle rounded a corner and appeared on the road ahead. It was a pickup truck, and it was travelling slowly, as if looking for a turn-off. The only one close was the driveway to the house.

Jonah had no reason to be suspicious, but something niggled in his gut, telling him that this wasn't the right ride to flag down.

If he missed it, it was an opportunity gone to get help quickly to Nancy. Still though, he hesitated, remaining in the shadows of the trees as the truck drew closer.

It was the kid with the baseball cap he recognised. He was sitting closest, the window wound down and his arm hanging out, his narrow eyes skimming over the trees, even though he didn't seem to be focusing. Still, Jonah stepped back, not wanting to be seen.

There wasn't enough time for him to see Baseball Cap's friends, but he could hazard a good enough guess that one of them was Kenny McCool, and it appeared that they were heading back to the house, back to where they would see Billy's car with the flat tyres.

They had to be responsible for that. There was no other explanation.

Jonah was glad they had put the seats down, hoped Kenny and his friends wouldn't pay close enough attention to the car to spot the bloodstains.

More worryingly though, if they were heading back to the house, Amelia and the others could be in trouble. While it was tempting to turn back, was it really a wise idea?

Could he really take on Kenny and both of his mates? It was doubtful. No, he needed to go and get help and he had to be close now. Maybe a mile to go.

Get to the neighbouring house, call an ambulance, call the police.

Yes, they had done a bad thing, but right now all Jonah really cared about was knowing that Amelia was safe and getting help for Nancy. If there were consequences over what they had done, he would deal with them.

As the truck disappeared around a bend, he pushed his way through the nettles back to the path and picked up pace.

Kenny and his friends were heading back to the house, he was sure of it.

Which meant he needed to get help, and he needed to get it fast.

15

AMELIA

Jonah had only been gone for fifteen minutes and already Amelia was missing him.

Although they hadn't had a chance to spend much time alone together, he had been a buffer, helping to stick up for her whenever Griffin went on the offensive.

She was wishing now that she had insisted on going with him. Instead she had walked back through from the garage to a sly look and snide comments from her ex-fiancé and a brief dismissive glance from Billy who was now preoccupied by TV.

Ignoring them both, Amelia went through to the hallway to check on Nancy, hating that she had agreed to come on this stupid weekend. Griffin clearly hadn't forgiven her, despite what he had said, Billy wasn't taking any responsibility for ending a man's life, Ross had been off with her ever since he had arrived, and now her friend was seriously hurt, and they couldn't even call a bloody ambulance. She hadn't asked or wanted to be any part of this, and it was bothering her that she didn't understand the circumstances of Nancy's accident.

Had she tripped and fallen, or had she been pushed?

It had to have been an accident, right? This whole situation was unsettling her and making her jump to conclusions.

Nancy was still lying at the foot of the stairs, unmoving, the cushion under her head now soaked in blood, while Ross sat on the bottom step, his face in his hands.

'Jonah has gone to get help.'

Ross knew that already of course, but Amelia felt she had to say something to cut through the silence. He would have heard her approaching, yet he hadn't looked up and asking if he was okay seemed a little bit ironic given that it was obvious none of them were anything close to being okay.

For a moment she thought he was going to ignore her, but then he did glance up, daggers in his eyes, and Amelia had to stop herself from visibly wincing at his blatant hostility. 'I take it she hasn't reacted at all,' she asked, trying to mask her reaction.

'No,' he muttered coolly.

'Do you want me to sit with her for a bit?'

'I've got it.'

'Okay, well I'm going to put the kettle on. Do you fancy a cuppa?'

He gave a brief shake of his head.

She wanted to ask him what his problem was with her, but it didn't feel appropriate, not with Nancy in such a critical state. Instead she looked at her lifeless friend, her olive skin pale, and her thick glossy black hair matted down with blood. They had wrapped a towel around the top of her head, but it was already a deep red.

Blinking back tears, determined not to look weak in front of Ross or Griffin, she went back into the kitchen, heading straight for the kettle. 'Do either of you want a tea or coffee?' she asked, forcing herself to sound breezy as she filled it with water. She wasn't actually thirsty but seeing Nancy motionless on the floor made her feel so helpless. She needed to keep herself busy.

Billy waved a hand at her, though didn't bother to peel his eyes away from the TV. 'I'm good.'

'Griffin?' Amelia was determined to be civil to him.

'Tea please, Mils.' Polite, but still there was something mocking in his tone.

As she made the drinks he came and stood beside her, a little closer than she was comfortable with. 'Do you remember how I take it?' he asked, as she took mugs from the wall cupboard and reached for the teabags.

'Milk, but strong, with two sugars.' Amelia didn't bother looking at him as she said it. Of course she remembered. She had made him tea for years.

'That's right.' He sounded pleased. 'Good to know you do remember some things about us.'

That last comment sounded like a bit of a jibe, so she decided to ignore it. He was still standing in her personal space and that annoyed her. 'Why don't you go sit down and I'll bring your tea over?'

Griffin was quiet for a moment, though made no attempt to move. 'So do you know how Jonah takes his tea?' he asked eventually.

Amelia's shoulders tensed. What was that supposed to mean? She decided not to bite. Two could play this game. 'Does he drink tea now? I always thought he preferred coffee. Black, no sugar. Same as Nancy. Billy was always the big tea drinker. Three sugars.' She nodded to the beer bottle dangling from Billy's fingers. 'Looks like his tastes have changed though.'

She fished out the teabags and stirred sugar into one mug, which she pushed towards Griffin. Then she picked up the other and took it with her over to one of the armchairs.

Billy was watching football, but Amelia had little interest. She took a sip of her too hot tea, scalding her tongue. She just wanted Jonah to hurry up, get help for Nancy and get back here so she didn't feel so out of place.

'Do you see much of Jonah these days?' Griffin's tone was conversational, innocuous enough, though Amelia's shoulders tensed again. Why did he keep asking about Jonah? Did he know what had happened?

She dismissed the idea. Of course he couldn't know. What had happened had been four years ago. If he knew, he would have said something before now.

He had been watching them in the hallway, when Jonah had held her. It had to be that.

'No.' She kept her tone even. 'This is the first time I've seen him in ages.'

'Really?' He sounded incredulous, though didn't push it. 'He's split up with Nicole.'

'He said.'

'Oh, I bet he did.'

This was getting ridiculous now, all these sarcastic little comments. 'How is Chantelle, Griffin? I'm surprised she isn't here this weekend.'

'She's busy. Wedding stuff. I invited her, but she knew it was uni pals and I don't think she wanted to intrude on that.'

'Does she know you invited me?' It was a loaded question, but one Amelia was desperate to know the answer to. She took another sip of her tea and waited. Certain that he was looking at her she purposely avoided eye contact.

Griffin answered after a longer than necessary pause. 'Of course. You are part of the old gang.'

'And she was okay with that?'

'What, you think she is threatened by you?' Griffin's laugh was deep and condescending and had Amelia looking at him. 'Don't flatter yourself. You're not even a blip on her radar.'

'That's not what I meant!'

'She loves me, and she can't wait to marry me. I waited a long time before I proposed again, Amelia. I wanted to be sure it was the right person this time and that there would be no hiccups.'

He left that last word hanging there and she inwardly cringed. No, he definitely hadn't forgiven her.

Amelia really wasn't sure what else she could say to him or what else he was expecting from her. She had repeatedly apologised to him, both at the time and also when they met up again recently. As far as stupid ideas went, thinking this weekend would work was probably her most foolish.

Griffin hadn't forgiven her, and she guessed deep down that she didn't blame him. Her biggest mistake had been not ending things sooner, but of course it hadn't been that easy.

Unfortunately, when it came to Griffin, nothing ever was.

16

THEN

They had met the day she arrived at university. Loud and overly confident Nancy Perez was her new roommate. She had intimidated the shyer and slightly overwhelmed Amelia at first, as she worried their personalities were too different. It was Nancy who had suggested they head out to the pub after unpacking and, throwing herself in at the deep end, Amelia agreed.

It was while up at the bar getting drinks that she had bumped, quite literally, into him, spilling his pint everywhere.

She had seen him when he had first walked in the pub. He had been with Billy, and as they headed straight to the bar, she hadn't been able to help herself checking him out. Long and lean, his hair a dark mess of curls, and his bum toned in worn but snug jeans.

'Do you want another drink?' she offered, noticing Nancy had just about finished her cider.

'Does a bear shit in the woods?'

Smiling, Amelia made her way to the packed bar, jostling to get a space. They had been told about this place by one of the girls in their corridor and it was a typical student dive, rammed full of bodies, the cacophony of excited first day chatter filling the room, and the air scented with beer and the odour of light teenage sweat. By some miracle they had grabbed a table, albeit they were sharing it with another louder group, and glancing back at Nancy, Amelia could see she had already struck up conversation with a couple of the girls.

Nancy was going to have no trouble fitting in and making friends and Amelia hoped it would be that easy for her.

It was as she turned back that he stepped away from the bar, two full pints in his hands and Amelia had walked straight into him. She knocked his arm and both drinks went everywhere, some of it on her top, the bulk of it over his T-shirt.

'Oh my God. I am so sorry.'

She thought he was going to be angry with her, so it surprised her when his lips curved into an appealing grin. 'Don't worry about it. It was just an accident.'

'I've soaked you though.' Amelia spotted a wad of paper towels on the bar, grabbing a couple and attempting an embarrassing mop-up job on his chest, heat rising in her cheeks when his grin widened further, and she realised what she was doing; that she could feel the heat and the hardness of his chest beneath her palm.

'I'm sorry,' she said again. Jesus, he must think she was a real geek. Her cheeks were burning now as he studied her, and when she forced herself to glance up, she could see his eyes were an earthy shade of green, almost olive in colour. 'I'll buy you another couple of pints.'

'Honestly, there's no need.'

'Please. It was my fault. I'd like to.'

For a moment she thought he was going to argue with her, but then he nodded. 'Okay. Thank you. What's your name?'

'Amelia. Amelia Abery.'

'First day, right?'

135

'Yeah. It's exciting, but all a little bit nerve-wracking too. What about you?'

He had nodded again, his eyes not leaving her face. 'It will be fun. You'll see. We'll soon settle into a routine.'

If he shared any of her first day nerves, they weren't showing, and the way he was smiling at her, his full focus on her, had her heating up a little inside. There was no boyfriend on the scene. Amelia's last relationship, which hadn't even been that serious, had ended a few months before she had left to come to university. Was he flirting with her or just being friendly?

'You never told me your name.' She smiled back, figuring she would go for flirty too.

'No, I didn't.' The grin cranked up a notch. 'I'm Jonah.'

Jonah and Billy had ended up joining Amelia and Nancy, the conversation light and fun, and when Jonah had looked at Amelia as he casually suggested they all swap numbers, she couldn't help reading into it, convincing herself he definitely fancied her.

She saw him a handful of times over the next few weeks, though they were never alone, much to her annoyance, and the one time he did text her, asking if she fancied meeting up for a drink, a drunken Billy had crashed their table ten minutes after they arrived at the pub and ended up staying for the remainder of the evening.

There were several texts between them. Mostly banter, though Amelia was certain a few were flirty, but she didn't dare make the first move herself in case she had read everything wrong and ended up looking foolish.

It was at a Halloween party that things reached a head.

It was being held at the house Jonah shared with Billy and another friend, and he had messaged Amelia asking her if she wanted to come. Nancy was invited too and the pair of them had dressed up as Batman villains – Nancy as Catwoman and Amelia as Poison Ivy.

This was going to be the night, Amelia decided. She would have a drink for Dutch courage then make a move. She took extra care with her hair and make-up, wanting to channel a sexy Poison Ivy that she hoped would catch Jonah's attention.

Once ready, Nancy poured them both a vodka and Coke (heavy on the vodka) then they set off to the party.

All the way there, Amelia's belly was jittery with nerves. New places and people did that to her anyway, but there was the added pressure of knowing she was going to make her move if Jonah didn't do so first.

The party was already in full swing by the time they arrived, the door answered by a drunken stranger who promptly disappeared. Finding the kitchen and not recognising anyone, Amelia poured herself a large glass of the wine they had brought, while Nancy went about making friends, quickly vanishing through to another part of the house. A second glass of wine started to steady Amelia's nerves, though by now she was a little drunk.

She really needed to go and find Jonah.

Instead she had her first encounter with Griffin King.

He intercepted her as she headed through to the lounge, the crowds of people and the noise of the music starting to suffocate her.

'Hey, you okay?' He was dressed as Superman. Oh, the irony, she would come to realise later. But here he was a friendly concerned face in a sea of uncaring people.

'I think we need to get you outside for some fresh air,' he told her, leading her by the hand through the crowd and opening a door at the back of the house. Outside it was blessedly cool, the music slightly muffled and there were no crowds to overwhelm her.

'Stay here,' he instructed, sitting her down on a low wall. 'I'll go get you some water.'

Amelia watched him go and at the time was so grateful. He had looked after her that night, but she hadn't realised it was with an ulterior motive.

'What's your name?' he asked, returning and handing her the water, which she sipped gratefully at.

'Amelia.'

He had momentarily looked surprised then quickly recovered. 'Ah, the famous Amelia. Finally we meet.' When she looked confused, he elaborated. 'Jonah has mentioned you a few times.'

He had? This was great. He had talked about her with his friends.

'I'm Griffin. His housemate.'

'Griffin! Yes, he has mentioned you too.' It had only been briefly in passing, but alcohol made her feel she knew him so much better, and she rather overenthusiastically gave him a hug. 'It's so nice to finally meet you.'

He seemed pleased with that, moving nearer, and had Amelia been sober, she would have realised that he was misreading all of her signals. 'Is Jonah around? I haven't seen him,' she asked as Griffin slipped his arm round her.

'He's inside somewhere. He never mentioned quite how pretty you are.'

Again that little surge of confidence even knowing Jonah had discussed her with his friends.

Griffin had shifted even closer now and was rubbing his hand up and down her bare arm.

'I guess I should go find him.' Amelia turned to look at Griffin. 'Thank you for looking after me.'

Why was he looking at her like that?

As she considered the question, his mouth crushed against hers, shocking the hell out of her.

Shoving him away, she saw the hurt, the confusion on his face.

Had he thought she liked him? Had she led him on? She considered him now. He was tall and filled out the Superman costume he wore, and he wasn't unattractive. Possibly under different circumstances she might have been flattered. She was crushing on Jonah though, who was so much more her type.

'I'm sorry. I didn't mean to give you the wrong idea.' She tried to get up, halted when Griffin caught hold of her hand.

'Please don't go. Just stay and talk to me.'

'I need to go find Jonah.'

'Why?'

Amelia looked at Griffin, unsure how to answer that. Did she confess that she fancied Jonah? She wasn't sure she wanted to do that to one of his housemates.

He took the decision away from her. 'Oh. You like him, don't you?'

Was that a hint of bitterness in his tone?

'I never said I–'

'You know you're wasting your time, don't you?'

'Why?' She had reacted too quickly, giving away her secret crush, and her cheeks heated, despite the coolness of the night.

'So you do like him.'

Amelia couldn't decide if Griffin was gloating or annoyed he was right. He was a difficult person to read.

'Do you know Katie Lassiter?'

'No.'

Griffin leaned closer, his tone conspiring. 'You would know her if you saw her. Tall, blonde, really pretty.'

'What about her?'

'Jonah is smitten with her. They met last week, and I know she's coming tonight. In fact, she's probably already here with him somewhere.'

Amelia must have looked crestfallen, because Griffin paused, studying her. 'Oh, you *really* like him.' He screwed up his face in a wince, as if regretting his words. 'Sorry. Better you find out now though, right? I mean, I'd hate for you to have walked in on him with his tongue down Katie's throat.'

Alcohol and disappointment weren't a good mix, especially with the images Griffin had conjured up now playing on a loop in her head. She was humiliated and crushed and no longer up for the party, wanting only to go back to the dorm and nurse her eighteen-year-old broken heart. When she told Griffin she was going to leave though, he had other ideas.

'Moping isn't going to help you.'

'I'm not moping. I'm just really tired.'

'Come on, Amelia. You're not fooling me. I can see you're gutted. It's written all over your face. You know what you need? What we need to do? We need to cheer you up.' He smiled at her then, and he had seemed kind and concerned, and she found herself warming towards him.

'Sod Jonah. You know the best way to get over him? Stay, have fun. Why don't you wait here, and I'll go get us some drinks?'

'I don't know. I think I'd rather go.'

'Give me half an hour, okay? If I can't cheer you up and you still want to go, I will walk you back to campus. What do you say? Do we have a deal?'

Amelia wavered. She guessed half an hour wouldn't hurt,

though she preferred the idea of staying outside, scared now of running into Jonah and Katie whatever her name was.

'Okay. But just half an hour.' She found a smile for him.

'That's better. Now what do you want to drink? Wine, lager, vodka, Bacardi?'

'Surprise me.'

Griffin's grin had widened at that. 'You've got it.'

She had ended up staying much longer than the half an hour, but that was down to Griffin and his overly generous measure of vodka and then tequila.

Amelia was slurring her words and her legs weren't working properly, but she no longer gave a shit about Jonah, her new best friend being Griffin King, who was doing his best to keep her entertained. The second time he tried to kiss her, she didn't stop him and eventually she let him lead her back into the party, where they finally encountered a stony-faced Jonah.

Amelia barely acknowledged him, as Griffin threw his arm around her possessively and made a show of kissing her again. At the time she thought Griffin was doing it to help her, had no idea that it was all a show to fuel his ego.

The following day she woke up with a sore head and a ton of regrets, wishing she had never gone to the party, but then Griffin had shown up with a huge bunch of flowers, begging her to go have lunch with him, and his charm drew her back in.

He was confident and considerate and made her smile, and even though she still had some reservations, wasn't sure that he was really her type, his keenness to impress her came across as endearing rather than desperate. Before Amelia knew it, they were in a steady relationship.

Jonah had been off with her the first few weeks. She wasn't sure what it was she was supposed to have done to upset him, unless perhaps he didn't like her dating his housemate. Whatever was supposed to have happened with him and Katie

Lassiter had obviously fizzled out, because Amelia never saw them together.

Eventually he got over whatever was bugging him and he had slowly thawed towards her and given that he was Griffin's friend and Amelia was Griffin's girlfriend, they inevitably spent time in each other's company, which helped their friendship get back on track.

Over the years, Amelia figured that was perhaps what they had always been destined to be. Yes, she had liked him and wanted more, but Jonah had never seen her that way.

At least that was what she thought for several years. Until the fateful night when they had been out for Griffin's birthday. It was just a couple of weeks before Amelia was due to become Mrs King and the nerves had taken over big time.

She had never meant to get into a long-term relationship with Griffin; it had just happened, and he could be very persuasive when he wanted to be. Yes there were good times, and the happy memories mostly outweighed the bad, but things had just meandered along comfortably. Although she loved him, if Amelia was completely honest, she had never actually been in love with Griffin, and it had shocked the hell out of her when he had asked her to marry him.

Griffin being Griffin couldn't propose intimately, instead asking her to be his wife in front of a room full of family and friends.

Amelia had never even considered him being her 'forever', even if they had been together for several years and he had caught her off guard. She had said yes, because let's face it, she was hardly going to say no with everyone looking on, but as the date was set, and the wedding arrangements were quickly sorted, claustrophobia took over.

It was going to be okay. It was just pre-wedding jitters.

That's what she kept telling herself, but then Jonah had dropped his bombshell and it had changed everything.

Griffin was drunk and propping up the bar as he engaged in a brag-off with one of the other personal trainers from the gym where he worked and he had been completely oblivious to Amelia, who had been collared by his mother and aunt for another one of their wedding chats. Maxine King had tried to take over planning the whole event and Amelia had reached the point where she felt it was easier to go along with her.

Boxed in and needing to escape, she had eventually excused herself to go to the loo, relieved to find the ladies' room of the posh hotel empty. Away from the noise of the bar she had spent a few blessed minutes alone, steadying her breathing and reminding herself she had got this, while all the time a nagging little voice kept asking why she was going through with something she wasn't sure she even wanted.

When she stepped out of the loos, she had been surprised to find Jonah in the corridor. Had he been waiting for her? He was a little drunk and she knew he had been knocking back the whisky, seeming distracted all evening.

'Is everything okay?'

'Yeah.' He glanced around the empty corridor. 'Fancy getting some air?'

Amelia wondered where Nicole was, though she didn't question it. The idea of slipping outside and away from Griffin's mother was far too appealing. 'Yeah, sure.' She followed him out of the door.

It was mild for April, but there was still a nip in the air, which was a relief after the heat of the bar. 'Are you having a good time?' she asked, conscious that he seemed a little preoccupied. Something was on his mind.

Her question drew his attention to her, and she found herself caught in the intense gaze of those olive eyes. Even after all this time they still managed to heat her up inside. Griffin was classically chiselled and handsome, but Jonah had that edge, attractive but more in an interesting way, from his slightly crooked nose to the faded scar that slashed across his cheek (a result of a childhood accident), cutting into his dimple when he smiled.

'Are you?' He arched a brow, throwing the question back.

'I've had Griff's mother on at me about table plans for the last forty minutes.' Amelia rolled her eyes. 'Would you be having a good time?'

He gave a faint smile. 'No, probably not.' He seemed deep in thought for a moment, as if trying to figure how to say whatever was bothering him. 'Does he make you happy, Amelia?'

She must have looked surprised at his question. 'Griffin? Why would you ask that?'

'You're marrying the guy. I want to be sure.'

'Okay, well it's an odd thing to ask, don't you think?'

'Is it?' he pushed. 'You haven't answered. Are you? Are you happy?'

Amelia considered the question as she stared at him, trying to figure out where this was coming from, and not quite sure how to answer. She was happy, wasn't she?

Then something in his expression softened, his gaze dropping to her mouth, and when he met her eyes again, he was looking at her differently, hungrily even. Amelia's breath hitched, and a little voice in the back of her head warned that perhaps now would be a good time to go back inside. It was too late though and the next thing she knew he had stepped closer, catching her off guard, his palms cupping her face as his mouth pressed against hers.

She protested, mostly through surprise, for all of about half a second, but then she was caught up in the moment, urgently kissing Jonah back. The years of her unrequited crush rolled away in that explosive moment as she greedily took what she had craved for so long.

When Jonah eventually eased back, his eyes were heavy with lust, his lips curving into a satisfied smile at her obvious surprise. 'I've wanted to do that for a long time.'

When Amelia found her voice, it was croaky and a little shaken. 'You have?'

'I have. Since when we first met.' His expression grew serious. 'Don't marry him.'

'What?'

'Don't marry Griffin.'

'It's a little late for that.' She attempted a laugh, but it came out humourless.

'Do you love him?'

What the hell was Jonah playing at? 'I agreed to marry him, didn't I?'

'That wasn't an answer. Are you in love with him?' When she hesitated, he reached out, cupping her face with his hand and grazing the pad of his thumb down her cheek. 'I know you felt that kiss just as much as I did,' he told her, as tiny sparks of heat fused in her belly.

She had, and it had been everything she had dreamt of, plus more. She couldn't tell him that though. It was too late. She was about to marry his best friend.

Why now, Jonah? Why the hell wait until now!

He said he had been in love with her since they had first met, but if that was true, why hadn't he asked her out? Why had he gone after Katie Lassiter instead? She was about to ask both questions when they heard the footsteps, and she quickly pulled away from him, anger and frustration burning inside her. They both looked towards the pathway, but no one appeared.

'It's too late!' She snapped out the words, as she turned her attention back to Jonah. 'You've had years to say this to me. You can't do this to me. Not now, not just before my wedding. It's not fair.'

'And if I had said something before, would it have made a difference?' His tone was heated now too.

Would it? She knew she would be a liar if she said she wouldn't have left Griffin for him. Still, she didn't say the words out loud. It was irrelevant now. She had made her decision and there was no backing out of it now.

'I can't do this, Jonah. Not now. It's too late.'

When he reached for her again, she stepped away, quickly turning and fleeing back into the hotel before he could say anything else.

He didn't contact her again or try to change her mind, and he didn't end things with Nicole. Everything seemed to reset back to normal, as if the conversation had never happened, but his words stayed with her, his declaration of love tearing away at her, and if it achieved anything, it was that it made her realise she wasn't in love with Griffin and that she couldn't go through with the wedding. Four days later she returned the big flashy diamond engagement ring he had given her.

Staring out of the window at the woodland path that led down to the loch, Amelia absently rubbed the skin around her finger where the ring had once been, her face heating up when she realised Griffin was watching her.

It was stupid to think he could read her mind, that he knew

she had called their engagement off back then because of Jonah. But still it was unnerving.

Not that anything had happened with Jonah. He had sobered up and probably realised he had overstepped the mark and Amelia never reached out to him after breaking things off with Griffin, instead fleeing to Cornwall to stay with her aunt, keen to lie low until things blew over.

'What's up?' she asked sharply.

'What?'

'You're staring at me.'

'I wanted to ask your opinion on something actually.'

'You do?' Amelia was both wary and intrigued as he approached her, his hand disappearing inside his pocket. When he produced her topaz ring, the one he had given her back in university, holding it out towards her, her throat tightened. Was he going to admit stealing it? Or did he know she had been through his things.

'I bought this for Chantelle. I wanted her to have a little gift ahead of the wedding. I wondered what you thought of it. Didn't you used to have one similar?'

Is he fucking kidding? 'I had one identical,' she answered him, trying to keep her voice level.

'Really?' Griffin's lips twisted. 'Now what are the chances of that?'

'You bought it for me, Griffin. Our first Christmas together.'

'Did I? You'd think I would remember something like that. Do you still have it?'

Amelia gritted her teeth. 'I lost it.'

'That's a shame. You really should be more careful.'

They stared at each other for a moment, the goading look on Griffin's face, that tiny tug of a smile twisting his lips, and she knew. It was definitely her ring.

But what could she do? She couldn't prove he had taken it.

'I really should,' she agreed genially, though she was fuming inside when he handed it to her to look at. The ring had been in the jewellery box in her bedroom. She was sure of it. Had Griffin broken in to steal it?

'Do you think she will like it?'

Amelia turned the ring over in her fingers. 'One of the clasps is damaged,' she pointed out. 'I would take that back and get it sorted.'

'You're right. So it is.'

'Where did you say you bought it from?'

'I didn't.' He snatched the ring from her, putting it back in the box and slipping it into his pocket, and the smile returned to his face.

Amelia recognised it well. It was one he used when he knew he got the better of someone. He was aware the ring was hers, just as he knew she recognised it too, though he understood her well enough to know she wouldn't challenge him on it as she couldn't prove it. So just how the hell had it fallen into his possession and what exactly was this game he was playing with her?

As she toyed with the question, Ross appeared in the doorway, his face paler than usual.

Amelia's heart thumped. Had something happened to Nancy?

He shook his head before she could ask the question. 'It's not her. We have a bigger problem.' As he spoke, she heard voices outside.

'What?' Griffin's tone was terse, but Amelia could see his jawline had tightened. Knew he had heard them too.

'A truck's just pulled up outside.' Ross told them. 'There are three men inside and they look pissed off. I think one of them is Dougie's brother.'

17

GRIFFIN

Griffin carefully drew back the curtain and peered out into the driveway.

So far the men had parked the truck, but they were still sat inside talking, and tension rippled through him as he wondered what their conversation was about.

No one had seen them disposing of the body down at the loch, he was certain of that, just as he knew no one had seen McCool at the house last night. So why were they back?

'Amelia, I left the key in the front door. Go make sure it's locked. Ross, you check the back door and windows.'

The fact that neither of them argued with him, immediately doing as told, suggested that they were as anxious about Kenny McCool's return as he was.

Even Billy, who hadn't been given a job because Griffin knew he wouldn't be capable of doing it without fucking it up, had risen from the sofa, hands shoved in his pockets and his face pale, as he sought reassurance. 'What are we gonna do, Griff? You can't tell him what happened. You wouldn't do that to me, would you?'

His voice was a whine that pierced through the headache thumping against Griffin's skull.

'Shut up, Billy. I'm thinking.'

'Are we going to hide? We could pretend we're not here. Or maybe we should sneak out the back.'

'Shut up, Billy.'

'Let's do that. Let's go out of the back door and get the hell out of here.'

'And what happens to Nancy?' Amelia asked, hearing Billy's last comment as she walked back into the room. 'We can't leave her here.'

'She might not even wake up! We can't do anything to help her right now and we need to think of ourselves.'

'She's your friend, Billy! We can't just abandon her!'

'We won't leave her,' Griffin told them both. Nancy was an inconvenience that they didn't need, but Amelia was right, they had a responsibility to look after her.

Billy's nostrils flared and he looked like he might argue the point, but he knew better than to say anything further. He was probably annoyed with Griffin for siding with Amelia, which was bemusing in itself. Griffin couldn't recall the last time he and Amelia had agreed on anything.

Of course, he had played nice to get her to agree to come on this weekend, but truth was, even looking at her twisted his insides. It would be a cold day in hell before he forgave her for calling off their engagement just two weeks before the wedding.

The mind games, the subtle digs, wrong-footing her by showing her the ring that they both knew was hers, it was only supposed to be the beginning, but fucking Billy, fucking Dougie McCool, and now Dougie's fucking brother were messing everything up.

Griffin had plotted everything so carefully, taking some huge risks, and his big revenge plans that would show Amelia up to the others and expose her for what she had done and let them see exactly who she was were finally about to come to fruition. This interference was now ruining everything.

'Everywhere is locked,' Ross confirmed, coming back into the room. 'Are they still sitting in the truck? What the hell are they doing out there?' His tone was tight, panicked, and he looked even more jittery than Billy, who Griffin kept half expecting to bolt for the back door.

He glanced through the curtain again, the thump of his heartbeat quickening when he saw the door to the truck open and the driver – a bald man he assumed to be Kenny McCool – climb out. He was joined by the other two men, one of them reaching in the bed of the truck for something.

Shotguns, Griffin realised, watching in horror as he handed one each to Kenny and the other man.

Fuck! Maybe Billy was right. Perhaps they should just leave Nancy.

Except that was no longer looking to be an option as two of the men were heading for the front door, the third disappearing from view, and Griffin was pretty certain he was going round to the back of the house, which would effectively cut any escape route off.

'What are they doing?' Ross repeated. 'Can you see anything?'

'They have guns.'

'What?'

The loud rap on the front door had Griffin jumping, his bowels loosening as panic sliced through his gut. He was aware his hands were trembling and shoved them in his pockets, determined not to show the others how scared he was.

Where the fuck is Jonah?

He had left at least twenty minutes ago and should be at the neighbours by now. If he had done as he was told, the ambulance must be on its way, so why hadn't Jonah come back?

Griffin already knew better than to trust the man he had thought was his best friend, but even so, Amelia was here. Jonah might not give a shit about letting Griffin down, but was he really going to betray Amelia?

'What the fuck are we going to do, Griff?' Billy was clasping his head like he thought it might roll off his shoulders if he let go, his eyes wide with panic, and Griffin for the first time questioned why the hell he had helped this pathetic husk of a man cover his crime.

Deep down he knew the answer. He hadn't done it for Billy. It had been for himself. He had spent so long plotting his revenge on Amelia and he had been determined nothing was going to spoil the weekend. Not even a dead body.

What the fuck had he been thinking?

Of course, it was too late now. Dougie McCool's body was in the loch and somehow his brother had figured out what they had done.

'We all stay quiet and hopefully they will think we've gone out somewhere.'

'My car is sitting outside,' Ross pointed out, the tremor in his tone doing nothing to calm Griffin.

'So what? Who says we took the car? Maybe we went for a walk or something.'

'I still say we make a run for it,' Billy pushed again.

'We can't. One of them went round the back.'

'What?' Amelia's eyes had widened. 'Why would they do that? I told you all. You should have listened to me. I warned you they would come back.'

'Yeah, well we didn't think it would be so soon.'

Another knock, this one sounding more impatient, had them all exchanging worried glances.

'Maybe we should just talk to them,' Amelia suggested. 'We look guilty if they find out we're hiding inside.'

'That's not a good idea.'

'We can't just ignore them. What if they don't leave? I'll go talk to them again.'

'Don't you dare open that door,' Griffin hissed. 'We stay quiet and hopefully the ambulance will be here soon. I'm sure they will leave when they see that arrive.'

'Shouldn't it be here by now?' Ross pointed out. 'Jonah's been gone a while.'

'Maybe he's not coming back.'

Griffin rolled his eyes at Billy. 'Of course he's coming back. He's driving round in your blood-spattered car. He's hardly going to want to hold on to your one-man death machine.'

'Yeah, but what if something has happened to him?'

Griffin glanced at Amelia as Billy asked the question, saw the flicker of anguish on her face as she considered that possibility.

Fucking traitorous bitch.

Much as he wanted to twist the knife, this wasn't the time, plus he didn't want to panic Ross and Billy. If anything actually had happened to Jonah, it was bad news for all of them.

'Can you open the door please?' The voice came from outside. Polite enough in tone, though Griffin could hear the underlying threat. 'We know you're in there. We can hear you.'

They had been talking in hushed tones, but clearly not quietly enough, and he signalled to the others to keep their mouths shut.

A few seconds ticked by before the voice spoke again. 'We just want to talk with you. We're not looking for any trouble.'

They didn't want any trouble. Of course they didn't. Griffin thought of the shotguns, wondering if they were planning to use them as a threat or worse.

Dougie McCool had a criminal record for violence, so chances were his brother was a lawbreaker too.

'I really think we should talk to them,' Amelia hissed. 'They know we're in here, so they're not going to leave.'

Griffin wanted to tell her to shut up, but he knew she was right. He glanced at Billy and Ross, both of them pale-faced and sweaty, looking to him for leadership, and knew that they would be no good if Kenny McCool and his men attacked. Ross was short and skinny and likely had no idea how to defend himself, while Billy was just a coward. Griffin was pretty certain neither man had ever been involved in a fight. If Jonah was here with him they might have a chance, but he wasn't, so right now they were screwed.

'Okay, you go,' he told Amelia. 'But don't open the door. They might force their way in. Go speak to them from one of the upstairs windows.'

'Yeah, pretend it's just you here still,' Billy suggested.

'They know I'm not alone. They heard you talking.' Shaking her head, Amelia left the room.

Griffin glanced between Ross and Billy. 'Stay here,' he ordered, before hurrying after Amelia.

Nancy hadn't moved from her position, still unconscious at the foot of the stairs, her face now deathly pale against her dark hair. The bleeding seemed to have stopped, but Griffin wasn't sure if that was a good thing. Was she even still alive?

He caught Amelia's look of anguish and wondered if she was thinking the same. There wasn't time to stop and check on Nancy though. Somehow they had to persuade Kenny McCool and his mates to leave the house.

He hurried upstairs after Amelia, directing her to his bedroom at the front of the house.

She hadn't questioned why he had followed her, which

made him wonder if she appreciated him being with her for support.

Of course that wasn't the case at all. Oh no. If she was going to talk to Kenny McCool, he wanted to be sure she didn't fuck it up.

'What are you going to say to him?' he demanded, getting down on his hands and knees and crawling to the window, where he settled himself against the bedroom wall.

'I'm going to try and reason with him.'

'By saying what? You'd better not fuck this up, Mils.'

'You know, you could always talk to him.'

'No, it's better if you do. He might go easier on a woman.'

Amelia gave him a cool look, but ignored the comment, instead pushing open the window and peering out. 'Can I help you?'

There was a moment of silence then Griffin heard McCool's voice. 'Can you come downstairs and open the door please?'

'If you're looking for your brother, I already told you, we haven't seen him.'

'Look, I just want to talk to you.'

'We are talking.'

'Not like this. I mean privately. Just give me five minutes, please.'

He sounded convincing. Griffin hoped Amelia wasn't going to be stupid enough to fall for his bullshit. He tugged on the leg of her jeans to get her attention, but she nudged him hard with her knee, otherwise ignoring him.

'I'm sorry, I don't feel comfortable letting a stranger in the house.'

'Look, lady. We've already spoken once today and I was polite and civil, so I don't understand what the problem is.'

'My friend is badly injured. There's an ambulance on the

way. I'm sorry about your brother, but I need to go look after her.'

Yes, that was good. Use Nancy as an excuse.

'You've called an ambulance?' McCool sounded a little unsure.

'Yes. They will be here any minute.'

'Right.'

There was silence for a moment then Griffin could hear whispering coming from outside.

'What's going on?' he hissed.

'Keep quiet!' Amelia shot him an annoyed look.

Easier said than done. Griffin didn't like not being in control of situations. Had her ambulance story worked? Would McCool and his thugs leave? Hopefully an ambulance was on its way, but they didn't know that for certain. It was all dependent on Jonah. She had sounded convincing though.

Perhaps that shouldn't surprise him. She had already proven herself to be an adept liar.

'I think they're going to leave,' she whispered eventually.

Thank fuck for that.

Griffin's mind was made up. As soon as Jonah returned, they were all getting the hell out of here. Even if there was no ambulance, they would use Billy's car. Worry about the blood spatter later. It was a shitter because it meant his plans were ruined, but he would forego his revenge on Amelia for now rather than risk being interrogated and possibly left for dead by Kenny McCool. If they returned a third time, he didn't plan on being here.

Some kind of commotion down below had his ears pricking up. *What the hell?* It didn't sound good, and he saw Amelia's eyes widen before she leant further out of the window.

'What's going on?'

She ignored Griffin, instead shouting down to McCool. 'What are you doing? Let him go?'

Yelling then, along with plenty of swearing. Was that Billy's voice? Unable to resist knowing what was happening, Griffin pulled himself up from the floor, shoving Amelia to one side as he poked his head out of the window.

Fuck!

One of the goons, a heavyset man with sandy-coloured hair, had hold of Billy by the scruff of his neck.

Why was Billy outside?

He got the answer to that moments later when the goon spoke. 'Caught this little weasel as he climbed out of a window round the side.'

'Let me go.' Billy was struggling again, lashing out violently and provoking more swear words from McCool and his friends. He looked up at the open window. 'Griffin! Help me. Griff, please!'

McCool turned to look up at the window too, a smile widening on his face when he saw he now had an audience of two. Raising his shotgun, he pointed it at Billy's head, before looking back at Griffin and Amelia.

'No! Please don't hurt him,' Amelia begged.

'Well, I guess that all depends.' McCool's smile widened to a sharkish grin. 'Are you ready to come downstairs and open the door?' When neither of them replied, he gave a half shrug. 'No? Okay, let me make this simple. I am going to count to ten. If the front door isn't open by the time I reach ten then it's not going to end well for your friend here.'

18

JONAH

The neighbours weren't home.

Jonah had found the place easy enough, though it was definitely further along the road than Griffin had made out. Unlike the Airbnb they were staying in, it was visible from the road, which was good as he may have gone straight past it if not.

His heart had sunk when he saw there were no cars out front. There were no windows open nor any sign of life, but he told himself that didn't mean anything, and went to the front door and pressed the doorbell. He waited a minute before ringing again, impatient for an answer. When he didn't get one he circled the property, a small but well-maintained bungalow, in case the owners were working in the garden. Unfortunately the place appeared deserted, the curtains all drawn at the back windows and the patio table and chairs with covers on.

No one home meant no chance of using a phone to call for help, which would mean he had made the wrong decision. He should have gone back to the house and warned the others that McCool was on his way.

The man had already threatened Amelia and she and Jonah had heard him talking down by the loch. He knew that he believed Dougie had been at the house because that was where his phone signal had died.

That was still bothering Jonah. Was McCool mistaken or had one of the group found Dougie's phone? He was certain it wouldn't be Amelia, but Griffin, Ross, Billy, Nancy, had one of them taken it? And if so, why?

He didn't like that little sliver of distrust that was nestling in his gut. And it made him consider Nancy again. How exactly had she fallen down the stairs? Had it been an accident or was she pushed?

Were the phone and Nancy's fall connected?

Jonah had always thought they were a pretty tight group, and what had happened this morning should be pushing them closer together. Instead, though, he could feel them fracturing.

Of course he wanted to get help for Nancy, but if he was brutally honest, right now, the only person in the house he really gave a shit about was Amelia. And he had left her alone there with people he was no longer sure he trusted.

Stupid, Jonah. Stupid.

He ran his fingers through his hair in frustration, unsure what to do. Without his phone, he had no way of figuring out if there was another house nearby. Should he head back or keep going?

Returning to the house would stick them firmly back at square one, trapped without phones and now without a car, but if McCool and his mates were there, if they did anything to Amelia...

Fuck!

He went back round the front of the bungalow, pressing his face against the one window that wasn't covered, saw it was a kitchen. The room was dated, with pine units and decorative plates adorning the walls, but it looked neat and clean. Maybe the owners were away, as there was no clutter on the worktops, no dirty crockery or glassware by the sink waiting to be washed up. On the far wall counter, Jonah spotted a telephone. Like the rest of the room it was old-fashioned and attached by a cord. That didn't matter though, as long as it worked.

What was he saying? Whether it worked was irrelevant. The owners weren't home, which meant he couldn't access it.

Unless there is a way in.

No. He halted that line of thought straightaway. He was not that person. He didn't break into people's homes.

It was an emergency though. Nancy was badly injured. And McCool was heading back to the house. If anything happened to Amelia... It wasn't like Jonah was planning on robbing the place. He simply wanted to use the telephone.

He could check the doors and windows, just in case any of them had been left unlocked. If there was a way in, he could call for an ambulance. The owners would be none the wiser.

Tentatively, he tried the window, part annoyed, part relieved when it didn't open.

Biting down on his frustration, he made his way round the bungalow, checking for another way in, the relieved part of him gradually working itself into frustration when he realised he couldn't easily access the place.

So what now? He was just wasting time. First in even coming to this place, now with trying to get inside it. He should have just left when he realised no one was home.

But that telephone was so tantalisingly close.

In order to break in though, he would have to smash glass or kick in a door. That was a whole step up from sneaking through a window.

If it saved a life though, it was justified, wasn't it?

He desperately needed a telephone and there was one just ten feet away from him.

Okay, so he would have to cause criminal damage to the

property, but it was for a good reason. He would leave a note with his contact details and when this was all over he would pay for the damage caused and send a hamper or something to apologise for the inconvenience. The owners would understand. He would if he was in their situation.

Mind made up, he glanced around, looking for something he could use, spotting the large stones in the rockery. There was no time to think about his actions. He was in a desperate situation he reminded himself as he picked one up.

He was about to smash it against the kitchen window when the crunch of a footstep had him pausing.

Before he could react, a voice yelled behind him. 'Freeze.'

19
―――――
BILLY

For an awful moment there, Billy had thought the door wasn't going to open; that Griffin had finally tired of him and was going to feed him to the wolves.

He had been told to stay in the house, as Griffin went upstairs with Amelia, but then Ross had gone to check on Nancy and Billy had panicked. It hadn't been his fault. It was the pressure of the moment and he had simply buckled. He needed to get out of the house, to remove himself from this situation. The others would cope better without him.

Remembering the downstairs bathroom looked out to the side of the property he went to see if the window was big enough for him to climb through. It had been a tight squeeze, but he had almost made it to the safety of the trees when a burly hand had landed on his shoulder. Moments later he had found himself face to face with the man he assumed was Dougie McCool's brother, with a shotgun pointed at his head.

When McCool started counting, Billy had lost control of his bladder, much to the amusement of McCool's ugly baseball-cap-wearing mate, who had pointed and laughed.

Billy didn't care. He just wanted to get back in the house.

Please open the door. Please open the door. He had repeated the mantra under his breath, his teeth chattering in fear, convinced by the time McCool reached eight that Griffin was going to abandon him, but then the door had opened, and he had sobbed with relief, even as he was roughly pushed inside.

Griffin was going to be angry with him, but at least his head was still on his shoulders.

Now they were all sat on the sofa and Baseball Cap and the lout who had caught him stood guard as McCool paced in front of them. Billy was uncomfortable, his jeans damp from where he had pissed himself, but he didn't dare ask if he could go change his clothes.

And he had noticed that Ross, who was beside him, had been sniffing disdainfully, and – unless it was Billy's imagination – trying to shuffle away. Not that it was really possible. It was a large sofa, but still with four of them sat on it, it was a bit of a squeeze.

'What do you want?' Amelia repeated the question she had already asked twice, her tone clipped, and her steely gaze locked on McCool. 'You have just broken into our house, threatened to shoot one of my friends. What the fuck do you want?'

Billy had never seen her so angry, was surprised she was taking the lead over Griffin.

But then Griffin seemed to have lost his voice. Normally he was their leader, the one who made all the decisions. Why wasn't he speaking up? Why was he letting Amelia take charge?

Griffin was the one who had always protected Billy. He wasn't so sure he liked Amelia being their spokesperson. What if she decided to tell McCool what he had done?

She had never been on board with any of this, had sulked because they didn't call the police.

How could he be sure she wouldn't hand him over now?

'Don't antagonise him,' he whispered across to her, where she was tucked between Griffin and Ross. 'He has a gun.'

'Shut up, Billy. This is all your fault. All of it.'

Fuck.

'What do you want us to do with them?' That was from Baseball Cap, his question directed at McCool. He sounded excited and Billy suspected he was enjoying scaring them.

'Hold on, Greg. I'm thinking.' McCool glanced at the four of them then stepped back out into the hall where Nancy was.

Did he plan on doing something to her?

Amelia obviously thought the same. 'Leave her alone,' she demanded, trying to get up.

Baseball Cap... Greg stepped in front of her, his shotgun raised. 'Stay on the sofa,' he hissed.

When McCool returned to the room he was wiping the palm of his gun-free hand on his jeans. Billy noticed it was stained red. Was it Nancy's blood? Had he hurt her?

Fuck, that doesn't bode well for the rest of us. Sweat beaded on his top lip as sickness churned his stomach. They were being held at gunpoint by the brother of the man he had killed. Somehow he had to get away from here.

But how?

'What happened to that woman at the bottom of the stairs?'

Amelia glared at McCool. 'She has a name. It's Nancy.'

'That wasn't my question. What happened to her?'

'She fell. I told you she was badly injured.'

'You have to let us go get help for her,' Griffin said, finally finding his voice.

There was a moment of silence as McCool shifted his attention from Amelia to Griffin, a sly smile slowly spreading across his face. 'I thought you said when you were upstairs that an ambulance was on its way?'

Oh shit. It was unlike Griffin to mess up. Billy guessed it was the pressure of having a gun on them.

'So which is it?' McCool pressed. 'Do you need to go get help for her or is an ambulance coming?' He glanced back at the hallway. 'Honestly? She's not in a good way, so it doesn't really matter.'

'She's still alive, you arsehole,' Amelia snapped, ignoring his question. 'Of course it matters.'

McCool took a step towards the sofa, raising his gun and pressing it against Amelia's forehead. Billy nearly shit himself on her behalf, amazed that she was still holding McCool's glare, a challenging look on her face.

'You have a big mouth, lady. I would be careful if I was you.'

Amelia said nothing in response, but Billy could see she was trembling. Though he got the impression it was as much with anger as with fear. She looked like she wanted to murder Kenny McCool.

Eventually he eased the gun back, studying each of them in turn. Billy pressed his lips together, terrified that if he spoke he would say the wrong thing.

Why was Griffin being so quiet? His silence was scaring the crap out of Billy. Griffin was the one who always bailed him out of trouble. Billy needed him to figure this whole mess out.

The gun settled briefly on him, and he squeezed his eyes shut.

Don't ask me anything. Don't ask me anything.

'You!'

Terrified to look, but also scared what might happen if he didn't, Billy forced one eye open. The relief when he saw the gun had moved and that it, plus the question, was now directed at Ross made him want to burst into tears.

'I want a straight answer. Is there an ambulance on its way here?'

165

Ross's eyes were bulging, the colour drained from his face, and Billy was aware he was sweating heavily. He didn't immediately answer, instead letting out a faint murmur that reminded him of a hurt or frightened animal.

McCool's scowl deepened. 'I am going to count to five. One.'

'Please.' Ross also sounded on the verge of tears.

'Two. Three.'

'We don't know!'

'What do you mean, you don't know? It's simple enough. You either called an ambulance or you didn't.'

'Don't say anything!' Amelia ordered.

'Oi, Mouth! Shut up,' McCool spat at her, refocusing on Ross. 'What the fuck is going on here with you lot? Talk, now.'

'Our friend went for help. We don't know where he is or if it's coming.'

'Who is your friend?'

'Jonah.'

'So, there's this Jonah, plus the four of you, and Half-Dead Girl in the hall—'

'NANCY! She has a name.'

'Mouth! I warned you to shut up!'

Amelia glowered as McCool refocused on Ross. Billy scowled at her across the sofa. She needed to stop winding him up. She was going to get them all killed.

'Who else is with you?'

'No one,' Ross insisted.

'No one?' McCool repeated. 'You're sure about that? If I find out you're lying to me, you'll regret it.'

'I swear. There's no one else. It's just the six of us, I promise.'

'So when did this Jonah leave?'

'I guess nearly an hour ago.'

'Kenny, the Golf.' That was from the lout who had caught Billy.

How had he known Jonah was driving Billy's Golf?

'What car was this Jonah driving?' McCool demanded; his question directed to all of them.

Billy shifted his gaze along the sofa. Amelia was the only one looking at McCool. Ross was studying his clenched hands, while Griffin was staring into space. Billy noticed for the first time how pale he was, his bottom lip trembling, and his gut churned faster.

If Griffin was scared then they were all in deep shit.

'Was it a black Golf?' McCool pushed when none of them answered him.

How did he know that?

There seemed little point in pretending it wasn't, so Billy nodded tentatively. Maybe if he cooperated, the thugs would go easy on him.

'Was that a yes? Speak!'

'Yes.' Billy found his voice, the nerves making it reedy and high-pitched. 'That's the car.'

Had McCool connected the car to Dougie? Maybe if he thought it belonged to Jonah...

No, he couldn't lead them to believe the car was Jonah's.

But then again, Jonah wasn't here with a gun being pointed at him. Desperate times and all that.

Would the others back him up? Griffin and Ross possibly, but Amelia would sooner throw Billy under a bus than betray Jonah. He was certain of that.

'There was no one in it,' Greg assured McCool. 'I checked.'

What was he on about? Had they found his car? If so, where was Jonah?

Amelia was obviously having the same concerns, though unlike Billy, she chose to voice them out loud. 'What do you mean there was no one in it? Are you saying you've found the car?' Her tone was angry, her amber eyes blazing at Greg, who seemed amused by her outburst. 'Where's Jonah?'

'Mils.'

Oh at last. Griffin had finally found his voice. The word was hushed though. He clearly wanted to shut Amelia up.

'If Jonah went to get help, I think we can safely say he didn't get it.'

'What do you mean?'

McCool smirked at Amelia. 'He never made it off the property.'

'What do you mean? What the fuck have you done to him?'

'Language, *Mils*.' McCool's tone was sarcastic as he used Griffin's nickname for her. 'That's no way for a pretty lady to talk.' Whereas he had been annoyed with her before, now he looked like he was gloating and enjoying winding her up.

Billy's heart started racing. Had something happened to Jonah?

'Where is he?' Amelia demanded.

'We have no idea, but he didn't leave by car. The front tyres are both punctured.' McCool nodded to his loutish mate. 'Those spikes worked a treat. That was a good idea, pal.'

'You forced his car off the road?'

'Such a judgemental tone, Mils. We couldn't have you leaving now, could we?'

'You're an arsehole.'

'Mils!' Griffin hissed again.

'Yes, *Mils*. Listen to your boyfriend. I told you I needed to speak with you and your friends. I know you know where Dougie is.'

Billy's bowels knotted at the mention of Kenny's brother's name. How did he know? And what the hell was he planning on doing to them? Was he going to torture them to get answers? If one of the others let on what had happened, Kenny was going to kill him. He was sure of it.

'We have no idea where your brother is.'

That's good, Amelia. Convincing.

Please believe her.

'We need to find out where this Jonah is.' McCool was talking to his mates now. 'He can't have gone far.'

'Leave him alone.'

Jesus, Amelia. Shut up.

'Want me to go look for him?' Greg offered.

McCool glanced between the two of them, seeming unsure. 'Nigel, you go.'

'Don't you trust me?'

'To not fuck it up? No, Gregory, I don't. Not particularly.'

Nigel, the lout with the sandy hair and the thick neck, nodded. 'I've got it, Kenny.'

As he left the room, Greg pouted. 'So what do you want me to do?' He looked about sixteen with his turned-around baseball cap on his head, his ugly face full of pimples, but Billy still wasn't sure he would want to take him on in a fight. Knowing Kenny thought he was something of a fuck-up and that Greg had hold of a loaded gun also terrified the crap out of him.

'What I want you to do is stand there with your gun and keep an eye on our friends here. You think you can manage that without whining?'

'Yes, Kenny.'

'If any of them try to get up from the sofa, shoot them in the kneecaps.'

What? Billy had been thinking that with just two of them there he might be able to make a run for it, but would they really shoot him? Beside him, he could feel Ross shaking. Reassuring. And looking past Ross, even Amelia had paled, while Griffin appeared to only just be holding it together.

169

McCool pulled up a chair from the dining table, placing it before the sofa, the splat in front of him, and sat down facing the group. One arm rested on the chair back, while his free hand held on to his gun.

He smiled cruelly. 'I think it's time we all had a little chat about where my brother, Dougie is.'

20

JONAH

'Look, laddie.' PC Murray sighed. 'I've spent my night chasing a runaway Border collie. I'm tired and I need a hot cup of coffee, so I'm just going to arrest you.' He had been on his way home from work, still in uniform but now in his own car, when he caught Jonah trying to break into the bungalow.

'I know you're doubting what I'm saying,' Jonah tried again, doing his best to sound reasonable, 'but could you at least call for an ambulance. My friend has a serious head injury, and we really need to get her some help.'

PC Murray had insisted on handcuffing Jonah though, and putting him in the back of his Volvo, even as Jonah had protested bitterly. He had briefly toyed with resisting arrest but knew that wouldn't end well. Besides, Murray had a car and a phone. Jonah needed his help, so it was better to try and talk him round rather than make an enemy of him.

The problem was, Murray was far more interested in talking about Ralph the collie, rather than listening to what Jonah had to say and it seemed that, despite being told about Nancy and the pickup truck with McCool and his friends, Murray wasn't willing to trust or believe him. He seemed to think that Jonah was trying to pull some kind of trick to get himself out of the cuffs. He had seemed sceptical about Jonah's reason for trying to break into the bungalow, unwilling to believe that none of his friends had access to a phone.

Jonah admitted that it did sound pretty unbelievable.

Murray studied Jonah through the open window, as if trying to get a measure of this non-Scottish burglar. He struck Jonah as very localised and set in his ways, and Jonah suspected that if he had come from north of the border they may have been having a very different conversation.

'I'll drive you back to the house,' he said eventually. 'I can check on this *friend* and if she does need an ambulance, I will make the call, okay?'

It was a compromise that wasn't ideal, but Jonah would have to accept it. 'Okay,' he agreed, eager to get back and make sure Amelia was all right, and, of course, sort the ambulance for Nancy.

'I am taking you in afterwards though,' Murray insisted. 'You can't go round breaking into people's houses.'

Jonah resisted the urge to roll his eyes, wishing the officer would understand the urgency of the situation. Diplomacy was the way forward though, so instead he nodded. 'I understand. I won't cause you any trouble, I promise.'

He was quiet on the short ride back, letting Murray do most of the talking, already thinking ahead, mindful that McCool might be back at the house.

Jonah had no proof that Dougie's brother would hurt anyone, but the conversation he and Amelia had overheard in the woods, plus the spikes on the driveway (which he knew he couldn't prove was McCool's doing, but seriously, who else would it be?) suggested he was best to be prepared.

He needed to persuade Murray to take these cuffs off before

they reached the house. He could be wrong about McCool, but it just wasn't worth the risk.

As Murray pulled into the driveway, he spotted Billy's car up ahead. 'That your vehicle?'

Jonah had already told him about the spikes on the driveway, but the man had been preoccupied with the dog he was looking for.

'Stop the car,' he warned. 'You don't want to puncture your tyres on the spikes like I did.'

'Spikes you say?'

'Just stop driving... please.' Jonah resisted the urge to swear or lose his temper, and was thankful when Murray brought the car to a halt.

'Stay here,' the police officer ordered, and Jonah had no choice but to wait in the vehicle.

Murray approached Billy's car, and the faint ripple of unease in Jonah's gut that the officer might unfold the seats in the Golf and realise it was a fucking crime scene was overshadowed by the worry that he would shortly be approaching a potentially dangerous situation with someone who was going to be of no use whatsoever.

In another world, he would probably like Murray. He was affable and inoffensive, and okay, he might be a little too laid-back and dated in his ways, but he seemed like a decent man. But if McCool and his goons were at the house, seriously, how was he going to react? What could he do if they were threatening his friends?

Murray found the spikes further down the drive, alerting Jonah to this by stepping on one and yowling in pain as he hopped around on one foot.

Jesus fucking Christ. Jonah had warned him. The man simply didn't listen though.

The worst bit was they were no longer across the drive.

Someone had moved them to one side and Murray had still managed to step on them. While that had Jonah biting his lip in frustration, it also had his heart rate increasing. If the spikes had been moved, it suggested another vehicle had been through here, and there was only one he could think of.

McCool's.

He flexed his fingers, yanked his wrists against the cuffs. Murray needed to free him, and now. If he didn't, he needed to call for backup.

Yes, if he did that, chances are the police would find Dougie McCool's blood in Billy's car, but right now, Jonah didn't care. He would face the consequences of that, as long as he knew Amelia was okay.

'You need to uncuff me,' he told Murray, as he climbed back into the Volvo, a grimace on his face.

'Those things are sharp.' He winced, ignoring Jonah's comment. 'It went right into my foot.'

'Call an ambulance,' Jonah suggested dryly.

'I'll be okay. I just need a minute.'

Something they didn't have. *For fuck's sake, Murray!*

'Look. My friends are in trouble. Whoever put those spikes down has moved them, which means they are likely up at the house.' Jonah was trying to keep his tone calm and rational, but it wasn't easy. 'If I'm right and they are, you're gonna need my help, so please, do us both a favour and uncuff me.'

Murray finally glanced at him, seeming to register what Jonah was saying, and for a moment Jonah thought he had actually got through to him.

'It's going to be fine,' Murray told him, smiling. 'You just stay back there and behave yourself. If I need assistance I will call for backup.'

For fuck's sake! The man simply wasn't getting it.

As Murray restarted the car, Jonah bit down on his

frustration, hoping to hell he was the one who had this wrong, that Murray would actually be right, and everything would be okay at the house.

They would call an ambulance for Nancy, the whole Dougie McCool incident would go away, and he would talk to Amelia, tell her again how he really felt about her, as he should have done a long time ago.

'Mrs Campbell could do with getting some of these trees cut back,' Murray commented, conversationally, peering up at where the top branches intertwined to make a tunnel. 'None of the sunlight can get through.'

Jonah didn't give a shit about the trees right now, but he forced himself to stay quiet, wishing the PC would drive a little faster. He was going slower than a bloody milk float.

Eventually, they drove round the final bend and saw the house up ahead. It was an impressive two-storey building, part covered in white cladding, part exposed brick.

Only the best for Griffin.

Jonah spotted the pickup parked out front. McCool hadn't approached discreetly, and Jonah wasn't sure if that was a good sign or not. Just the fact he was back here and nowhere to be seen was unsettling.

Had Griffin really let him inside the house?

'That's the truck,' he pointed out to Murray. 'You might be best to pull over here. You don't want them to see you.'

He was expecting Murray to ignore him again, so was surprised when the officer actually did as requested. Murray's next words had his heart sinking though. 'You wait here. I'm going to go look around.'

'I really don't think that's a good idea. I don't trust these guys one bit.'

'I'm sure everything is fine.' Murray's tone was a little condescending, which wound Jonah's coil tighter and as the PC unbuckled his seat belt and climbed from the car, he tried again.

'Look, just uncuff me, okay? You know where I'm staying, and I promise I won't run. There are three of them and one of you.'

'I already told you. If the situation requires it, I will call for backup.' For the first time, Murray was getting a little huffy. 'Now you stay here and let me do my job.'

Do your job? He was about to walk unarmed and alone into a potentially explosive situation, and Jonah didn't like it one bit. 'Why don't you call them now? Just let them know you need help.'

Murray looked at him through the open back window as if Jonah was the one who needed help, more of the straightjacket variety. 'Just wait here please,' he repeated.

Frustrated, Jonah watched the officer approach the house, relieved when he didn't go to the front door. At least he had some sense. Murray tried the garage door and finding it locked, disappeared round the side of the property. Jonah peered through into the front of the car, looking for any sign of the cuff keys. Murray wasn't completely stupid though. He would have those on him. Instead, he twisted himself on the seat, so his back was towards the door, reaching for the handle. It wasn't easy with his hands cuffed behind him, but after a couple of attempts he pulled it open.

He would stay in the car. He didn't want to totally trash Murray's trust, but at least with the door ajar, he could move quickly if there was any trouble, not that he could do much with the cuffs on.

The bang, when it came, made him jump.

Murray had been gone for over five minutes and Jonah was already edgy, wondering if something had happened to him.

Now, with the unmistakable sound of a gunshot ringing through the air, his mind went into overdrive.

Maybe he was panicking for nothing. He had no idea if the woodland surrounding the house was used for hunting. It had sounded like a shotgun, so it was possible.

The sound had been close, though, and the timing was too coincidental. If anything had happened to Murray, whoever had shot him, or at him, was going to come looking for his car.

Jonah needed to get out of here before that happened. Kicking the door fully open, he wriggled out, then used his elbow to shut it. He looked towards the house trying to decide on a plan of action.

Priority was getting the cuffs off, but he would have to find Murray to do that.

Second priority was finding Amelia and learning what was going on inside the house.

Was she with McCool? It was possible the gunshot was fired in warning, but what if it had been intended to injure or kill? Was McCool really that crazy?

For the first time it occurred to Jonah that his friends might not just be in trouble. They could actually be dead.

No, he wouldn't think that way. Amelia was okay, and so were the others. He had to believe that.

Hearing a cough behind him, his head shot round. There was no one there, but he could hear approaching footsteps. Was help on the way? Maybe it was someone Murray had called.

The property was isolated though and there was no way anyone would have arrived so quickly. Besides, who the hell would be on foot? Following his gut he stepped off the driveway, positioning himself behind one of the large oak trees, as McCool's mate, the one with the sandy hair, came into view. The first thing Jonah spotted was that he was holding a shotgun.

He had approached from behind, though, so it couldn't have been him who had fired.

Did all the fuckers have guns? This was not good.

The man was breathing heavily, sounded like he had been running, as he continued to cough and splutter, and he was looking towards the house.

Had he come to investigate the gunshot?

Jonah saw his eyes narrow as they fell on the Volvo and he approached the vehicle cautiously, peering inside, before hurrying towards the house.

Think, Jonah.

He needed to get to Murray. Find out what had happened to him and somehow he needed to do that without being seen.

The oak trees ran along the edge of the driveway and were mature enough to conceal him until he was just a few yards from the house. There was then an open space before he could slip into the woods and follow them round to the back of the property.

He approached cautiously, not wanting to take any unnecessary risks, though conscious that he needed to find out what was going on.

When he reached the end of the drive, he glanced around to check the coast was clear, before running to the safety of the trees. Just as he reached them the front door opened and the man he had seen in the driveway stepped out of the house again. He was rattling something in his hand. Did he have the key fob? He was heading back down the drive towards the Volvo, so it appeared.

Jonah didn't wait to find out. He needed to find Murray.

As he approached the rear of the house, he spotted the police officer on the ground. He was lying on his side, facing away from Jonah. Blood stained his uniform and the patio slabs beneath him.

Dammit. He had told the man to either release him or to call for backup. Why hadn't he listened?

Was he dead?

The back door opened and the skinny guy with the baseball cap stepped out. He approached Murray's body, rolled him onto his back and patted down his pockets. He took the officer's phone, slipping it into his own pocket. If he had found the keys for the cuffs, he showed little interest.

Leaning down and grabbing Murray by the wrists, he started to drag him backwards towards the house, leaving a snail trail of blood as he went.

Fuck, this isn't good. I need the cuff keys.

He watched as Baseball Cap jerked Murray's body roughly over the step to the door, then Murray's legs and feet disappeared inside, before the door was slammed shut.

A minute or two passed, and as his scrambled brain tried to plot his next move, from within the heart of the house came a blood-curdling scream.

21

THEN

S haring a house with Griffin King was mostly a lot of fun.
Griff was good at getting to know people and always willing to talk to anyone, which meant Jonah and Billy's social circle grew quickly.

He also knew all of the best pubs and clubs to go to and could be very generous when it came to stocking up the fridge and cupboards with beer and other alcohol, as well as with letting his housemates share all of his stuff.

Unfortunately, as Jonah soon learnt, he had no scruples when it came to borrowing back.

Amelia Abery hadn't been his to share, but Griffin had known that Jonah liked her.

After meeting on the first day of university, Jonah and Amelia had struck up an easy friendship, and Jonah was keen to escalate things before he was relegated to the friend zone.

He was confident Amelia was interested in him and he was definitely interested back, attracted to her appealing mix of naivety and enthusiasm. She had led a pretty sheltered life, he could tell, and university was proving to be a real eye-opener for her. It could have been overwhelming, but she wanted to fit in, and she wanted all of the experiences that her new student life would bring. And Jonah wanted to share them with her.

At first it was difficult. Other people were always about, and even the one time he had got Amelia out for a one-on-one drink, Billy had crashed their date and hadn't picked up on Jonah's subtle hints that he needed to fuck off.

He and Griffin both knew the score. Jonah hadn't kept his Amelia crush to himself and both of them kept ribbing him about it.

The Halloween party was supposed to be the night things changed. Yes, they would be in a crowd, but it would be easier to be intimate and Jonah hoped to pull her to one side and let her know exactly how he felt.

She had texted him a picture before leaving, a drunken selfie of her and Nancy dressed as sexy Batman villains. Amelia's normally straight copper hair fell in waves around her shoulders, the green eye make-up made her amber irises sparkle, while her tight satin dress showed off every curve of her appealing body.

Griffin – who unlike Billy had yet to meet her – peered over Jonah's shoulder and whistled.

'She is gorgeous, mate. I totally get why you like her.' He had nudged Jonah with his elbow. 'Best you get in there quick before I make my move.'

At the time Jonah had laughed, not threatened at all, but later, when the party was in full swing, that was when he learnt of Griffin's betrayal.

Griffin had decided they needed more spirits, and generously he offered to pay, dispatching Jonah down to the off-licence to get them. Amelia hadn't arrived yet, so he had gone willingly. When he arrived back, he had found Nancy in the hallway talking with friends.

'Is Amelia here?'

KERI BEEVIS

'She's about somewhere.' Nancy was waving her bottle of WKD around. She looked as though she was already plastered.

Jonah had gone through to the kitchen and dumped the bag of drinks on the counter. Feeling a hand touch his shoulder he assumed it was Amelia. He had swung round with a wide grin, and was disappointed when he found himself face to face with Katie Lassiter. She was dressed as a sexy Freddy Krueger, in an extremely short and tight red-and-green jumper dress teamed with fishnets and knee-high boots, her blonde locks spilling out of the trilby she wore tilted on her head.

'Jonah, hi.' Katie was beaming, seeming thrilled to see him.

They shared a couple of lectures together and Jonah had been told that Katie thought he was cute. It was flattering, because she was really pretty and most of the first-year students were lusting after her. He wanted Amelia though.

'Hey, Katie. Thanks for coming.'

'When Griffin invited me, I was so excited. I love your costume.'

Jonah wasn't big on dressing up, so he had borrowed an orange body warmer from a friend and was channelling his inner Marty McFly. 'Thanks. You look great.'

'Do you think so? I love fancy dress, but I didn't know what to wear. You know how it is.' Katie laughed, as she rolled her eyes dramatically. 'In the end I decided to go with this old thing.'

Jonah didn't doubt that 'this old thing' had probably been carefully planned to raise the blood pressure of every male at the party, but he didn't say that. She did look great. He hadn't been lying. She just wasn't Amelia. He asked Katie if she had seen her.

A little crestfallen at the question she answered, 'No, I haven't. Would you be a love and get me another drink?'

'Sure. What do you want?'

It was just after he had handed her the vodka and Coke that Griffin and Amelia walked in through the back door.

The smile on Jonah's face dropped when he realised that Griffin had hold of Amelia's hand, that she was laughing at something he had said. His mind was reeling as he tried to register what he was seeing, but then came the lowest, most crushing blow, Amelia glancing briefly and dismissively in his direction before his supposed friend pulled her in close, sticking his tongue down her throat.

For a moment he stared in stunned silence, but then he blinked, shaking his head back to reality, and abruptly left the room.

He didn't speak to either Griffin or Amelia that night, seeking solace with Katie Lassiter and a bottle of whisky. The next day though, while fighting the hangover from hell, he had got into a fight with Griffin.

Jonah had been relieved when he finally rolled out of bed to find that Griffin had gone out. After helping Billy clear up, he retired to the sofa, where he spent the afternoon drinking black coffee, eating bacon sandwiches and feeling sorry for himself.

It was later when Griffin returned and had the nerve to ask him what his problem was that things blew up.

'This is about Amelia?' He had looked so surprised that Jonah might be angry about that, as if it was a really stupid trivial point. And then the fucker had laughed. 'I'm sorry, mate. I didn't realise you were quite so hung up on her. You're right though, she is great. I like her a lot. I think she likes me too.'

'You're a shit. You knew, Griff. You fucking knew I liked her.'

'What can I say? You hadn't made a move, so she was free pickings.' Griffin had smirked. 'You snooze, you lose.'

That was when Jonah had hit him.

He didn't speak to Griffin for two weeks after that, trying to sort moving out to other accommodation. It wasn't easy though, as there were no other free rooms within his budget, and eventually he had accepted he would have to stay.

At first it was difficult, because Griffin and Amelia weren't just a one-night thing; and they began seeing each other on a regular basis. Jonah kept his mouth shut and stayed out of their way, but eventually he moved on, dating other girls, accepting Griffin and Amelia's relationship, and slowly thawing towards them both. By the end of the first year, they were all friends again and he had accepted that he hadn't been in a relationship with Amelia, so she was free to date whoever she chose.

Of course Amelia knew none of this and he had never planned to tell her.

She was always his first, albeit secret love, though, and his feelings for her never went away.

Then he got drunk at Griffin's birthday party and had put his heart on the line. This time she had told him straight. She wasn't interested and she was marrying Griffin.

She couldn't be more final than that and Jonah resolved to move on. But then she called off the wedding and his head had been so far up his arse feeling sorry for himself, he hadn't realised it was a sign.

Because she didn't reach out to him, Jonah had walked away. He was now realising that might have been one of the biggest mistakes of his life.

Four years had passed. Four years without her in his life. Now he had another chance with her, and he was not going to let anything fuck that up.

Right now she was in a potentially dangerous situation. A police officer had been shot, and McCool and his mates were wandering freely in and out of the house. They had guns and Jonah had no idea where Amelia, Griffin, Ross and Billy were or if they were okay.

He needed to get in the house without being seen, and to do that he needed a plan. Get inside, unlock the cuffs, save his friends, tell Amelia he was still in love with her.

It sounded simple in his head, but somehow he doubted it would be.

22

AMELIA

Being held prisoner by thugs with shotguns would be frightening for most people, and yes, Amelia was scared. What surprised her though was just how angry she was too.

This weekend had been a huge mistake and she deeply regretted coming. Griffin was being an arse, Ross seemed to have a problem with her, and Amelia had no idea what it was she was supposed to have done to upset him; Nancy was badly injured, and Billy, who generally was a good laugh, had behaved like a selfish and irresponsible dick. Only Jonah was worth being here for. And he had disappeared. Amelia didn't know if she should be worried or annoyed about that. Instead she was mostly frustrated.

She hadn't wanted any of this and she had refused to partake in any of the foolish decisions the others had made this weekend. So why the fuck was she now stuck on a sofa, pressed between a sweaty Ross and her odious ex-fiancé, while some bald Scottish lunatic and his thug friends tormented them for fun?

Kenny McCool was the kind of man she was finding it easy to dislike. He thought he was omnipotent and that the world owed him a favour. It was a dangerous combination and she really needed to stop pressing his buttons.

It had mostly been mind games; McCool making it clear that he knew Dougie had been at the house and mentioning his brother's phone again, intimating that one of them had it. He had been trying to turn them on each other and Amelia could see from their faces that paranoia was creeping over Griffin, Ross and Billy.

But then there had been a noise outside and after going to investigate, McCool's little twat friend, Banjo Boy Greg, had fired his gun. Amelia hadn't known who was outside or what had happened, but the gunshot had her taking things a lot more seriously.

Her first thought was that Jonah had returned. If Banjo Boy Greg had shot him, she was going to fucking kill him. She wasn't sure how, but somehow she would get revenge.

The relief when she heard Greg and Kenny whispering, and Kenny berating Greg when he saw the uniform, was tempered with fresh fear. Banjo Boy had shot a cop. While that meant it hadn't been Jonah, a dead police officer made things all the more serious, and a hell of a lot scarier.

Kenny McCool had four witnesses here. Was he seriously now going to let them go?

Nigel (or Shrek as Amelia preferred to call him) had returned and been dispatched again to take care of the police officer's car and Greg sent outside to move the cop's body into the house, so they obviously weren't planning on turning themselves in, and McCool was now pacing furiously, muttering to himself and swearing a blue streak about Greg, who when he returned to the room had lost his cocky smile and was now looking positively terrified.

Amelia wasn't sure if it was because he realised how much trouble he would be in for shooting a police officer or because he was fearful of Kenny. Likely the latter she decided.

His excuse to McCool had been that he had panicked. Seriously, why had he been trusted with a shotgun?

Meanwhile, Griffin seemed to have lost all of his bravado, while Ross was quivering like a frightened puppy, which was doing nothing to help her nerves. She could tell they were going to be absolutely no use whatsoever.

She kept her eyes trained on McCool, watching his every move, conscious that their lives were now very much in danger and that somehow they needed to escape from the house.

As McCool came over to where Greg was at the kitchen sink scrubbing the blood from his hands, his back briefly to the others, Billy clearly had the same idea, though being Billy, he was thinking only of his own neck.

One moment he was on the sofa, the next he was making a mad dash for the hall.

No! Billy, you idiot.

'Kenny!'

McCool's head had already shot round before Greg had alerted him and both men were charging across the room. Billy might actually have made it out of the house, but the pocket of his jacket caught on the door handle, jerking him back.

McCool dragged him back into the room, threw him to the floor and kicked him in the gut. Billy let out a blood-curdling, and quite frankly, embarrassing scream.

McCool kicked him again, the thump of his boot making Billy whoosh and Amelia wince. Then he hit Billy around the head with the butt of the shotgun. He seemed to be taking his frustration out on Billy, who had curled himself up in a ball, trying to protect his head from the blows.

'Griffin!' Amelia whispered, poking him in the ribs. 'Do something.'

'What exactly do you expect me to do, Mils?' he hissed back. 'They have guns.'

Yes, Griffin was going to be absolutely no help whatsoever.

'Stop it. You're hurting him.' To be fair, Billy probably deserved it, but even so, she couldn't just sit back and watch McCool beating on him. 'I said STOP!'

McCool glared at her, but said nothing. She must have got through to him, though, as he let up on his assault. 'Go find some rope or something to tie them up with,' he demanded to Greg, who immediately nodded, leaving the room.

No, this wasn't good. 'You don't have to do that,' she protested. 'I promise we won't try anything.'

McCool glanced at Billy lying on the floor then back at Amelia, scowling. 'You already did.'

'What are you going to do to us?' Amelia didn't want to ask the question, but the not knowing was worse. Ross took a sharp intake of breath beside her and she suspected he wished she hadn't said anything.

'What am I going to do?' McCool seemed to consider the question before his lips curved into a sharkish smile. 'Well, for starters I am going to find out where my brother is. I know you've seen him, and I know he was at this house last night, so no more lies. We will turn this place upside down if we have to, though I would rather it didn't come to that.' He rubbed his chin thoughtfully, cruel dark eyes on Amelia. 'As to what happens to you, well, I guess it depends how willing you are to help me. If you give me answers then I'm sure we can come to an arrangement, but if you don't, well, there's a good chance it won't end well for any of you.'

'We don't know your brother.'

Oh, hello. Griffin has finally found his voice. Unfortunately he was using that slightly preachy tone, the one Amelia hated. She really wished he would shut up. But no such luck.

'I don't understand why you think we do,' he continued.

'Really?' McCool pulled his chair up again, straddling it so they were all eye level, though his focus was now on Griffin. 'So how do you explain his phone signal coming from this house last night?'

'I can't. We only arrived yesterday. Maybe he had been passing by.'

'Passing by?' McCool laughed harshly. 'In case you hadn't noticed, posh boy, we're in the middle of fucking nowhere.'

'Could he have been hiking?' Griffin was going for nonchalant, but not really pulling it off.

'Hiking? My brother? That's actually quite funny. Dougie isn't a nature lover and he's the laziest fucker going. I would say from that comment you've never met him, but of course we both know that's a lie.'

'It's not a lie.'

McCool shook his head in frustration. 'You're not understanding me. I deal in facts and the facts are, Dougie's motorcycle broke down about eight miles south of here last night. He called Nigel here,' he told them, nodding at Shrek who had just walked back into the room, 'and said to come get him. He would be walking towards the village. When Nigel arrived, he wasn't anywhere to be seen. I have a tracker on his phone. About half an hour after that call, it put him at this house, then the signal died, which tells me either his battery ran out of charge, or it was switched off. So, posh boy, answer me this. How the fuck did my brother end up here and where the fuck is he now?'

'I don't know.'

Griffin's tone was more hushed now and Amelia heard the fear in it. None of them had considered that Dougie McCool had been on an empty stretch of road in the middle of nowhere because he'd been stranded and waiting for help. Of course people were going to be looking for him.

Still lying on the floor, clutching at his bruised face, Billy whimpered.

They had messed up badly. No, not Amelia. She had never wanted a part of this. Griffin and Billy had messed up badly. They were the ones responsible. Billy for getting behind the wheel of his car when he was pissed, for not doing the responsible thing and taking Dougie to a hospital, and Griffin for bullying the rest of them into covering Dougie's death.

Now they were screwed. McCool knew he had been here and wasn't going to leave without answers. They were dead if they didn't give them to him and dead if they did.

'Look, Mr McCool,' Griffin began. 'I understand you're upset...'

Mr McCool? Was he fucking serious? Amelia couldn't listen to this. Did he really think he was going to smarm his way out of this mess he had made? Trying to block him out she focused on the hallway, wondering how Nancy was, double blinking when she saw the figure in the shadows.

For a moment she thought it was one of McCool's goons, but then whoever it was stepped closer, and she recognised the dark curly hair and long lean build. Jonah.

No, don't come in here. As his eyes locked on hers, she tried to warn him, shaking her head very slightly and mouthing the word *no*.

McCool was preoccupied with Griffin; and Shrek had gone over to the kitchen, but if either of them saw him or if Banjo Boy Greg returned and got trigger-happy again...

Jonah already seemed to realise the score though, nodding back. Had he called for an ambulance? Was help on the way? He indicated the cloakroom, and she understood he wanted her to get inside there so they could talk. *Easier said than done*, she thought, watching him disappear, before refocussing on McCool, catching the tail-end of his reply to Griffin.

'And of course he's my brother. So yes, Mr Posh Boy, I am upset.'

If they weren't being held at gunpoint then Amelia might have found the nickname funny. While Griff had always been quick to poke fun at others, he had never been able to take a joke himself, and she knew that inside he would be seething. She supposed he did sound a bit plummy, especially when he was talking in his smooth condescending voice.

The sound of a door opening pulled her attention back to the hallway, her heart thumping when she saw Greg. Jonah was nowhere to be seen though, and Greg didn't know he was in the cloakroom.

Please let help be on the way.

Greg threw a coil of rope to McCool, then picked up his shotgun again and aimed it at the four of them. This made Amelia distinctly uncomfortable. She didn't trust Greg and his trigger-happy finger one bit.

'Stand up,' McCool ordered Griffin, producing a knife and cutting off a section of rope.

'Look, you really don't need to–'

'I said stand the fuck up.' This time Griffin jumped at McCool's raised voice, as he snapped out the words. 'I won't ask again.'

Griffin was six foot three, but Amelia had never seen him so small. He appeared to shrink in stature, doing as asked, bottom lip quivering and the colour drained from his face, as McCool yanked his arms behind his back and tied his wrists together. It finally seemed to be getting through to him that he couldn't negotiate with these people.

Shoving him back down on the sofa, McCool turned his attention to snivelling Billy next.

'So, the six of you have been friends for a while, have you?'
he asked conversationally, ignoring Billy's cries of 'Ow' as he
pushed him on his stomach, using his knee to hold him down,
and yanked the rope tight.

When none of them answered, he looked at Griffin, raising
a brow. 'Cat got your tongue, Mr Posh Boy?'

'No.'

'Then answer the question.'

'We met at university,' Amelia answered for him.

'University, eh?' McCool exchanged a grin with Shrek. 'No
wonder they all think they're so clever.' He pulled Billy up from
the floor, ignoring his cries, and sat him back on the sofa, moving
to Ross, who stood compliantly, apparently not fancying being
rough-handled.

'So you all go back a long way then? I guess you must have
some secrets and some old grudges between you.'

How would he know that?

'I told you Dougie broke down, but what I never told you
was why he was up this way in the first place.' McCool glanced
at each of their faces. 'He was going to do a job for someone.'

Why is he telling us this?

'He owed me a lot of money and I kept chasing him for it;
thought I was going to have to get nasty with my own brother.
He promised he would have it tonight though. Said he had a job
that was paying cash. One of you hired him.'

What?

'No we didn't.'

'Yes you did, Mils. He told Nigel and Greg he had a job for
them. The three of them were supposed to be coming here
tonight and staging a break-in. Roughing up everyone in the
house and giving you all a scare.'

'You're lying,' Griffin challenged.

'I'm not lying.'

'Then who?'

'If I had a name this situation might not be happening. Dougie never said who he was meeting.'

This had to be another mind game. McCool was trying to turn them on each other. Yes, things were a bit fraught between them all, but none of them would do anything like that.

Amelia scowled at him. 'If that's true, why are we all here? Whoever had hired him would have left or not come in the first place.'

'And miss all the fun?'

'I don't believe you.'

'You don't have to believe me, sweetheart. I know it's the truth, just as I know that one of you has done something to Dougie. Did you change your mind about the plan? Try to get out of giving him the money?'

'You're wrong.' Ross sounded like he was going to burst into tears. 'No one hired him. You must have the wrong house.'

'I don't think so.' McCool squashed him back onto the sofa between Amelia and Billy, raising a finger as he went along the line of them. 'Eeny, meeny, miny, moe. Catch a liar by his toe. I wonder which one of you it could be? Is it Posh Boy here, or our feisty little Mils?' He looked at Ross, appraising. 'You've not had much to say until now. Were you planning on doing the dirty on your friends and my brother?'

'No!'

'Or what about you, Sniveller?'

'It wasn't me,' Billy protested. 'I didn't do anything.'

'Maybe it was your friend in the hallway then? Or what about this Jonah? He seems to have abandoned you. Was this always his plan?'

'He wouldn't do that,' Amelia snapped, feeling the weight of Griffin's stare.

'You seem pretty certain about that.'

194

'I am.'

'I think he's the most likely,' Griffin said after a moment of hesitation.

'What?'

'He went to get help, Mils, and he never came back.'

Yes he did. Of course she couldn't say that. 'He would not leave us.'

Beside her, Griffin bristled. 'What you mean is, you don't think he would leave you. That's right, isn't it?'

'What are you trying to say, Griffin?'

'Oh come on, Mils, stop being coy about it. You and Jonah have been fucking each other behind my back for years. Do you seriously think I am stupid?'

'No we have not!' It was the truth though, seriously, how did Griffin know anything about what had happened that night with Jonah?

McCool was watching their exchange with a smirk. 'Now this is an interesting development. I figured you two were a couple, but I didn't realise you were cheating on Posh Boy Griffin here, Mils.'

'We're not a couple,' Amelia snapped, still reeling that Griffin knew. 'Not for a long time.'

'Because of Jonah,' Griffin pointed out.

'Not because of Jonah.' Okay, so that time she was lying. Well, partly lying. She had left Griffin because she realised she wasn't in love with him, but yes, what had happened with Jonah had triggered that. How had he found out? 'I never cheated on you.'

'Well it seems we have plenty to chat about,' McCool told them, nodding to Amelia as he held the rope out. 'Now are we going to do this the easy way, Mils? Or do I need to give you a hand getting up?'

She couldn't let him tie her up, knew she needed to play for time. 'I really need to use the bathroom.'

McCool rolled his eyes. 'No bathroom breaks. If you get desperate you'll just have to do what your friend did.' He glanced at the damp patch on Billy's jeans, laughing.

Fuck. She needed to see Jonah. 'I'm on my period. Please.'

Beside her, Griffin grimaced. He had never been good with any female issues, freaking out when she'd once asked him to pick her up some tampons. McCool seemed to consider her request, looking pretty grossed out himself. Typical bloody men.

'Please?' she asked again. 'This is humiliating to have to ask. I really need to go.'

Eventually he let out a huff, shaking his head and glancing at Greg. 'There's a cloakroom down the hall. Take her there.'

'I need my bag. It has my tampons in it.'

Another huff. 'Where is it?'

'On the kitchen counter.'

'This one?' Shrek asked, picking up her black tote bag.

Amelia nodded, taking it from him when he brought it across, her mind skimming the contents as she considered what she and Jonah could use in there for a weapon.

McCool must have read her mind though, snatching it from her. 'Not so fast.' To her dismay he emptied the contents on the floor, picking through her cosmetics, purse and other bits, removing her nail scissors, deodorant, pen and keys. Satisfied there was nothing of concern in there, he handed it back. 'Make it quick,' he snapped.

Amelia didn't waste any time getting up from the sofa, going compliantly with Greg. She spotted Nancy still motionless in the hallway next to the body of the police officer and shuddered. Was her friend even still alive? How the hell were they going to get out of this mess?

'Come on.' Greg roughly took hold of her arm, dragging her towards the cloakroom.

No, he can't come inside with me! Jonah is in there. 'Let go of me, I don't need you to follow me in,' she protested, trying to pull free.

'You're not going in there until I've checked it out, sweetheart.' He opened the door and Amelia held her breath, waiting for him to spot Jonah.

'Ha! I see what you were planning.' Pulling her into the room behind him, he positioned her in front of the window. Amelia had forgotten that it was still open from when Billy had made his bid for freedom, which had ultimately resulted in McCool getting in the house.

The fuckwit.

'Thought you were going to be smart and crawl out of there, didn't you?'

'I just need to use the loo,' Amelia insisted, so relieved he was focused on the window and not Jonah. Where was he? He had definitely come in here, right? She glanced warily around the room, her eyes falling on the cupboard in the corner, and she understood.

Greg pulled the window closed and Amelia noticed there was a key in the lock, which he turned before pocketing it. He glanced towards the cupboard and her heart thumped as he tried to open the door. Relief spilled over when he found it locked. At least he seemed satisfied she couldn't get out.

'Can I have some privacy please?'

He studied her for a moment, and she thought he was going to insist on staying in the bathroom with her. 'You have three minutes,' he said eventually, pulling the door shut behind him.

Three minutes was barely any time. She went straight to the cupboard, pressing against it and whispering, 'Jonah?'

For a brief moment there was silence and she second-guessed herself. Maybe he hadn't come in here. But then there was shuffling on the other side of the door and the sound of a key turning in the lock.

She waited impatiently, willing him to hurry up, as he seemed to be taking bloody forever. She glanced back at the main door to the cloakroom, aware Banjo Boy Greg was just outside.

Damn it, Jonah. Hurry up.

Eventually the cupboard door opened, and Jonah stepped out. Amelia threw her arms around him, hugging him tightly. 'I was scared they had hurt you,' she whispered, wondering why he wasn't returning her embrace.

'I'm fine, though I've had a few issues of my own.' He stepped back from her, twisting away, and to her shock she saw he was wearing handcuffs.

'What the hell happened?'

'Long story and we don't have time, but you see the copper in the hallway? He has the keys for these cuffs, and I need you to help me get them.'

'How? They have guns, Jonah.'

'I know, but I can't do anything to help you like this.' He was silent for a moment. 'Do you think you can persuade them to move his body in here?'

'I don't know. I can try. But can you get the keys while you're cuffed?'

Jonah shrugged. 'I have to. Get him in here and I will figure out a way.'

'There's no help coming, is there?' Amelia finally asked the question she was dreading the answer to, her heart sinking when he shook his head.

'The neighbours weren't home. I tried to get to their phone, but this happened.' He gestured to the cuffs. 'PC Murray out there was insistent he didn't need backup.'

A knock on the door had Amelia jumping.

'You have one minute left,' Greg shouted.

'Okay,' she called back. 'I'm nearly done.'

She went through the motions of flushing the toilet and turning on the tap, before turning back to Jonah. 'I will try my best to get them to move him in here, I promise.' She hesitated, her mind going back to McCool's revelation that one of them had hired Dougie. It was possible that he had been trying to get a reaction, wanting to make them turn on each other, but what if he was telling the truth? Why had Dougie McCool been here in the middle of nowhere, with a rucksack of money?'

Jonah frowned. 'Is everything okay?'

'McCool says one of us hired Dougie. That he was supposed to be staging a break-in here tonight.'

'What? Why would we do that?'

'I honestly don't know, and it makes no sense. But what if it was true?'

'McCool is playing with you. Don't listen to anything he says.'

'There's something else too.'

'There is?'

'Griffin knows.' She didn't have to elaborate exactly what Griffin knew. Could see from Jonah's expression that he understood.

He nodded slowly. 'Well that explains a few things.'

She wanted to ask him what he meant by that, but another knock on the door told her she had to go.

'Time's up.'

Shit. 'Two seconds, I'm just finishing up,' Amelia answered Greg, pushing Jonah back into the cupboard.

'Amelia. I'm going to figure out a way to get us out of this, I promise. You and me. And we'll get help for Nancy too.'

She nodded, knew he meant it. Leaning up on tiptoe, she bunched his T-shirt into her fist and pulled him close, kissing him firmly on the lips, needing him to know how she felt about him, in case it was the last chance she had. 'I know.' She pressed her mouth to his ear. 'And just so you know. It was always you. It always will be you.'

Before he could react to that, she eased the door shut, sucked in a breath, needing an extra moment she knew she didn't have.

As the cloakroom door opened, she made a show of looking in the mirror, smoothing her fingers over her hair.

'Come on, you don't need to worry about looking pretty. By the time Kenny has finished with you, you'll never want to look in a mirror again.' Banjo Boy Greg laughed at his own comment and Amelia scowled at him, ignoring the sliver of fear that trailed down her spine. Not knowing what Kenny McCool planned to do to them was frightening the hell out of her.

Kenny was waiting for them back in the living room, the rope in his hands, and she frantically tried to think of another excuse, anything to buy more time. 'My friend needs help. She's lost a lot of blood.'

McCool shrugged. 'There's nothing I can do about that.'

'Yes there is. You could do the right thing and call an ambulance.'

'And miss out on having some fun with you? I don't think so.'

Fun? What the fuck does he have in mind?

'Anyway, I thought an ambulance was on the way?' he questioned, his tone mocking. They both knew one wasn't.

'We don't know where Jonah is,' she reminded him. 'If he finds help, one might show up. And you're going to have four hostages, plus a dead cop and my badly injured friend in the hall. At which point you will be fucked.'

'Such ladylike language, Mils. Now come here.'

When she didn't move, Greg pushed her forward with the

gun. McCool took her bag from her and turned her round so her back was to him, yanking her hands behind her. She sensed she had struck a nerve with her Jonah comment, as he spoke to Shrek. 'Nigel, what did you do with his car?'

'I moved it off the road. No one will see it.'

'Maybe we should move him out of the hallway, just to be on the safe side. Mop up that blood too.'

'I can help you,' Amelia offered, ignoring the look Griffin was giving her. 'I don't mind mopping up. And you could put the body in the cloakroom. It's out of the way there.'

'And why would you want to do that?' McCool still had hold of her wrists, twisting them behind her and pulling her back against him.

'Because I'm scared, and I just want to try and get through this in one piece.' She kept her tone demure, the note of fear in it genuine. 'I will help you if you promise not to hurt me.'

It sounded like she was throwing the others under a bus, but they had no idea about Jonah, and she couldn't tell them. Instead she tried to avoid looking at their faces.

'You want to know what I think?' McCool's mouth was right up against her ear now, his hot breath making her skin crawl. 'I think I preferred Mouthy Mils. Docile doesn't suit you, sweetheart. Now hold still.'

She winced as he lashed her wrists together, giving a sharp tug on the rope and tightening it more than she thought was necessary. Her heart sunk. How was she supposed to help Jonah now?

He twisted her around, the look on his face suggesting he knew exactly what she had been trying to do and wanting her to know that he had beaten her.

'That's better,' he told her, pushing her back down on the sofa between Griffin and Ross. 'Now you stay there and behave.'

As he went over to the kitchen to join Shrek and Banjo Boy, Griffin leant towards Amelia, hissing in her ear.

'You traitorous bitch. If we get free, I'm going to get you for this.'

Amelia glared at him, though didn't attempt to explain her actions. If she told Griffin that Jonah was in the house, she didn't trust him not to tell McCool.

Instead of coming together, the group had fractured, and it seemed they were hiding more than the secret of what had happened to Dougie McCool.

Amelia no longer trusted Griffin and she wasn't sure Ross or Billy would have her back either. It was each for their own now and she was going to do whatever it took to survive.

23

THEN

Griffin King was used to getting his own way. His father was an ambitious man whose first rule of business was not to involve his feelings when it came to building his business empire. His mother was a trophy wife who had been driven by her own parents to marry for status rather than for love. Griffin had lacked the general ambition part, happy to take handouts from his father, and very occasionally his heart ruled his head, but he had learnt to bulldoze his way through life, taking what he wanted, and if that meant using a little creative storytelling, then so be it.

He liked Jonah Flint and the pair of them had hit it off when Jonah first came to look at the room Griffin was letting in his house. Well, okay. His dad had bought the place, but he still thought of it as his, and had been allowed to choose who he lived with.

Laid-back Billy Maguire had been an easy pick. He seemed fun, plus he knew people and played in a band. Griffin had approved of him straightaway, knowing Billy could help expand his social circle.

Jonah had been different: sharp-minded and quick-witted,

but with an easy-going nature that had drawn him in. He wasn't quite as sure of himself as Billy, but there was an appealing honesty about him, and Griffin soon learnt that he wore his heart on his sleeve.

While he was keen to make connections through Billy, it was Jonah he bonded with most. Griffin could be overconfident at times but beneath his hard exterior was a more fragile side he hated showing to people. Jonah was one of the few people who had come close to seeing beneath the surface.

All bets were off, though, the night Griffin met Amelia Abery.

He already knew of her because Jonah never stopped talking the fuck about her. Jonah had it bad for Amelia and Griffin had expected her to be one of the pretty but empty vessels that wandered about campus, walking the walk and talking the talk, but never delivering when it came to substance.

How wrong he had been.

Amelia had been the most vulnerable-looking Halloween villain he had ever seen when he had found her a little dazed and confused in his kitchen. Her Poison Ivy outfit had caught his attention, but it was her innocence that sucked him in, and he immediately understood why Jonah was smitten with her. And that there was a problem, because now, so was Griffin.

Perhaps he should have considered his friendship with Jonah, just as perhaps he shouldn't have duped Amelia, but he was used to getting what he wanted, so he lied without even thinking about it.

Jonah was mad at him for a while, though he eventually got over it. But Amelia, bless her, was never any the wiser.

Griffin had what he wanted, the woman he planned to marry, and everything was on track in his life, even if he hadn't achieved quite the results his parents had been hoping for when he graduated university, despite Ross's help. He found a job as a personal trainer and Amelia worked as a graphic designer on magazines before going freelance. They had bought a house together and she had accepted his marriage proposal. Griffin expected the next step would be babies. He wanted heirs to his family name. But then she had broken up with him, calling off their engagement just weeks before their wedding, and he had been mortified.

To some he guessed, Amelia had acted honourably, given the circumstances. She had sat down with him privately, returning the expensive engagement ring with the huge flashy diamond, that he had paid a fortune for, and telling him she was making a mistake. It wasn't him; it was her and that while she loved him, she wasn't in love with him. There was no one else; she just needed to be alone. She had apologised for her timing, offered to contact everyone and pay for anything that couldn't be refunded.

Griffin had reacted by kicking her out of the house they shared, calling her a string of vile names and telling her he never wanted to see her again.

Amelia had gone to stay with her aunt, refusing to fight him when he played hardball over the house and its contents, saying he could have it all.

She had broken him.

Scraping up what little dignity he had left, he had spent the next few years playing hard and fast, seeking solace in the fact that at least he had friends he could rely on.

How fucking wrong he had been.

Sat on the sofa in the luxury house he had hired for the weekend, where he had planned an extravaganza tonight fitting of his birthday, he rued those friendships, realising that the only person in the room who had his back was Ross.

Sure he had played pally with Jonah and Amelia to get them here, but it had all been a charade, while Billy fucking

Maguire, the one person who Griffin had bailed out time and again, was only thinking about himself.

Ross, on the other hand, had shown his loyalty time and again, yet he was probably the one person Griffin had always taken for granted. He didn't really fit in with their circle of friends and Griffin likely wouldn't have given him the time of day if he hadn't needed his brain.

As it was, he kept him close and part of him was ashamed for how he had manipulated the man over the years. Ross never seemed to mind though and Griffin knew he was assured of his unwavering loyalty when it came to Amelia. Probably because on the occasions he wanted to do stuff without him, he had led Ross to believe it was Amelia who didn't want him around.

It was lucky he had, as Ross had witnessed Jonah's declaration of love to Amelia, just before she had called off the wedding – had seen them kissing – on Griffin's birthday just to add insult to injury.

And okay, Ross should have spoken up sooner instead of waiting years to tell Griffin, but the important thing was he had eventually told him the truth.

Griffin had been consumed with rage, both towards Amelia and Jonah. His lying ex-fiancée, who had told him there was no one else, and his supposed best friend who had commiserated with him in the days after Amelia moved out.

They had humiliated Griffin and he was determined he was going to pay them back. Tonight was supposed to have been his big reveal, toasting the pair of them over dinner as he told them he knew what they had done; then playing a video he had made of Amelia, back when they were together. One he knew would devastate her and infuriate Jonah. He had intended to humiliate them both before kicking them out of the house.

Instead he was tied up next to his lying, cheating, two-faced ex-fiancée, while a lunatic with a shotgun was holding them hostage. He had known Amelia was cold, cheating on him with his best friend and humiliating him the way she had, but she had just shown another crueller side, ready to sell Griffin, Ross and Billy out.

How could he have ever loved her?

If they ever got out of this mess, he was going to teach her a lesson once and for all.

24

JONAH

With his wrists cuffed, Jonah couldn't see his watch, so had no idea how long he had been waiting in the cupboard, but it felt like forever. He had locked the door behind him again and the only light came from the gap underneath it.

Had Amelia failed in persuading McCool to move Murray's body into the cloakroom? If so, he was going to need a Plan B, which might involve getting out of the house again. He was reluctant to leave her behind, even if it did mean he might eventually be able to help her.

The minutes ticked by, and he strained his ears, trying to figure out what was going on in the other room. Other than the occasions when McCool raised his voice or one of the goons laughed, though, the sounds were muffled and often barely audible.

The problem was, the longer he waited here, the worse things could be for the others.

There had only been one scream, a sound he was fairly certain had come from Billy, who could be melodramatic at the best of times, but how patient was McCool going to be? Would he eventually turn to torture to get answers? And if he did get them, what then?

If he learnt what had happened to Dougie, Jonah was certain he would kill them all.

Which he might well do anyway. The gang already had a dead police officer on their hands.

Deciding that he couldn't wait any longer, he turned so his back was facing the door, fumbling for the lock. His fingers had just made contact with the key when he heard the creak of the main door opening, and froze.

Was it one of them coming to use the loo?

But then he heard the voices arguing and the distinct sound of something being dragged.

'Be careful. You're making a mess.'

'It's fine. We'll just mop it up.'

'What about the girl? Are we moving her too?'

Were they referring to Nancy or had something happened to Amelia? It made sense that it was Nancy, but that didn't stop his heart thudding.

'Kenny just said the cop. Leave her where she is for now.'

'Is she dead? She looks dead?'

'Fuck knows. Does it matter?'

'Be careful with his feet.'

'Why? He can't feel anything.'

'Yeah, but you don't want them sticking out of the door.' Silence, then, 'I can't believe you shot a cop, you silly bastard.'

'I already told you it was an accident. I panicked.'

'Fucking liability. That's what you are.'

'Come on. Let's get back out there. I think Kenny is ready to start having some fun with them. See how loud he can make them squeal. I don't want to miss that.'

'I tell you who I would like to make squeal. That hot little redhead.'

'She has a mouth on her.'

'I know where I would like to put her mouth.'

They both grunted with laughter at that as Jonah fought to keep his breathing steady. He balled his hands into fists, pulling against the cuffs. If either of them did anything to Amelia he was going to find a way to fucking kill them.

He heard the cloakroom door close, their voices becoming more muffled, then he waited a couple of minutes just to be certain they weren't coming back. He reached for the key again, turning it in the lock and easing the door open.

Murray was propped up between the sink and the toilet, head tipped to one side and eyes shut. His face was drained of colour. He may have been a little set in his ways, insisting he knew best, but he hadn't deserved this. Jonah had told him to call for backup. Why hadn't he listened? If he had, McCool and his mates might be in custody right now and Amelia and the others would be safe.

Instead, he had to find the key to these handcuffs then figure out a way to either get help or stop McCool himself.

He dropped to his knees beside Murray's body, trying to angle himself so he could reach inside the pockets of the officer's work trousers and jumping like hell when a cold hand clutched at his arm.

What the fuck?

A low groan followed, as the hand eased its grip, and Jonah somehow stopped himself from yelling out. He rolled over though, quick to use his feet to push himself back across the floor, keen to put distance between himself and Murray's body.

He stared at the dead police officer as his heart thumped, his mind briefly going to *The Walking Dead*.

Fuck no. This was real life.

The man looked dead. Had it been some kind of cadaveric spasm?

But then he noticed the police officer's chest. The movement was faint, but he appeared to be breathing.

He's alive?

One eye fluttered open, staring at Jonah. 'You need to get help.' Murray's voice was weak, but he spoke with enough clarity to suggest that maybe he had been conscious for a while.

'I thought you were dead.'

'I feel like I should be. Lost a fair bit of blood.' The other eye cranked open now. 'Thought I told you to wait in the car?'

'Lucky for you I didn't listen,' Jonah told him, moving closer again.

'That's true.' Murray was silent for a moment, a grimace indicating he was in a lot of pain and struggling to breath properly. The bullet had gone into his stomach and while he was alive now, he might not be for long. 'They took my phone. You need to get out of here and find help.'

Jonah indicated the cuffs. 'That's a little difficult right now.'

Murray nodded, the dismay on his face suggesting he was wishing he hadn't used them now. 'Keys are in my shirt pocket, if you can get to them.'

It wasn't easy, especially with how Murray was positioned on the floor and Jonah was conscious not to hurt him, but after half a dozen attempts he retrieved the keys.

Unlocking the cuffs was fortunately easier and he slipped them off, rolling his shoulders and rubbing at his wrists, relieved to finally have full movement back.

Squatting by Murray, he looked over the man's wound. Although he had no medical training, he could tell it was bad.

'How close is it to the nearest neighbour after the bungalow?'

'About four and a half miles.'

That would take over half an hour if he ran.

He needed to get help quickly and the only way to do that

was by phone. McCool and his idiot mates would each have one, plus they had Murray's too. If he could somehow steal one... His best chance of doing that was to overpower one of the men.

The guy with the baseball cap, the one he had seen dragging Murray into the house, would be the easiest target. He was young, small and wiry, but if Jonah caught him off guard and alone, he was certain he could take down any of the men easily.

He would then have access to a gun and hopefully a phone.

If this was going to work though, he would need a distraction, to separate the men.

'I'll be back as quickly as I can,' he told Murray, who seemed to be drifting in and out of consciousness. He wasn't sure if the officer heard him or not. Slipping the cuffs and the keys into his jeans pocket, he eased open the cloakroom door a crack, seeing the hallway was empty. The voices from the living room were no longer muffled, and he listened for a moment, trying to gauge the situation, checking the men were still in there.

He was fairly certain it was McCool doing the talking, his tone authoritative and a little mocking.

'I think we all know help isn't coming. Just as we all know this place is in the middle of nowhere. What are we? Saturday afternoon. If you only arrived last night, I'm guessing you have this place until at least Monday; maybe the rest of the week? Now I'm willing to wait if I have to, but I do get bored easily, so if you want to drag this out, we will, but I'm going to need to find ways to amuse myself. That could become quite uncomfortable for you.'

There was a beat of silence then an anguished yelp before Ross spoke. 'No, please! Please stop!'

'Don't hurt him. Leave him alone.' That was Amelia, and Jonah's gut tightened at the thread of fear in her voice.

Then there was laughter at her comment, he guessed from McCool's two friends.

'So you see, you have a choice. You can tell me what I want to know, or we can do things the hard way.'

Ross – at least Jonah assumed it was Ross – was sobbing hard now and McCool sounded a little disgusted. 'For God's sake, man, pull yourself together. It was only a scratch. Things are going to get much worse than that if you don't start talking.'

As the threats continued, Jonah slipped out of the cloakroom into the hall. Nancy was in a bad way; the bleeding having stopped and she was unnaturally still. Was she even breathing? It was too risky to stop and check and he tried to ignore the stab of guilt as he stepped over her body, heading for the back door.

Outside, he made his way round to the front of the house, crouching low when he approached the living-room window, peering inside.

One of the kitchen chairs had been dragged to the centre of the room and that was where Ross sat as McCool circled him, and Jonah could see the vicious blade in McCool's hand was stained red.

Amelia was sandwiched between Griffin and Billy on the sofa, all three of them watching McCool, who seemed to be berating the sobbing Ross, while the other two men looked on from the kitchen area. Baseball Cap sat on the island counter, his short legs dangling, while his thick-necked mate leant against it, elbows on the marble work surface, both thoroughly amused. Their guns were resting on the countertop.

Jonah dropped to the ground, his back pressed against the wall, his mind ticking over as he tried to figure out a way to gain an advantage. He couldn't access the locked garage and going back in the house was tricky. There was no way he could enter the living room without being seen. That meant he needed to lure one of the men outside, take him by surprise.

But how?

A scream from inside cut straight through him, followed by more laughter.

Think, Jonah.

The rear garden was circled by the woods. To the back of the lawn was a patio with a wooden overhead trellis that covered the outdoor bar and hot tub. If the bar was unlocked he could smash a couple of bottles on the patio. Maybe use another one as a weapon. If he made enough noise it would bring the men out to investigate. But probably only one or two of them. McCool wouldn't want to leave his hostages unguarded.

He made his way round the back again, not missing the irony that had Billy not run over Dougie McCool, they would have probably been using the hot tub and bar for a very different purpose this afternoon. As it was, Jonah had only seen it once, when Griffin had given them a brief tour after they had first arrived.

The hot tub was covered and the shutters down on the front of the bar. As he suspected, the door leading into the bar was also locked, but he broke in easily, this time without hesitation, using one of the stones from the rockery.

Inside were dozens of bottles of spirits, both on shelves and in optic bottles, while an under-the-counter fridge hummed as it kept cans of lager and bottles of white wine cool.

Figuring he would smash the glass on the patio then hide in the woods and wait, he started to reach for a large quarter-full bottle of gin. But then he spotted the radio and had a far better idea.

25

BILLY

Billy Maguire was beginning to worry that his luck had run out.

No one had ever hit him before. They had tried, but he always ran away from trouble or talked his way out of it. Or when things were really desperate he made someone else take the fall for his cock-ups.

While Kenny McCool's back was turned, he had seen an opportunity and taken it, bolting for the door and fully expecting to get away. He hadn't even considered the others. At this point it was every man for himself. He just knew he had to run. And he would have made it, he was sure of it, had it not been for his stupid jacket and its stupid pocket and that stupid bloody door handle.

And now he was bruised and battered, sat on the sofa, his hands tied uncomfortably behind his back, so he couldn't even check his split lip or wipe away the blood that had been dripping from his nose, his gut aching like hell from where he had been kicked, and wondering how the fuck he was going to get out of this mess.

At the moment McCool seemed focused on Ross, having picked him at random, perhaps because he looked the easiest to break, tying him to the dining chair and circling him like a shark, alternating between asking him questions and taunting him with threats, occasionally using the knife he was holding to make Ross squeal.

Only superficial cuts, nothing that was going to kill him, but from the amount of screaming and sobbing Ross had been doing, each slice had hurt like hell.

It was a miracle that Ross hadn't yet completely broken down and confessed what they had done to Dougie. At some point he would either talk, or McCool would put another one of them on the chair. Griffin and Amelia were stronger. Billy knew he would never cope.

As though he had heard Billy's thought, McCool cut the ropes, dragging Ross off the seat and pushing him back down on the sofa. He picked Ross's glasses up from the floor, one lens cracked from where they had fallen off when McCool had earlier punched him, and pushed them back on to his face. As McCool stepped back, Billy shot a glance at Ross. If this whole situation hadn't been so bloody dire he might have actually laughed at how ridiculous he looked with the twisted frames making the glasses hang lopsided.

Beneath the glasses though, he could see the swelling and the cuts to his face, felt the fear as Ross trembled against him, and he yanked at the rope binding his wrists, panic closing in, aware he was trapped.

When McCool turned to face them again, waving his blood-splattered knife at each of them in turn, silently selecting his next victim, Billy squeezed his eyes shut. *Please pick Amelia or Griffin. Please pick Amelia or Griffin.*

'You!'

He didn't have time to react, as McCool yanked him off the sofa, dropping him on to the chair. Tears leaked from his eyes when the man grinned at him.

'Now you look like a man who's ready for a chat.'

'Please don't hurt me again,' Billy begged, as McCool fastened him to the chair, so he had no chance of getting away.

Behind them, one of the goons laughed. 'Don't make him piss himself again, Kenny.'

Shame might have heated Billy's cheeks, but all he could focus on was getting himself out of this situation. He shot a glance at the hallway. From the angle he was sat he could see Nancy's leg and booted foot, knew that beyond that was the door that would lead to freedom.

It was so close, but he knew he couldn't get there.

McCool raised his knife, caressing it against Billy's cheek, and fear sweated out of every pore. Beyond the knife, beyond McCool, he could see the horrified faces of Griffin and Amelia and he wasn't sure if their expressions were filled with terror about what was now going to happen to him or panic that he might blab.

Ross, who was still quietly sobbing, sat broken and bleeding beside them, and Billy wasn't prepared to suffer the same fate. He would tell McCool whatever he wanted to know before he let the man cut him with his knife.

Well, within reason. He could say that Dougie collapsed dead on their doorstep. No way was he admitting to Dougie's psycho brother that he had hit him while drink-driving.

That wouldn't end well for him.

'What's your name, son?'

'B-B-Billy.'

'And are you going to be a little more cooperative than your pal, Ross, Billy?'

Wincing as the point of the blade moved higher so it was just below his eye, Billy sucked in a breath, ready to confess. 'It was—'

'What the fuck is that?' One of the goons interrupted Billy, moving over to where McCool had paused, his knife still hovering way too close to Billy's eye for his comfort.

'Is that music?'

McCool's question was answered for him as the volume doubled, Neil Diamond belting out *'Sweet Caroline'*. It was coming from outside.

What the hell?

'Go check it out!'

The wiry guy with the baseball cap didn't need to be asked twice, charging down the hallway with his shotgun and out of the door.

McCool didn't seem overly concerned about what might be happening, instead turning his attention back to Billy. 'Right. Where were we?' He moved his knife down to Billy's ear, slipped the tip through the silver hoop that pierced his lobe and gave it a painful tug. 'Where's my brother?'

Billy didn't respond, again squeezing his eyes shut, as he focused on the lyrics of 'Sweet Caroline'.

Make it go away. Make it go away.

'My brother was at this house last night and he has my money. I know you know where he is. Tell me.'

'I don't know.'

'You don't know?' McCool tugged harder on the ring.

'Ow. Please stop.'

'Tell me!'

'Okay! I don't know where your brother is, but your money's upstairs.'

There was a sharp intake of breath from the sofa. Billy

thought it might have come from Griffin, though he didn't dare look.

McCool didn't ease up on the pressure. 'Upstairs where?'

'In Ross's room. We put it under the floorboards. Please let me go.'

'Which room!'

'Please stop!'

'WHICH ROOM?'

'Second door on the left. The floorboards by the bed are loose.' Griffin sounded resigned and Billy suspected he was probably swearing about him under his breath.

'I'll go look,' the other goon muttered.

'Okay, I've told you. Let me go now. Please.'

'Not until you tell me where my brother is.'

'I don't know where your brother is. I swear.'

'Then why the fuck do you have his money?'

'I don't know!' Billy squeezed his eyes shut again, trying to block him out.

McCool twisted his knife in the ring and yanked hard, and a bright white light of pain shot through Billy's ear, making him scream. It all went quiet and when he finally dared open his eyes again, his tormentor was holding his knife up in front of Billy's face, the bloody hoop caught on the end.

He was going to be sick.

As his ear throbbed, McCool leant in close, one hand yanking his head back, the other with the knife now pressed against Billy's throat. 'What have you done with my fucking brother?'

'Step away and drop the knife.'

What?

The pressure of the blade eased, though McCool still had a hold of a clump of Billy's hair.

He glanced through tear-blurred eyes towards the voice, saw Jonah in the doorway; he was holding one of the shotguns and had it aimed at the ugly baseball-capped goon in front of him.

Jonah was back. He hadn't left them, which meant help must be on the way. And he had taken control of the situation. Billy's tears turned to sobs of relief.

As Jonah pushed the goon – Greg, Billy was sure McCool had called him – further into the room, he saw the man was handcuffed, subdued, not daring to make eye contact with McCool, as he realised he had fucked up.

McCool's shotgun was on the kitchen counter, and he only had the knife. Realising he had no choice, he did as asked, releasing his grip on Billy and backing up, though he still kept hold of his weapon.

'I said, drop the knife.'

'Look, let's just talk about this, okay?'

Seriously, now he just wants to talk?

'Jonah, are the police on the way?'

Jonah gave the briefest of glances at Griffin, though didn't answer his question. Instead he kept his focus on McCool. 'Put the knife down or I'll shoot him.'

'You wouldn't have the bottle.'

'Is that a challenge?' Jonah aimed the gun at Greg's temple and waited for McCool to respond.

'Kenny, please.' Greg wasn't sounding quite so cocksure now.

McCool hesitated, seeming unsure whether to call Jonah's bluff. Reluctantly, his actions slow, he set the knife down on the floor.

'Kick it away from you.'

Another hesitation before he did as asked.

Jonah glanced at Billy then his focus went straight to Amelia, sandwiched between Griffin and Ross. 'Are you okay?'

She nodded, holding his gaze, as Griffin grumbled, 'You need to untie us.'

'In a second.' He turned his attention back to McCool. 'Get down on your hands and knees and then put your hands on your head.'

Billy was pretty certain McCool rolled his eyes. He did as asked though, looking thoroughly pissed off.

'Sorry, Kenny,' Greg whispered.

McCool shook his head at the kid, though said nothing.

What happened next was so quick, Billy barely had time to register. He had forgotten all about the other goon – Nigel he thought his name was – who had gone upstairs to find the money.

Amelia was the one who spotted him first, her amber eyes widening in horror as she yelled out a warning. 'Jonah!'

Jonah reacted, but wasn't quick enough, as the heavy vase came crashing down onto his head and he crumpled to the ground.

Amelia was screaming and Billy started sobbing again, the freedom that had moments ago seemed so close, cruelly torn away.

As the goon retrieved the shotgun, aiming it at Jonah's unconscious body, McCool climbed to his feet, a smug look on his face.

'Good work, Nigel.'

'Can someone please uncuff me?' Greg pleaded.

McCool ignored him, picking up his knife and going over to the kitchen counter. He cut off another section of rope before returning to the group.

'Did you get the money?' he asked Nigel, as he used the rope to secure Jonah.

Billy could only hope Jonah had managed to call the police before his attempt at playing hero. If not they were fucked.

But he soon discovered there was a whole new level of fucked when Nigel answered.

'He was dicking us around, Kenny,' he told McCool, shaking his head. 'I found the rucksack, but there's hardly any money in it. It's mostly stuffed with clothes.'

M cCool had positioned Jonah against the wall next to the now closed door that led through to the hall. His head was slumped forward and he had been unconscious for several minutes now. Amelia was frantic to check on him, needing to know he was okay.

It was just the five of them with McCool in the living room. McCool had dispatched his goons upstairs to try and find the missing money and she could hear floorboards creaking as they stomped about, the various bangs of falling furniture telling her they weren't being at all careful.

Although Amelia had wanted no part in keeping the rucksack, she knew the others had agreed to put it under the floorboards in Ross's room; so where the hell was the cash?

According to McCool, one of the group had taken Dougie's phone and had also hired him to stage a break-in. The money had now gone missing too. Plus, of course, there was the question of whether or not Nancy had been pushed down the stairs.

One of them couldn't be trusted, but Amelia wasn't sure who it was.

She had already ruled Jonah and Nancy out of the equation, so that left Griffin, Billy and Ross. The money missing was a fact, and it was hard to doubt McCool about the phone and the break-in. He was holding them hostage and had no reason to do so unless what he was saying was true.

Which of the three people she had classed as friends would do this?

If Griffin wanted revenge, it would be on her and Jonah. As far as she was aware, he had nothing against the others. Billy was selfish and a fuck-up, but he wasn't calculated. That left Ross, but he was the most successful and financially secure of them. Plus she struggled to see him moving in the same circles as Dougie McCool.

She looked at them now. Billy sobbing quietly as he sat on the chair facing them. The side of his face and ear lobe were caked in drying blood from where McCool had ripped out his earring.

Ross looked defeated, covered in cuts and bruises from where he had been tortured.

If the thugs couldn't find the money, it would be her turn next, or Griffin's.

McCool had already shown that he was happy to hurt them. For as long as they couldn't give him what he was looking for, he wasn't going to leave. Was he a murderer though?

Just how far would he push this?

She shuddered at the thought, looking at her ex-fiancé. Griffin tried to make out he was tough, but truth was he was more of a bully. Amelia didn't think he would hold up well under McCool's questioning. He sat beside her, his face like stone, and she suspected he was still seething about her perceived betrayal. Well, that and the fact that Jonah was back in the room.

Even in this dire situation she couldn't see Griffin working with them to get out of this. He had too much damn stubborn pride.

She glanced over at Jonah again, wanting him to wake up so she knew he was okay, but at the same time she was scared of what McCool might do to him if he regained consciousness.

When she turned back, she realised Griffin had been watching her.

And so had McCool. He had been in the kitchen, casually making a coffee, acting as if he lived here and hadn't just been torturing the occupants of the house he had invaded. 'So tell me,' he asked, coming over with the mug between his hands. 'What exactly is the deal with this little love triangle? This is Jonah, right?' He nodded to where Jonah was slumped by the door.

When neither Griffin nor Amelia answered, he sipped at his drink, studying them both. 'So you and Posh Boy here used to be together, right, Mils?'

'We were supposed to get married,' Griffin told him, his tone bitter.

'But she cheated on you?'

'Yes.'

'With Jonah?' McCool pushed.

'I did not bloody cheat on you!'

'Don't lie. Ross saw you!'

What? 'What are you talking about?'

'Ross told me! He saw Jonah with his tongue down your throat at my birthday party, just before you told me you wanted to call off the wedding.' Griffin turned on the sofa, so he was facing Amelia. His face twisted with anger. 'You lied to me, you callous fucking bitch.'

Amelia's skin heated and she thought she was going to be sick. 'Is that true?' she demanded of Ross, noticing that he kept his head down, refusing to meet her eye. When he didn't acknowledge her at all, she asked him again. 'Ross? Is it true? Did you really tell Griffin that?'

His head snapped up. 'Yes, and don't try to take the moral high ground. You're the ones who betrayed him,' Ross sneered. With his wonky glasses, cut face and swollen eye he looked both pitiful and furious. 'You were his fiancé and Jonah his best friend. At least I was honest with him.'

'Well, well, well. This is a real soap opera situation we have going on here,' McCool commented, amused that they were fighting between themselves. 'Mils, that is very naughty, cheating on poor Posh Boy here. So you and this Jonah are planning on running away together, are you?'

'I didn't cheat on Griffin, and Jonah and I are not together,' Amelia growled.

'Liar!'

'It's true,' Amelia protested at Griffin. 'I never cheated.'

'So you didn't kiss Jonah?'

'He kissed me. I told him no. We've barely seen each other since.'

Griffin shook his head, clearly not believing her. 'Well it seems you've picked up right where you left off. Do you think I'm stupid?'

'What do you mean?'

'When Ross first told me, I struggled to believe him. I hated you for leaving me, but I honestly believed your reasons. And even travelling up here, knowing what you had done, there were still moments I doubted myself. But then I saw you two together. You probably thought you were being sneaky. Those sly little glances and disappearing off together. And here on my birthday again, you traitorous bitch.'

'Nothing is going on. I promise.'

'Does Mils love Jonah?' McCool asked, though the question seemed to be directed at himself. He seemed fascinated by the politics between the group. 'Let's settle this once and for all, shall we?' He set his coffee mug down on the kitchen counter and picked up his shotgun, sauntering back over to the group.

What the fuck is he doing?

'I'm going to kill one of the men in your life, Mils. You can choose who lives. Posh Boy or Jonah?'

What? 'I'm not picking someone for you to kill.' Her heart was thumping. He was joking, right?

'I'm not asking you to pick someone for me to kill. I'm asking you which one you want to save. So who's it going to be? Posh Boy Griffin here or Jonah?'

When she didn't answer the question, he raised the gun, aiming it at Griffin, who flinched. 'You're in love with Jonah, so I'll shoot Griffin, right?'

'What? No, please don't do this.'

'So you do have feelings for Posh Boy. Interesting.' He nodded, lowering the shotgun and moving over to where Jonah was.

'What are you doing?' Amelia heard the panic in her voice. 'Stop!'

McCool didn't answer, again pointing the gun. 'Jonah or Griffin, Mils. Pick. Which one are you going to save?'

'Please don't.'

'Jonah or Griffin.'

'No, stop it! Put the gun down!' Her heart was thumping too fast, her palms sweating, and everything felt too claustrophobic sat here on this sofa.

'Okay, if you won't choose, I will. Let's give Posh Boy a chance to win you back. I say... bye, Jonah.'

'No, NO! Not Jonah. I save Jonah.' The words were out before she could take them back and she saw the smirk on McCool's face, heard the utter betrayal in Griffin's tone as he cursed her. She squeezed her damp eyes shut so she didn't have to look at him, wishing she could swipe away the stray tear that leaked down her cheek.

'Sorry, mate. I think you have your answer as to who she's in love with,' McCool was saying, his voice growing closer.

'Please don't hurt me,' Griffin begged.

'Look, Posh Boy, I have some good news and some bad news for you. You want to hear the good news first?'

'Yes.'

Amelia could hear the tremble in Griffin's voice. Still her eyes stayed shut. She could not watch McCool killing him.

'The good news is you get to live. Well... at least for a while longer.'

'Thank you.' Griffin sounded like he was about to cry.

'We still have to talk about the bad news of course.'

There was no reaction to that, other than a sharp intake of breath.

'The bad news is, I still need some answers, so I can't promise I won't hurt you. I think it's time to give your snitch friend here a break, don't you think? Give you a turn in the hot seat, Posh Boy Griffin?'

Amelia finally opened her eyes, the relief at knowing she hadn't signed Griffin's death warrant was tempered by their predicament. They were still tied up and McCool was still going to torture them for answers they could never give him. She had tried so hard to stay angry at the situation and she still was, but despair was now kicking in, as she realised there was no way out of this.

Billy was sobbing with tears of relief and Griffin was shaking with fear.

'I bet you'd all like to give Snitch here a kick,' McCool told them as he cut Billy free, dragging him up by his good ear and shoving him back down on the end of the sofa, as Ross hurriedly tried to squeeze up to make space. 'I was seventy per cent certain you knew about Dougie, though bluffing it a bit. Snitch here was my golden ticket. I would have probably let you go if you'd have kept protesting your innocence, but he's sealed your fate.'

Billy's sobbing became louder, his voice whiny. 'It's not my fault,' he insisted to the others and Amelia hated him so much in that moment.

All of this had been his doing. He had showed up at the house with Dougie's body in his car and shirked responsibility for his actions since he'd arrived. And now he was making things ten times worse for them all.

McCool picked up on her expression, grinning at her, and she realised the game he was playing. He was trying to turn them all against each other and right now, he was succeeding. He had forced her hand to favour Jonah over Griffin and now reminded them that Billy was responsible for their fate going forward. By dividing them he knew he would break them down and weaken any united front.

Not that there was much of one left.

McCool had just pulled Griffin up from the sofa and sat him in the chair when Amelia caught movement from the corner of her eye.

Jonah.

He was awake, though looked a little too pale, and had eased himself into a seated position. 'Let him go,' he snarled, drawing everyone's attention.

'Well if it isn't the leading man himself,' McCool commented dryly. 'Nice of you to finally rejoin us.'

Jonah scowled at McCool before dragging his attention to Amelia, scanning her face for signs of injury. She gave a brief shake of her head, wanting to sob with relief that he was okay. It was best not to react though. She didn't want to give McCool any ammunition.

Too late, unfortunately, as he had already seen.

He patted Griffin on the shoulder. 'Sorry, Posh Boy. I think we can safely say Mils here is over you. Did you just see her making eyes at Loverboy over there?'

Griffin was scowling at Amelia, but he didn't get a chance to reply, as Banjo Boy Greg and Shrek Nigel returned to the room, both with big grins on their faces. Greg was carrying a huge box and Amelia recognised it as the one with Nancy's sculpture inside.

'Did you find it?' McCool demanded, losing interest in Griffin.

Shrek shook his head. 'We've looked everywhere, but nothing. I don't think it's in the house.'

'Fuck! So why the hell are you both looking so happy then? And what the fuck is in that box?'

'Wait until you see this.' Banjo Boy set the box down on the table and lifted the lid, carefully easing the sculpture out.

As everyone focused on it, she watched Griffin, wondering how he was going to react, unsurprised when his face darkened, his lips drawn in a tight line.

'What the fuck is that? Is that you, Posh Boy? Fuck me, it is.' McCool laughed, a deep rumbling sound that came straight from his belly, his goons joining in.

Amelia might have laughed too had their circumstances been different, but it was difficult to find the humour in their current situation, plus she hadn't expected the rush of sadness that Nancy couldn't see Griffin's reaction to her gift. She wondered how he would have reacted if she was here in the room with them. Would he have tried to fake liking it? Griffin King had a terrible poker face.

'This is brilliant! Look at his big nose. Did one of you fuckers do this?'

'Our friend Nancy made it. You know, the one in the hall

who urgently needs medical assistance.' Amelia's tone was sarcastic, but she couldn't help it.

McCool's smile turned ugly. 'Maybe you should have thought about that before you took my money.' He turned his attention to Shrek and Banjo Boy, all business again. 'Are you sure you've looked everywhere?'

'We turned the place upside down,' Banjo Boy insisted, though McCool pretty much ignored him. He had been mostly giving Banjo Boy the cold shoulder since letting him out of the cuffs.

Shrek added, 'I don't think it's up there.'

'Well go look again. It's got to be here somewhere.'

'Okay, Kenny. We're on it.'

McCool bared his teeth, as he picked up his knife again. 'Meanwhile I'll try to be a little more persuasive.'

27

AMELIA

As the goons disappeared back upstairs, McCool glanced at Jonah and Amelia, then back at Griffin. 'How about I give you a choice, Posh Boy?'

Griffin's eyes went wide, part suspicious, part hopeful. 'Okay.'

'You've seen how this works and you know I'm going to rough you up a little, get creative with my knife. Make you squeal a little. Maybe a lot. It depends. Or perhaps maybe not at all.' He gave a sharklike grin. 'How about I give you a chance to swap your place with one of your friends? You get to pick who. You can either stay here and take one for the team or I will give you a get-out-of-jail-free card and you can let someone else come sit in my hot seat for a while. What do you say?'

Griffin's quivering bottom lip was twisting into a cruel smile before McCool had even finished asking the question and Amelia struggled to hold his gaze as his dark eyes bore into hers, understanding her fate before he had even spoken, her stomach dropping.

'I'd like Mils to take my place.'

'No!' Jonah was trying to get up, though without success.

He was still weak, the task too difficult with his hands tied. 'Griffin, man. Don't do this.'

Amelia attempted to give him a reassuring smile, wanting him to know she was okay, though it wobbled as McCool let Griffin out of the hot seat then manhandled her off the sofa.

She tried to keep her chin up as he tied her to the chair, understanding this game. He had known Griffin was going to pick her out of retaliation. He had divided Billy from the group, just as he had driven a further wedge between Amelia and Griffin. Now he was going to use her to split Griffin and Jonah once and for all.

She told herself to be strong, that she would not be his pawn, as he stepped behind, smoothing his hands over her head, cringing at the touch of his fingers combing through her hair and brushing it back from her shoulders.

'You have lovely hair,' he commented, pulling it into a ponytail, his grip tight, yanking her head slightly back. Fear churned inside her belly when his free hand produced the knife and she couldn't help the shaking that started when he caressed it down her cheek.

She stared ahead, trying her hardest not to react, refusing to meet the eyes watching her from the sofa. Billy and Ross had both already endured this and were too busy licking their own wounds to show her any sympathy, while Griffin was smirking, making no secret that he was enjoying the show. Jonah was the only one getting agitated, and she willed him to shut up as he alternated between pleading with, swearing at and threatening McCool to let her go, offering to take her place, while shooting daggers at Griffin.

This was what McCool wanted and Jonah needed to understand that the more upset he became, the worse it would be for her.

'Tell me where my money is, Mils.'

Amelia didn't answer him, not trusting her voice to remain steady. Instead she opted for a steely silence, while inside she cursed him to hell. *Fuck you, McCool. Fuck your brother and fuck your arsehole friends.*

She tried not to flinch as the knife point dug into her chin, biting into her bottom lip when he moved it up, waiting for it to slice at her cheek. Instead he caught her off guard, gripping her hair tighter and yanking her head further back.

What the hell is he doing? Is he going to cut my throat? Her heart thumped as she fought the urge to beg for her life.

But then she felt the blade hacking at her hair and it hurt like hell. It was shock though, not pain, that had her crying out. He couldn't cut her hair off.

'No! Stop it. Please!'

It was too late and he held up the clump of copper hair in front of her before dropping it to the floor.

For a moment Amelia couldn't react, a flood of emotions hitting her, as she felt the coolness of the room on her bare neck. She was bereft; too shocked to even cry. He had taken her hair. Her pride and joy. How could he do that to her?

'I know you and your friends did something to my brother. Where's the money you took?'

Ignoring McCool's question, ignoring Jonah's furious and frustrated stream of expletives as he again tried to get up off the floor, Amelia concentrated on her strongest emotion, finally focused her attention on Griffin, meeting his gaze full on. 'I will get you back for this,' she hissed.

'Fighting talk,' McCool commented. 'I like your tenacity, Mils, but pay attention please. I'm going to need some answers to my questions, or you won't get the chance to punish Posh Boy for anything.' He leant down, putting his mouth to her ear and she thought he was going to whisper something to her. Instead he screamed at her. 'Now where the fuck is the money!'

Caught off guard, Amelia jerked against the chair in shock.

It took a moment to compose herself, her heart beating too fast, and she almost missed seeing McCool stride over to Jonah, who had managed to get to his feet and was looking mad as hell. He punched Jonah in the face, the crack of his fist against bone making Amelia wince. As he knocked Jonah back against the wall, pushing him to the ground, she pleaded with him to stop.

'Leave him alone, please!'

Ignoring her, McCool kicked Jonah in the gut. 'You'll get your turn.'

On the sofa ahead of her, Billy was fidgeting, and Amelia could see him checking all exits. With the doors now closed though, he couldn't make his escape. Ross seemed to have retreated into himself, possibly in shock at everything McCool had done to him, while Griffin was now enjoying himself, the sadistic bastard. She glanced at Jonah, and he met her gaze. His nose was bloody, but he was still coherent, and he mostly looked okay.

'Where's my money, Mils?' McCool demanded, the knife glinting in his hand as he headed back to the chair. 'You don't want me to cut that pretty face of yours too.' He glanced briefly back at Jonah. 'Or maybe I should use my knife on Lover Boy back there. See if that will make you talk.'

No, not Jonah.

'I don't know where your money is. It was up in Ross's room, I swear.'

'And I know that's a lie. So where is it?'

'She's telling you the truth. Let her go,' Jonah demanded.

'The rucksack is there, but most of the money has gone. Someone took it? Who?'

The sound of voices distracted McCool as Banjo Boy and Shrek headed back into the room. 'Still no luck?'

'It's not up there,' Shrek confirmed. 'They must have put it somewhere else.'

'Well that's tough luck for Mils here unless she starts talking. What's that in your hand?'

Shrek held up the disc and Amelia recognised it as the one she had found in Griffin's room. 'It was in one of their bags.'

'A CD? What's on it?'

'It says it's a compilation for Mils.' Shrek laughed a little self-consciously. 'I thought I'd nick it for the car.'

'You mushy bastard,' McCool joked as Shrek reddened. 'You're the only fucker I know who's happy to break someone's nose then go home and listen to Celine fucking Dion.' He looked at Griffin and then at Jonah. 'So which one of you soppy gits made our Mils a mix CD?'

'It's mine,' Griffin told him, looking pleased with himself.

'Oh, yeah? Trying to win her back, are you?' When Griffin didn't answer, he winked at Jonah. 'Looks like you still have competition. You need to up your game, pal. So, Posh Boy, you got any Celine on there for our Nigel?'

'It's not a CD.'

'It's not?'

'No, it's a DVD. I made it as a little weekend gift for Mils.' Griffin's tone was taunting, which had Amelia dreading what it was. 'Play it if you like. I think you chaps might enjoy it.'

Shrek and McCool exchanged a glance, seeming intrigued. McCool looked to Amelia for her consent. 'Want to watch it, Mils?'

Seriously? He was asking for her permission? A couple of minutes ago he was threatening to cut her face. She was tempted to point out the irony, though didn't want to remind him. While she worried what might be on the DVD, at least it bought her time. Jonah too.

'Sure.'

It took a couple of minutes of setting up. The house didn't have a DVD player, but it turned out Griffin had brought one with him, though it wasn't plugged in yet.

Why had he brought a DVD player and what the hell was on the disc?

As Shrek switched on the TV and slipped the disc into the player, McCool twisted Amelia's chair slightly so she was facing the screen. As he did so, Griffin caught Amelia's eye, giving her a smug smile. 'Enjoy the memories.'

Oh God. What was she about to watch?

The screen went grainy for a moment before clearing and she noticed two things. There was a timer in the corner, suggesting this was a home movie, and it had been filmed in the bedroom of the house she used to share with Griffin.

A sick feeling swirled in the pit of her stomach as she recognised their bed.

He hasn't. Please say he hasn't. Amelia's face burned as she recognised herself walking, no staggering, towards the bed, kicking off her shoes, then stripping out of her clothes, before pulling back the duvet. She was talking to Griffin, but the sound was too low, and she couldn't hear their conversation.

'Turn it up,' McCool urged, as though reading her mind. Both he and his two mates were glued to the screen.

Shrek did as asked, and Amelia cringed at the conversation happening on-screen.

'I'm really tired, Griff. Let's just go to sleep.'

Watching herself climbing into bed, completely naked, her bum facing the camera, then her breasts, Amelia wanted the ground to swallow her up. How had she not known that Griffin had a camera in their bedroom?

'Oh, come on. It's my birthday. Are you seriously going to go to sleep and not give me my real present?' Griffin's tone was petulant and sulky, and she realised what night it was.

It was just before she broke up with him. The night of his party. The night Jonah had kissed her.

Watching him bully her into getting out of bed, she honestly thought she was going to throw up. She remembered how she had felt that night, her head reeling with Jonah's badly timed admission. She had been in love with him for years, but had accepted he didn't feel the same, so she had tried to move on. How could he do this to her, tell her how he was really feeling, just a couple of weeks before she was due to marry someone else?

After she had left Jonah outside, she had gone back to the bar and ordered a succession of shots. By the time she had arrived home, her head had been hazy, and she had craved sleep.

Griffin had other ideas though.

He had been begging her to try anal ever since they had first got together, and it was the one thing Amelia wasn't comfortable doing. Eventually though, he had worn her down and she had been a little too drunk to protest. It hadn't been a memorable night, though fortunately her memories had been blurred. Right now though, she got to see them playing out on the screen.

She watched horrified, her face burning when McCool and his mates started laughing and making jokes to each other. She cursed Griffin and didn't dare look at Jonah as she watched herself on all fours on the bed, Griffin pounding into her.

How fucking dare he humiliate her like this?

How fucking dare he film her?

Had he done this before? She quickly realised the answer to that, as after a couple of minutes, the screen cut, going to another clip, and then another.

The DVD lasted for about ten minutes, and she watched it all, wanting to yell at him, but the fight was lost in her. It sickened her to the stomach that he had done this to her. And he couldn't claim it had been done in revenge. He had been videoing her for years. All of these intimate moments where she had thought it was just the two of them.

How fucking dare he?

She wanted to rip his head off, tell him that he was pond life, but anger wasn't an option for her right now. Instead she sat and wept, hot silent tears burning her cheeks as she understood his betrayal.

It was the commotion behind her that drew her out of her self-pity.

Along with McCool and his friends, she had been so focused on her sex tape, she hadn't spotted Jonah getting to his feet, hadn't seen that he had charged at Griffin, somehow knocking him to the floor.

It might have been comical under different circumstances, the two of them wrestling with their hands tied behind their backs.

McCool and Shrek pulled them apart, though with difficulty, as Banjo Boy grabbed his gun, and both of them were forced back down onto the sofa, though at opposite ends, still furiously fighting to get at each other across Billy and Ross.

'Sit the fuck still.'

'A sex tape? Seriously, you perverted fuck? Why would you do that to her?'

'Don't try to take the moral high ground, Jonah. Not after what you did. I know all about what happened before the wedding. I know that you were fucking my fiancée. You're supposed to be my best friend.'

'Jesus. Will you both shut up!' McCool snapped the words. 'We have more important things to talk about.'

'I've never slept with Amelia,' Jonah snarled, a scowl on his battered, but still handsome face. 'And don't give me that crap about being a good friend. You knew what you were doing when you went

239

after her at the Halloween party. You fucking knew how I felt about her. But you had to swoop right in, come up with some bullshit reason to get me out of the way, so you could make your move on her, because Griffin King always wants what everyone else has.'

'What?' Amelia stared at Jonah, then at Griffin. Jonah had been with Katie Lassiter the night she met Griffin. He hadn't been interested in her at that point.

'She was never yours in the first place!' Griffin spat. 'I just threw my hat in the ring, and she chose me! Get the hell over it.'

'Women,' McCool grumbled to Shrek. 'It's always about a bloody woman.' He disappeared out of Amelia's peripheral vision, and she was vaguely aware of the banging of drawers and doors opening and closing in the kitchen.

'I never chose you.'

Jonah and Griffin were so focused on each other that at first Amelia's words were lost. She tried again, louder. 'I never chose you, Griffin.'

Both of them paused fighting to stare at her.

'I never chose you,' she repeated. 'Not over Jonah. You knew I liked him. You said he was seeing Katie.' She turned to Jonah. 'You were. You were with her that night. I saw you.'

Jonah's gaze was heated, but when he spoke his words were soft. 'I was never with Katie. At least I wasn't until I realised I couldn't have you.'

Amelia fell silent as she processed this. Had Griffin really manipulated her right from the start? She remembered being in the garden with him, her teenage heart breaking when he told her Jonah wasn't interested in her.

She wasn't the only one shocked by the news. Jonah seemed to be piecing things together too, while Ross was finally paying attention, the revelations surprising him also. Meanwhile Billy looked bored, while Griffin's pout had turned to a scowl.

'I never forced you to go out with me,' he reminded her. 'We were together for years and you never complained, so don't try to make out you didn't have it good.'

'You had a fucking hidden camera in the bedroom.'

'Well, thank God I did. At least now everyone can see what a dirty little slut you are.'

That set Jonah off again as he tried to get to Griffin.

Amelia was so focused on watching them argue that she didn't see McCool come up behind her. Her eyes widened as the plastic bag covered her head. As she screamed, the bag tightened around her neck, and she thrashed in the chair in panic, each breath making the plastic stick to her mouth and nose.

She could hear someone yelling, telling McCool to stop. But instead he twisted the bag against her throat. 'As you're all arguing over Mils here, maybe we should use her to focus on the more pressing situation of my money.'

'Take the bag off her head!'

'You want it off her head, Lover Boy? Tell me where my money is, and I'll let her go.'

Perspiration dripped into Amelia's eyes and down her face as she tried frantically to shake herself free, a small part of her brain telling her not to panic as she was making it worse. She couldn't help it though.

If she didn't get the bag off her head she was going to die.

'Stop it!' A different voice.

Instead McCool clamped his hand over Amelia's face, making it even more difficult to breathe. The lack of oxygen was making her light-headed.

'STOP IT! It was me.'

The hand disappeared and then the bag was being ripped from her head. Amelia gulped greedily at the air, the damp ends of her slashed hair sticking to her forehead and cheeks, as she tried to calm herself.

It took her a moment to realise it was Ross who had spoken. His mouth was trembling as he held McCool's gaze. 'I was the one who hired Dougie and I took the money. Let her go and I will tell you everything.'

28

THEN

Ross had always been the brainy one in the family, while his younger brother, Tim, was the brawn.

Things came easier for Tim. He had been blessed with the looks Ross had missed out on and had an easy-going, charming nature. People gravitated to him and throughout school, girls had wanted to date him, while the boys had all wanted to be his friend.

While Ross hid away behind his computer, Tim was a star on the football pitch and also on the school rowing team, and the trophies he won filled the shelves in the family home.

Perhaps the shy and socially awkward Ross should have been jealous of him, but Tim was so kind, so giving, he was impossible to dislike. Besides, Ross still had a promising future. He was getting good grades and hoped to go to university. He just lacked the charisma, muscle and looks of his brother.

It turned out that Tim did have an Achilles heel though. His health.

The nagging knee injury that had kept him off the football pitch for much of the season was finally diagnosed as bone cancer and following the devastating news that it had spread throughout his body, it seemed maybe Ross was the lucky brother after all.

He was with his brother at every appointment, spent time with him when he was too sick from chemo to go out. And even after Ross went to the university of his choice, they still spoke by phone a couple of times a week, with Ross trying to get home at least once a month to see him.

While Tim received palliative care, his once strong muscles weakening and his good looks fading; his skin pale and yellowing and dark circles of exhaustion haunting his eyes, Ross was finally making his way in the world, having already been singled out by his tutors as a rising star of the future.

It was during that time that he met Griffin King. He knew of Griffin, was aware how popular he was, but they didn't move in the same circles and Ross would never have expected them to become friends.

At first he had been surprised he was even on Griffin's radar, wary when Griff started making attempts at a bit of banter. They shared a couple of lectures and he noticed that Griffin would often hang back after class and walk out with him.

Initially Ross was flattered, but then he realised that it was his brain Griffin was interested in, not his friendship. It had felt like a slap in the face. Griffin just wanted to use him. But Ross was smart enough to turn the situation to his own gain.

Griffin and his pretty girlfriend, Amelia, and their friends Jonah, Billy and Nancy, were the popular students, and having sat on the sidelines watching his brother for so long, Ross yearned to have a slice of their life, even if it was just for a short while.

Griffin had actually offered to pay him for helping with his coursework, but Ross had a better idea. He would do the work for free, but he wanted a way into Griffin's world. He wanted to be invited to all the cool parties.

At first Griffin had seemed amused by the idea, but it didn't take much to get him to agree, and eventually Ross had somehow worked his way into Griffin's inner circle.

Griffin's idea of help was to actually have Ross do the work for him, but that was fine. For a while there, Ross was living his best life and honestly didn't care that what he was doing was morally wrong, or that Griffin was taking advantage of him.

They even spent so much time together that Griffin had started to confide in him, telling him about his sex life with Amelia and how he was convinced Jonah was jealous of their relationship. Griff was paranoid that Jonah had a thing for Amelia and might try to make a move on her. He had made Ross promise that he would watch the pair of them like a hawk.

Of course, when Griffin wasn't confiding or using Ross's brain to keep his grades up, he liked to use him as his stooge.

At first the jokes were harmless enough and Ross could laugh with him, but as time went on, he became crueller and more relentless with his taunting. Ross forced himself to harden to it, as he knew if he walked away from Griff, he would have to give up this coveted new lifestyle and the friends he had made.

It didn't matter that those friendships were mostly superficial. They were like nothing he had ever experienced, and he wasn't prepared to lose them.

The last time he saw Tim was two weeks before he died.

His nineteen-year-old brother, now a shadow of his former self, had been in a hospice and was looking frailer than Ross had ever seen him, having lost over five stone. He was so weak, he even struggled to sit up by himself.

The family had been warned the end was near and Ross returned to university with a black cloud hanging over him. Tim was his best friend in the world and knowing that he wouldn't have him in his life for much longer cut him like a knife.

He kept his phone close, obsessively watching it for texts and missed calls, ready to hop on a train and make the two-hour journey home when the end was near.

When that call came, he had been round at Griff's, working on a paper for him. His phone had been sitting on the kitchen counter and he had been listening out for it, but it never rang, as unbeknown to him, Griffin had switched it off so it didn't distract him.

Tim had already passed away when Ross finally realised. He had eight missed calls and two texts from his parents, urging him to contact them. Both had been at his brother's bedside and, although neither of them had ever said anything, he could feel their hurt and the weight of their disappointment that he hadn't been there.

'He asked for you near the end,' was the only thing his mother had said to him. 'I think he kept holding on, hoping to see you. When he realised you couldn't make it to him, he told us to tell you he loved you.'

The worst bit of it all was Griffin King. He hadn't apologised; he hadn't shown any kind of remorse for what had happened. Instead he behaved as if Ross was overreacting.

For a while after the funeral, Ross had tried to avoid him. He was angry with Griffin, and he was annoyed with Amelia. She must have known what Griffin had done.

Griffin wasn't an easy man to avoid though, chasing Ross down, showing up at his dorm and relentlessly texting and calling him. They had eventually settled back into an uneasy friendship, mostly because Ross was so alone and didn't have anyone else.

The hatred he had for Griffin though, had gradually spiralled over the years and despite achieving success in his professional life, he had never got over the guilt that he hadn't seen his brother again before he had died.

It would have been easy to cut Griffin off after graduating, but Ross had been reminded of the old saying about keeping his enemies close. One day he was going to punish Griff for what he had done.

He had seen Jonah and Amelia kissing at Griffin's party. Had heard Jonah's confession that he was in love with her. At the time Ross had been reminded of Griffin's words back in university, that Jonah was trying to steal Amelia from him.

Although he had cursed both Jonah and Amelia for their lack of morals, figuring they were just as shallow, he hadn't said anything to Griff. Griffin hadn't told him about Tim, and he wouldn't tell him about the kiss. It was tit for tat.

But the rage continued to build. It was not the same thing at all. Ross had been denied the chance to say goodbye to his beloved brother.

Griffin needed to pay.

It was when Griffin announced this weekend away that the plan began to take shape.

Amelia hadn't even been on the guest list. An accidentally-on-purpose reveal of what Ross had witnessed led to Griffin discovering the real reason why he had been dumped and Amelia became a late addition.

Griffin had again become obsessed with Amelia, almost to the point where Chantelle was ready to walk out on him. He had been intentionally bumping into her and Ross was pretty certain he had broken into her flat, though Griffin never admitted to it.

He had presented himself as her ex-fiancé who had moved on and bore her no ill will and she even unwittingly agreed to have dinner with him, thinking the past was firmly in the past.

Then, when he had invited her on his birthday weekend, she had accepted.

With the guest list for the weekend away sorted, the six university friends reunited, it was the perfect time to exact revenge.

29

ROSS

What were the chances?

Seriously, what were the bloody chances?

Ross had met Dougie McCool in the woods near the house, having been put in touch with him through a friend of a friend, confident that there was no way a connection between them could ever be traced back.

After going over the plan and handing over the cash, he had made his way to the house, leaving Dougie to crawl back to whatever hole he came from until Saturday evening, by which time Ross planned to be long gone, and Dougie and his friends would be breaking into the house and giving Griffin King one hell of a shock.

What were the chances that Dougie's motorcycle would break down shortly after leaving Ross?

And what were the chances that he would be walking along the exact same stretch of road that Billy fucking Maguire was swerving all over, because Billy apparently believed the 'don't drink and drive' rule did not apply to him.

Dougie had been such a mess that Ross hadn't even

recognised him when Billy had shown up. But when he did realise who he was, he had panicked.

The first problem was Dougie's phone. The pair of them had been swapping messages and Ross's number would be stored. If Griffin and the others found it...

He couldn't even think about that. Knew he had to get the phone and destroy it.

Using the excuse of going out for a cigarette, he had quickly retrieved the phone from Dougie's body, unaware that Nancy, the one person in the group he actually liked and trusted, had seen him do so from the bedroom window.

The phone had been casually and discreetly dropped into the loch the following morning, along with Dougie's body, and, unfortunately, with Ross's key fob.

Now he was trapped here with the others, wondering if McCool's friends would come looking for Dougie or try to carry out the plan without him. Only Dougie knew who he was. If they broke in, Ross dreaded to think what they would do.

But of course, things were worse than that. How was he supposed to know that Dougie's brother had a tracker on his phone or that Dougie owed the money to Kenny?

'So where is it then?' Kenny McCool had a stoic expression, despite Ross pouring his heart out between sobs, admitting to everything that had happened.

He hadn't dared look at Griffin yet, though could hear him muttering under his breath about what shit friends he had.

The only one who seemed to have any empathy for Ross's situation was Amelia. Her eyes had filled with fresh tears as he spoke about his brother and it had him wondering if perhaps he had misjudged her. After all, he had been wrong about her and

Jonah. It had come as a shock to him that it had been Griffin who had betrayed Jonah, not the other way around.

He had known Griffin liked to manipulate people, but had he seriously been playing his friends off against each other all this time?

Ross was beginning to realise that he couldn't trust anything Griffin said.

'Hey, Four-Eyes. Focus please. My money. Where is it?'

Ross glowered at McCool's use of such an outdated nickname, though didn't say anything. He had already endured the man's wrath, could feel the sting of cuts to his face and neck, as well as the swelling of bruises. He didn't want to provoke him. 'I gave it to Nancy.'

'You gave it to Nancy,' McCool repeated. 'As in dead-girl-in-the-hallway Nancy?'

'She's not dead,' Amelia snapped.

McCool rolled his eyes. 'Calm the fuck down, Mils. Okay, almost dead girl. Happy?' He didn't wait for her answer, turning back to Ross. 'So, you gave her the money? Where is it?'

'I don't know.'

'You don't know? Are you fucking kidding me? You said you'd tell me where it is.'

'She was blackmailing me.' Ross thought back to how Nancy had waltzed into his room, so full of confidence, stating it exactly as it was going to be. She had seen him take Dougie's phone and she wanted him to give her the money.

Even though she had hinted that she might tell Griffin if he didn't do as asked, he still couldn't bring himself to hate her.

Her eyes had widened when she had seen he had already emptied the rucksack, instead handing her his briefcase, which was filled with the cash. 'You sneaky bastard,' she had said with a grin. 'You were planning on stealing it.'

She seemed impressed and Ross had shrugged his shoulders

a little self-consciously. 'You know you didn't have to try and blackmail me,' he pointed out. 'If you're now going to take the rucksack and dump it, you could have easily just taken the cash.'

'I could have, if I was going alone. Jonah's not going to let me get away with that though.'

True. But it led Ross to another question. 'So if you take the money now, how are you going to dump the rucksack? It's clearly empty.'

She had grinned again, looking pleased with herself. 'You underestimate me. I have a plan.'

He had gone along with her idea, not attempting to talk her out of it. He didn't need the money, and knowing Nancy would benefit the most from it, he had helped her fill the rucksack with clothes to bulk it out, laying four of the wads of notes on top.

If Griffin or any of the others checked, they would think it was all cash. Nancy had then left the room with the briefcase containing the bulk of the money, telling Ross to bring down the rucksack. There had been just a five-minute gap between then and when he heard her fall down the stairs. She could have put the briefcase anywhere.

He said this now to McCool, who didn't look impressed.

'Go check on the girl,' he ordered Nigel. 'We need to get her conscious, so she can tell us where it is.'

As Nigel did as instructed, McCool turned back to Ross. 'So you hired my brother to beat up Posh Boy here and give him a scare? That didn't quite work out for you, did it?' He glanced briefly at Griffin and grinned. 'Tell you what. Once I have my money, I will happily do the honours for you. He has the kind of face you want to hit.'

This time Ross did sneak a quick look at Griffin and, although he looked a little worried at McCool's threat, it annoyed Ross that so far Griffin was the only one of the group that McCool hadn't touched. The others all had cuts and bruises (or in Amelia's case, a lack of hair) from McCool's fist and knife. Why was Griffin King the one who always got away scot free? He never had to suffer.

McCool said he would beat him up, but would it really happen? Griffin always wormed his way out of things, and it was easy to feel bitter that he would probably do so again.

'Kenny, we have a problem.' Nigel's voice called through from the hall. Moments later he appeared in the doorway, and he looked annoyed. 'She's dead.'

There was a long pause as everyone took that in. Ross struggled to keep his composure as he felt Jonah tense beside him, heard Billy's sharp intake of breath, while Amelia paled considerably, shock on her face.

When McCool spoke, he sounded frustrated. 'Are you sure?'

'I've seen enough dead bodies to be sure. She's not breathing and she doesn't have a pulse. What do you want to do?'

What you should do is leave us the hell alone to grieve our friend. Ross wanted to shout the words, but he knew they wouldn't achieve anything. McCool didn't care about Nancy and whether she lived or died. If he gave a shit, he would have called an ambulance for her. He was only interested in his money, and no one could tell him where that was.

As the shock told hold, he began to cry, could see silent tears streaming down Amelia's cheeks too. 'Please leave. Please just leave us alone. We've just lost our friend.'

McCool stared at him, and Ross thought he saw a fleeting glance of sympathy, actually believed for a moment that McCool was going to take pity on them, but then his expression hardened. 'You want me to care about your friend, but you still haven't given me any answers about what happened to my brother.' McCool moved to stand behind Amelia's chair again, placing his hands on her shoulders. 'We know you hired him to have some fun roughing up your friends, yet now you're trying to tell me you care about them. Why would you do that to people you're supposed to care about?'

Ross choked on a lump of mucus sliding down the back of his throat and cried harder. He couldn't answer the question, knew that by seeking revenge on Griffin, the others were always going to be collateral damage, and he had been okay with that.

So okay, maybe he had told Dougie to go easy on Nancy, but still, she was going to be here, was going to be subjected to the trauma of the break-in. He was so tunnel-visioned on hurting Griffin that he had never really stopped to think how it would affect the rest of them.

'Your friend is dead, but that's not our problem. We're here for two things, to get my money and to find out what happened to my brother and things are going to get very bad for you all if I don't get some answers soon.' McCool turned to Nigel. 'Go move the girl's body out of the hallway.'

Nigel nodded, going off to do as instructed.

'Nancy had the money. We don't know where it is,' Griffin protested. His voice sounded a little strained, but Ross suspected that was from their situation and had nothing to do with Nancy's death.

'Again, not my problem. You'd better figure out where it is.'

'I'll replace it.' Everyone looked at Ross. He could afford it. Yes, he would need to get back to his office and move things around in his accounts, but he could get hold of the money easy enough. Why hadn't he thought of this before, buying his way out of the situation. 'Let us go and I promise I will get you the money.'

'Let you go? I don't think so. We both know you'll go running straight to the police and I won't see a penny.'

'I won't. I swear.'

'Why can't you get it now?'

'It's tied up in investments. I need a couple of days.'

'We could keep the others as hostages,' Nigel suggested. 'Let them go when he gets the money.'

McCool seemed to consider the idea. 'He paid my brother to rough them up. I'd say it's fifty-fifty whether he's good for it. Who's to say if we let him go that he just buggers off and leaves them?'

'I won't. I swear.'

'If I say yes, I want an extra ten grand for the inconvenience.'

Fuck! Okay, it was still doable. And it was going to be worth it to get out of this mess. 'Okay.'

'And Nigel would have to go with you. Agreed?'

Again, not ideal, but if it meant McCool would let them go. 'Agreed.'

'Greg and I will take your friends to more comfortable accommodation and keep them entertained. I'm looking forward to getting to know Mils here better, especially after watching her little video.'

McCool massaged Amelia's shoulders and Ross saw her flinch. Although she was doing her best not to react to that, he noticed she was trembling.

McCool had to be dicking around though. He wouldn't really rape her, would he?

He felt Jonah tense again beside him. From the other end of the sofa came a snigger and he turned to see Griffin had a smile on his face.

Seriously? Griffin hated her that much he would find it funny.

Ross was shocked, though he wondered why. He knew he wasn't blameless himself, but honestly, it never failed to amaze him how low Griffin would sink. This was the woman he was supposed to have been in love with, who still – according to

255

what he had told Ross – was the love of his life. How could he find another man talking about raping her funny? He was no better than the animals holding them hostage.

'I'll get the money to you as quickly as possible,' he promised, trying to push the idea of what might happen to Amelia out of his mind. 'We can leave right now if you untie me.'

Ross's heart was thumping hard as he tried to push himself up from the sofa. He was kicking himself. Why hadn't he just thought of this before? He could have saved them all going through this.

'Not so fast,' McCool ordered, and he tensed. 'Before you go anywhere, I need to know what happened to my brother.'

Fuck. Fuck. Fuck.

'I don't know.'

'You keep saying that, so why don't I believe you?'

'It's true,' Billy piped up. 'We've never seen your brother. Well, apart from Ross.'

'So how come you had his money?'

It was a relevant question and one none of them could answer.

When they all remained silent, McCool heaved out a frustrated sigh. 'Okay, so here's my problem. I could let Four-Eyes go; he could get me my money and we could all move on. But I won't have any answers to where my brother is, and the fact that none of you will tell me the truth suggests you have done something to him. Something bad.

'So until we get a confession, none of us are going anywhere. So I will ask again. How come you had his money?'

'We found it?' Billy's downfall was that he phrased his response as a question. No one was going to be stupid enough to believe him.

McCool gamely played along for a moment though. 'Oh,

really? You just happened to find a rucksack of money? Where was this then?'

Of course, Billy being Billy, was too stupid to realise that McCool was onto him. 'Um, it was down by the loch.'

'Just lying there, was it?'

'Yeah, yeah, it was.'

'So what happened, Snitch? Where was my brother?'

'We, uh...'

Ross was aware of Billy looking to him for help. He kept his focus straight ahead, wishing he would just shut the hell up before he said something he shouldn't.

No such luck.

'We think maybe he went for a swim.'

Ross attempted his best poker face, though he could feel the sweat beading on his upper lip. Amelia's eyes had gone wide. He knew they were all willing Billy to shut up.

'So, he was in the loch having a swim. Where is he now?'

Shut up, Maguire. Shut up.

'Maybe he got into difficulties?'

Fuck!

McCool studied Billy gravely. 'You think he got into difficulties and drowned?'

'I don't know.' Billy was sounding whiny now, as if he had just realised what he had said.

'Okay. Let me get this straight. So my brother's motorcycle breaks down, he calls Nigel to pick up and agrees to walk down the main road towards the village to meet him. But for some inexplicable reason, he decides to wander off down to the loch, where he leaves a rucksack full of cash, to go for a late-night swim – in his clothes I'm assuming, as we would have found them if he had stripped off – and he just happens to drown?'

'Um, I guess.'

'For fuck's sake.' McCool marched over to the sofa and

grabbed hold of Billy by the front of his T-shirt, yanking him forward and slapping him hard across the face. 'Stop lying to me. Where is Dougie?'

'I don't know.'

McCool slapped Billy again. 'If you don't tell me right now, I'm going to take a match to this house and burn it down with you all inside.'

When none of them responded to that, he let go of Billy and turned to Greg. 'They think I'm messing around. Go get the canister of petrol out of the truck. I've had enough of this.'

No. Ross could tell from McCool's expression that he wasn't kidding and fresh panic set in as he pulled at the rope binding his wrists. They had pushed him too far and now they were going to pay for it. The only way out was to tell him what had really happened, but that would also make things worse. Unless... 'Wait. I will tell you the truth.'

McCool paused, as did Greg, who was halfway out of the door. When McCool nodded at him, Greg came back into the room. Everyone looked at Ross and waited.

He swallowed hard, knowing he was about to take a huge gamble. 'Billy wasn't lying. He's in the loch.'

'For fuck's sake. I'm not stupid. Dougie would not have gone for a swim.'

'He didn't.'

'So why is he in the loch?'

Ross turned and looked across Billy at Griffin, the only one unscathed throughout this ordeal. He thought about how Griffin had laughed at the idea of McCool raping Amelia, how he had betrayed Jonah's friendship, and worst of all, he remembered how he had prevented Ross from saying goodbye to his brother.

He glanced back at McCool, knowing exactly how he was going to take revenge. 'Because Griffin put him there.'

30

GRIFFIN

Had Griffin actually heard him right?

Ross was trying to pin the blame for Dougie on *him*?

It was the most ridiculous thing he had ever heard, and he couldn't quite believe the made-up story falling from Ross's mouth about how Griffin had been the one driving the car, and how he had panicked after hitting Dougie, and put him in the loch himself, later confessing to the others what he had done.

Was Ross deranged? McCool wasn't stupid and when the others didn't corroborate his story, he was going to know it was a pack of lies.

Honestly, after everything he had done for the nerdy little weasel, allowing him into his circle of friends, trusting him to keep his secrets, and all this time, Ross had been holding on to a stupid grudge about his brother.

It had shocked Griffin to learn that Ross had hired Dougie. He hadn't realised how devious he was. But this betrayal was far worse. If his hands were free, he would be trying to wrap them round Ross's neck, wanting to strangle the lying little fucker.

McCool's expression was darkening by the second and when he scowled at Griffin, for a horrible moment, he thought he might be buying this bullshit. The most worrying thing was, Ross was starting to sound convincing.

The snivelling as he told his story then the complete breakdown at the end was Oscar-worthy. He almost deserved a slow clap.

'Is this true, Posh Boy?' McCool demanded.

'Of course it's not bloody true.' Griffin was aware he was blustering a bit, but honestly, Ross had thrown him with his betrayal.

'It's true.'

What was that? Had he heard Amelia right?

He looked at her now, his mouth opening and closing like a fish. 'What?'

She met his gaze head-on, and he saw the hatred in her amber eyes. 'Come on, Griffin, you know it's over. We tried to cover for you, but it's time to confess to what you did.'

Bitch!

Was this because of Jonah or the sex video, or because he had been amused by McCool's comments about getting to know her better?

'You people are deranged. Jonah, please be the voice of reason here.'

For a moment Griffin didn't think Jonah was going to respond. When he finally did, he wished he hadn't.

'We said you shouldn't have done it. You should have called the police, mate. I know you had been drinking, but it was your choice to get behind the wheel.'

'You were drunk?' McCool demanded.

'You fucking prick!' Griffin hissed the words at Jonah, looking to Billy, who was conveniently studying his crotch. All of the times he had bailed Billy out. Billy had no reason to betray him, as Griffin had been nothing but a true friend to him.

It was time for him to return the favour. 'Tell him what really happened, Billy.'

'I don't know what you want me to say, Griff. You know I'm a terrible liar. I tried to cover for you.'

'After everything I have done for you. You ungrateful son of a bitch.'

Billy refused to meet his eyes. 'Sorry, man.'

'Okay, that's enough.' McCool grabbed hold of Griffin's arm, roughly dragging him up from the sofa, and Griffin tried to pull away, a wave of panic hitting him as he realised he was trapped. They had all turned on him. After everything he had done for them over the years.

The fury surging through his veins was only tempered by the cold itch of fear that was creeping down his spine.

What was McCool going to do to him?

'Posh Boy is going to come down to the loch with me and help me find my brother. Nigel, you come with me. Greg, stay here and keep an eye on the rest of them.'

No, this wasn't happening. What would McCool do to him once they had located the body? 'They're lying to you.'

'What, all of them?'

'They're trying to punish me.'

'Do you deserve to be punished?'

Griffin ignored the question. 'It was Billy driving the car,' he said instead. 'He was the one who really hit your brother.'

'No I didn't.'

'Yes you did, Billy. Tell him the fucking truth.'

McCool rolled his eyes. 'Okay, bring him too.'

'No, get off me,' Billy protested as Nigel pulled him to his feet.

As the pair of them were marched from the room, Griffin glowered at the people he had thought were his friends. Ross,

Amelia and Jonah were watching him and none of them seemed in the slightest bit remorseful.

Fear and anger knotted together in his belly and he promised himself that if he got free he was going to get his revenge on all three of them.

McCool stopped rowing and looked at Griffin. 'So whereabouts is he, Posh Boy?'

Despite the size of the boat, the thug had insisted the four of them ride together. The heavy load had them rocking from side to side and Griffin was terrified the boat was going to tip over, knowing that if it happened he wouldn't survive.

He and Billy sat facing each other, while Nigel rowed and McCool watched over them with his shotgun, and as they went further out, the water lapping at the edges of the boat, Griffin had never felt more vulnerable.

The shore was so far away, the sun low in the cool sky, illuminating the tips of the forest trees that ran along the shore for as far as the eye could see, a reminder of just how isolated they were. McCool could do anything to them out here and no one would be able to help. That knowledge scared the shit out of him.

'I think it was about here.' If he was honest, he didn't have a clue. This far out, it was difficult to get his bearings. It wasn't as if they had put any kind of marker where the body was.

'I can't believe you dropped me in it,' Billy hissed at him as McCool and Nigel both peered down into the water.

'Dropped you in it? You all turned on me. Some friend you are.'

McCool pulled his oar into the boat. He looked at Griffin. 'Right, Posh Boy. Are you ready for a swim?'

'What?'

'You put Dougie down there. You can go and get him.'

Griffin's eyes widened. 'I can't.'

'No such word as can't. Now get in there.' To demonstrate he was being serious, McCool pulled him to his feet. The boat rocked violently, and Griffin gulped as he looked down at the water. It was sparkling on the surface where the sun was bouncing off it, but he knew it was deep and that terrified him.

'I can't swim.'

'You what? You're having a laugh.'

'Seriously?' Nigel laughed. 'Everyone can fucking swim.'

'I can't swim, honestly.' It was the truth. Griffin was sporty, but he had never really been interested in the water and despite his parents' best efforts, he just couldn't stay afloat.

There was no way he could go down to the bottom of the loch and find Dougie.

McCool pulled out his knife and Griffin's bowels knotted at the sight of it. Why had he brought that with him? What was he going to do? Stab him and throw him overboard? 'Please don't hurt me,' he begged.

Billy was watching too, wide-eyed and pale-faced, on the verge of tears.

When McCool turned Griffin round, reaching down and cutting through the rope binding his hands, relief flooded through him and he thought he was going to cry too. His arms ached from being pulled behind his back and he rubbed at his sore wrists where the rope had been cutting into them. 'Thank you, thank you.'

The relief, though, was short-lived.

'Right, get in.'

'What? No, you don't understand. I'm not lying. I really can't swim.'

263

'Maybe you should have thought about that before you put Dougie in a watery grave.'

'It wasn't me. I didn't–'

Griffin didn't get to finish the sentence as McCool gave him a hard shove and he toppled face first into the icy cold water.

31

BILLY

'Do you think he was telling the truth about not being able to swim?'

'I don't know. Maybe he's putting it on.'

McCool and Nigel were watching where Griffin had surfaced and was thrashing madly in the water, and Billy used the opportunity to work the rope around his wrists loose. He had pulled one of the knots free when they were back at the house. If he could just get the other one undone while they were distracted...

'He doesn't look like he's putting it on,' McCool decided. 'Maybe you'd better go in and get him.'

'Fuck that. I don't want to get wet.'

'Well we can't leave the prick to drown.'

'You go in then. You're the one who pushed him.'

'Not a chance. Here, use the oar. He can try and grab hold of it.'

Billy watched them, could see Griffin was struggling. His panic was sapping his strength and each time he disappeared beneath the surface he was taking longer to come up for air.

Nigel held the oar out to him. 'Here, grab hold of this.'

He was leaning so far over the edge of the boat, jeans pulled low to reveal a deep crack and the sun illuminating the blond hairs on his arse cheeks, Billy thought it was going to tip. When the oar did make contact with Griffin, it ended up bashing him in the face.

'Careful, Nige. You're supposed to be using it to pull him in, not knock the fucker out.'

Nigel tried again and this time Griffin's hand made contact with the oar, but instead of grabbing it, he knocked it clean out of Nigel's hand.

'You clumsy fuckwit,' McCool stormed.

'Hey, it wasn't my fault. At least I was trying.'

'Now we've lost an oar.'

'I'll get the other one.'

'No, fuck that. We need it.'

Billy pulled the second knot free, shaking off the rope. He flexed his fingers, carefully watching both men, terrified they might turn at any moment.

'So what are we going to do about him?' Nigel was asking.

McCool watched Griffin disappear beneath the surface again.

'I guess he's fucked.'

'You're just going to leave him?'

'You want to fish him out, be my guest.'

Billy glanced back towards the shore. He wasn't good at much in life. Drumming, drinking and swimming. In fact, swimming was something he excelled at. He could go help Griffin, bring him back to the boat, or he could save himself.

He already knew which one he was going to do.

'Sorry, Griffin,' he muttered to himself, kicking off his trainers before diving into the water and swimming furiously for the shore.

Behind him, he heard commotion on the boat.

'Shit, he's getting away. We need to go get him.'

'Fuck it. He knocked the other oar in.'

'What about Posh Boy?'

'I think he's gone. Go check. You can get the oars at the same time.'

'Fuck off, Kenny. You go in.'

The voices became fainter and Billy kept swimming. He refused to feel guilty. It was Griffin's own stupid fault that he had never learnt to swim.

It was each man for his own now and Billy was almost back to the shore.

He had got this.

32

THEN

Billy Maguire didn't consider himself to be selfish, but he would be the first to admit he did like things to go his way, and with the least amount of effort possible.

He wasn't academic like Ross, didn't have Amelia's empathy, Jonah's charm or Nancy's guile, and he certainly lacked Griffin's leadership, but that was fine, Billy wasn't bothered about leading anyone. He just wanted an easy life and he had no interest in putting himself out for anyone.

He liked to think that if he had a label, he was the cool one. He played in a band, was invited to all the best parties, and people seemed to gravitate towards him because he seemed so laid-back. What they didn't realise was that laid-back equated to not giving a shit.

If things were too much effort, Billy couldn't be bothered. He just wanted to live his best life and, if there were any bumps in his road, get someone else to smooth them out for him.

That was where Griffin King came in useful. Griffin liked to throw his weight around, but he was also good at fixing things, and Billy knew that if he had a problem, Griffin was the man to solve it for him.

They had settled into an easy pattern over the years with Billy screwing up his life and Griffin sorting things out again. And because he knew he could count on Griffin to help him, Billy turned a blind eye to how Griffin used and mistreated people, while playing along with him when he tried to paint Billy as a bit of a fool.

That was where people misjudged Billy. He might be lazy and a screw-up, but he was no fool, and he knew how to play people and use them to his advantage. He was also a survivor and always put himself first in any situation. If that meant being callous, deceitful or, even cruel on occasion, then so be it.

After university, Billy had bummed his way through life, living mostly off generous handouts from his parents, due to his inability to hold down a steady job.

He wasn't a pen-pusher or a clock-watcher. All he wanted to do was play his drums, go to parties and get stoned or drunk. Often both. And where was the issue with that? He wasn't harming anyone.

Being in the band meant plenty of female attention and Billy liked to overindulge. He wasn't good at relationships, given that he couldn't keep his dick in his pants, and had a string of angry exes that he mostly left Griffin to deal with. The one woman he had loved was Emily, but as always, she hadn't stuck around when she found out he had been unfaithful to her.

It was reeling from being dumped that had put him in such a hyper mood for this weekend away, and it was Emily who had driven him to drink on the way up. He had just wanted to blow off steam.

How the fuck was he supposed to know that Dougie McCool would be walking down the middle of the road? He blamed Ross for that, knowing that if Ross hadn't hired Dougie, the accident would not have happened. It was not Billy's fault.

Some great friends he had.

Ross, who had plotted for Dougie to hurt them, then Nancy who had tried to blackmail him.

He hadn't seen that coming. Had been shocked when she had knocked on his bedroom door, coolly suggesting an arrangement where he started paying her a monthly fee for her silence.

At first Billy had thought she was mucking around. She had been there with them on the loch and had watched them get rid of Dougie's body. Surely she would be implicating herself. But no, it seemed Nancy had been more manipulative than he realised, telling him she had recorded them from the shore, and that she would go to the police if he didn't cough up. While she might have been calling his bluff, he couldn't take that chance. The problem was, he didn't have any money to give her.

Of course he had agreed though, figuring he would buy time to work something out.

Panic had taken over though as she left his room, and he had followed her out onto the landing.

He hadn't meant to push her. One minute he was planning on reasoning with her, the next she was tumbling down the stairs and, realising what he had done, he had fled back to his room.

It was only later that he realised the recording she claimed she had was on her phone, which was locked in the safe, which he now couldn't access.

Nancy was dead, and now so was Griffin, and Billy honestly didn't know what fate was in store for Ross, Jonah and Amelia. They were still trapped in the house with Greg.

He guessed he could go back and help them, but unless he could get into the safe and retrieve Nancy's phone, it seemed futile. No, it was in his best interests to try and find a ride, then get the hell out of there.

33

JONAH

Luckily, Baseball Cap Greg didn't make a particularly good guard.

He had initially watched Jonah, Ross and Amelia like a hawk, marching around the living room and kitchen with his shotgun, which was a worry in case he decided to get trigger-happy again, but five minutes after his pals had left he seemed to grow bored of hostage-sitting, helping himself to a beer out of the fridge then fixing himself a sandwich.

'Are you okay?'

Jonah kept his tone low and Amelia glanced round to check Greg was preoccupied before answering with a nod.

Her eyes were raw-red from where she had been crying over the sex video, her hair a short choppy mess where McCool had cut it off, and even though she was still beautiful, he knew how much that had hurt her. He wished he could comfort her, guilt plaguing him, as he knew she hadn't asked for any of this and he should never have agreed to help get rid of Dougie's body.

'We're going to get out of this, I promise.' He knew he shouldn't tell her that, as he couldn't promise anything, but he was going to try his best to sort this whole shitshow out.

And he refused to feel bad for Griffin, knowing he had been a mug to go along with everything for so long. He should have fought for Amelia right from the start, telling her how he felt, instead of letting Griffin bulldoze his way in.

Griffin had betrayed their friendship, he had conned his ex-fiancée, and he had acted in the worst possible way where Ross was concerned. Hiding the news about Ross's brother from him wasn't just thoughtless or unkind. It was despicable.

Whatever McCool did to him now, Griffin deserved.

Despite Ross's involvement with Dougie McCool, Jonah couldn't bring himself to be angry with him.

Ross had barely stopped sobbing since confessing what he had paid Dougie to do and Jonah suspected his tears were more than regret about what he had done and fear of their current predicament. It was years of bitterness and pain that had been bottled away and were finally surfacing.

He hadn't been a good friend to Ross. He could see that now. Jesus. He hadn't even known the man had a brother who had died. How wrapped up in himself had he been to not realise?

Ross had always been the one on the periphery, he guessed. Yes, he hung around with them, but he was there by association with Griffin. There simply hadn't been that closeness he shared with the others.

How had that made Ross feel? Always on the outside looking in, with no one to turn to when he needed help or a true friend? 'How are you holding up, mate?' he asked now, silently promising himself that he would try harder if they got out of this situation.

He didn't think Ross was going to answer him. He had his head bowed, as if he dare not make eye contact with Amelia or Jonah. When he did eventually look up, shame haunted his face. 'I'm sorry,' he whispered then repeated a fraction louder, so Amelia could hear. 'I'm so sorry for all of this.'

When the pair of them made eye contact, Amelia nodded in understanding. 'I'm sorry too,' she murmured. 'I didn't know Griffin had switched your phone off that day. He never should have done that when he knew you were waiting for news.'

Something passed over Ross's face. Was that surprise? Had he not known that? Fresh tears fell as he struggled to compose himself.

'Pussy,' Greg mumbled through his mouthful at him, as he wandered back over, a plate in one hand and his beer in the other.

As he passed the papier-mâché sculpture of Griffin, he kicked it in the face, sniggering to himself when he saw he had damaged it. He put his plate down on the table, picking up the sandwich and taking another big bite, swearing when a huge dollop of ketchup dropped out of the bread, splattering his T-shirt. 'Fuck!'

Dumping everything down on the table, he went over to the sink where he tried to scrub the stain out of the white cotton. When he returned to the table, the T-shirt was sodden and the stain now pink and much bigger, and he didn't seem happy, muttering under his breath.

'I have spare T-shirts if you want one,' Jonah told him. 'Upstairs, fourth door on the left.'

It would be difficult to work on freeing themselves while Greg was in the room, but if he left them alone for a couple of minutes...

'Shut up,' Greg told him, picking up his sandwich and demolishing it in a couple of bites. As he swigged his beer, he pulled at the damp T-shirt where it was sticking to his skin. He really had soaked it in his pathetic attempt to get the stain out.

'Fourth door on the left you said?' he questioned Jonah, seeming to change his mind.

'That's right.'

'I'll be back in two minutes. Don't even think about trying anything.' He picked up his shotgun, eyeing them all suspiciously, before giving the sculpture another kick.

Jonah waited until he had left the room before turning to Ross. 'Put your back to me and see if you can loosen the knots.'

Ross nodded, giving a wet sniff before doing as instructed, and they both shuffled so they were back to back. It took a few seconds before they were lined up properly, then Jonah felt Ross's fingers tugging on the knot.

'It's tied really tightly,' he grumbled.

'Keep trying.'

Jonah kept his eye on the door to the hallway, well aware they had limited time.

'Okay, I think I've almost got one of the knots free.'

'He's coming,' Amelia hissed.

Footsteps on the stairs had both men straightening up and they were both sitting back in position when Greg returned to the room. The navy T-shirt he was wearing swamped his skinny frame.

If he could get his hands free, Jonah was certain he could overpower him.

It was a big ask though, he realised, yanking against the rope, disappointed to find there was still little movement. He felt around with his fingers, found the knot Ross had been trying to work loose and gave it another tug. It moved slightly and he kept pulling at the thread, all the while keeping his eyes on Greg.

He didn't trust the man one bit, especially as he seemed to be getting restless, and each time he went near the shotgun, once again resting on the worktop counter, it made Jonah jittery.

He thought of Greg's last casualty, PC Murray, in the downstairs cloakroom. He had been badly injured and Jonah had worried about how much time he had when he had last seen him. That had to be at least an hour ago, probably longer. Was he still alive?

The idea crossed his mind of asking Greg to let him use the loo so he could check. It was too risky though. Even if Greg agreed, he might insist on going into the cloakroom first and realise Murray was still alive. Besides, Jonah didn't want to leave Amelia alone with Greg. Okay, so technically she wouldn't be alone. Ross would be there. But no offence to Ross, he would hardly be able to help her if things turned sour.

And neither would you right now. Jonah ignored the irritating voice in his head, continuing to pull at the knot.

He hadn't missed the way McCool and his men had looked at Amelia or their lewd comments while watching Griffin's sex tape. No way was he leaving her side.

He looked at her now, determined to get her out of this mess one way or another, and when he did, there was no way he was going to be foolish enough to let her walk out of his life again.

She looked up at him and managed a smile, and he suspected that she was thinking the same.

Funny that it had taken a life-threatening situation to make them both realise what was important.

The moment was broken by Greg rustling in one of the kitchen drawers. He took something out, returning to the living-room area with a gormless grin and Jonah's gut tightened when he saw the box of matches.

What the fuck was he planning to do?

They all watched as he approached the sculpture of Griffin, that he seemed more than a little obsessed with. He had been kicking and punching it at various intervals and now it seemed he wanted to destroy it completely.

275

While Jonah had no issue with that, was happy for Greg to be preoccupied with something so juvenile, he didn't trust the man with fire and didn't like him holding the box of matches while they were all tied up.

'What are you doing?' he asked nervously.

'I'm going to burn the Guy, or rather the Griffin.' Greg laughed at his own rather pathetic joke.

'You know it's not November,' Amelia pointed out, her tone dry.

'So fucking what? If I want to burn it now, I will. Maybe you should shut your skanky mouth or I might put you and your bouncy little tits on the bonfire too.'

Jonah wanted to knock his head off. He forced himself not to react to Greg's vile comment though, not wanting to distract him. He had said bonfire. If he was planning on going outside to burn the sculpture, it would give them time to get free.

His heart sank seconds later though when he learnt Greg wasn't planning on going outside at all. As he watched him drag the sculpture across the room, he realised he was planning on using the fireplace.

He worked frantically and not particularly discreetly at the rope while Greg's back was turned as he concentrated on lighting the fire, and Jonah told himself to relax. So he was going to burn the sculpture. What could really go wrong?

The answer to that presented itself just a couple of minutes later when Greg pushed the sculpture onto the fire and the flames leapt up, consuming the paper. The mistake he had made was standing it upright and as the thing crumpled, it fell forward, the top of Griffin's head catching the edge of the rug.

Fuck, no.

The next few seconds were complete pandemonium as Amelia started screaming to Greg to stamp the flames out and

Ross pulled himself up from the sofa, stumbling for the door. His glasses slipped off his nose though and moments after they landed on the floor, his foot accidentally crunched them. Practically blind and with his hands tied behind his back, he had little balance, and Jonah heard him go down heavily on his knees.

He tried to stay calm as he pulled at the rope around his own wrists, feeling it loosen slightly. Amelia was watching him and he could see her doing her best not to panic, aware she was tied to the chair.

As the flames licked the curtains, spreading far too quickly around the walls of the room, Greg was staring at the fireplace, his head in his hands as he repeatedly yelled in frustration, 'No! No! No!'

'For fuck's sake. Help her!'

Greg ignored Jonah, continuing to stare at the fireplace.

At first Jonah thought he was reacting to the fire he had caused, but then he realised he was watching the sculpture burn. The plinth at the bottom had broken off and wads of fifty-pound notes were disintegrating in front of Greg's eyes.

That was where Nancy had hidden the money? Inside Griffin's sculpture?

It was almost poetic that the idiot had burned the money he had been hunting for and Jonah might have laughed, but right now he was conscious that they only had seconds and there was no way he was leaving Amelia.

As the last knot finally loosened, Greg seemed to realise he was actually standing in the middle of a burning room and was going to die very soon if he didn't act quickly.

Without a glance at his hostages, he fled the living room, only interested in saving his own skin.

Jonah pulled at the rope again, knew he was almost there. The room was full of thick smoke, the temperature unbearably hot. He could barely see Ross, though he could hear him coughing and spluttering on the floor.

'Go, Jonah. You can't save us both.'

He looked at Amelia through the filmy air, knew she was scared, though she was trying not to show it. 'I'm not leaving you.'

Fisting his hands, he yanked on the rope again, felt it loosen further, and tried to pull his hand though it. The rope cut into his wrists, but he kept tugging, relieved when he finally pulled his hand free.

Covering his face with his T-shirt to try and stop himself from choking, he went to Amelia, breaking the splat of the chair to free her from it, then he dragged her into the hallway before returning for Ross.

For a moment he thought it was too late. The smoke was too thick now and Ross wasn't responding over the roar of the flames. Jonah was about to give up when he nearly tripped over his body. Pulling him up from the floor, he carried the smaller man out of the burning house where a sobbing Amelia was waiting, alongside two bodies.

PC Murray and Greg.

At first Jonah thought they were both dead, but then Murray started painfully wheezing and raised his head slightly. He looked far too pale, but at least he was alive.

Beside him, face down and looking out of it was Greg.

'What the hell happened?'

Jonah's tone was incredulous and his mouth fell open as Murray explained that he had dragged himself out of the house. When Greg had come charging out of the house fleeing the fire, he had tripped over Nancy's body, landing flat on his face. Murray had used the opportunity to bash him over the head with a rock.

He was still alive, though currently out for the count, and Murray suggested they secure him as quickly as possible.

Jonah untied Ross and Amelia then used the rope to bind Greg's hands and feet. The man was stirring as he finished securing the final knot. Reaching into Greg's pocket, he was relieved to find a phone and wasted no time calling for help.

Knowing help was finally on the way, he wrapped his arms around Amelia, dragging her down to the ground with him and pulling her into his lap, while Murray let his head relax back on the grass, the exertion of dragging himself outside having taken its toll. Meanwhile, Ross put his face in his hands and silently wept. None of them spoke a word while they waited, all of them exhausted and overwhelmed by everything that had happened.

When the first sirens pealed through the air, Amelia lifted her head from Jonah's shoulder, brushing a kiss against his lips, before pressing her mouth to his ear. 'Whatever happens going forward, no more secrets,' she whispered.

Jonah knew she wasn't talking about what had happened here this weekend. She meant with them, and he nodded his agreement, resting his forehead against hers. 'No more secrets.'

34

BILLY

Hearing the sirens, Billy started to sob with relief.

He had no idea how long it had been since he had climbed from the loch. It was probably only an hour, but it felt like much longer. His wet and uncomfortable clothes were sticking to him and as the sun dipped lower in the sky, the coolness of the early evening was making his teeth chatter, and of course, he had kicked his trainers off in the boat, not anticipating how many spikey branches and stones there would be as he made his way through the wood.

Having cut away from the house, he had tried following a different path, but in doing so had become hopelessly lost. It had been darker in the trees and he had hated every second of it, as each crunch, every rustle of leaves, had him jumpy and paranoid.

He had left McCool and Nigel on the boat and when he had reached the shore they still appeared to be bickering. What if they had retrieved the oars, though, and were coming after him? And then there was the fear of what might be in the forest with him? Did they have bears in Scotland, or worse? Had they ever eaten anyone? Or maybe he would be stuck here forever like in that *Blair Witch* film Griffin had made him watch.

Oh my God. What if the woods were haunted by a witch?

Eventually he had reached the road and never had he been more grateful to see tarmac. Had he not been so exhausted and scared that he would not be able to get up again, he might have dropped down to his knees and kissed it.

You can do this, Billy. You've got it now.

But the road seemed to go on forever, with no houses and no traffic. It was like being in his own personal horror movie and he just wanted to curl up somewhere and make it go away.

Perhaps he should have gone back to the house.

Billy was coming to the conclusion that McCool and his goons were not quite as scary as being alone out here in the middle of nowhere.

He couldn't fend for himself and if he didn't find help, he would starve to death. And what about when it became dark? It was already dusk. He would never cope.

Maybe he should have saved Griffin. He would have known what to do. But instead, Griffin was dead and Billy was now all on his own.

Life was so unfair.

But then he heard the sirens and after sobbing with relief, his cockiness had returned. He was going to get rescued. Billy Maguire was back in the game.

He could hear them growing closer, knew they were on the same road. He would carry on walking towards them and when they saw him, they would have to stop. Emergency or not.

Was it an ambulance or a police car, maybe even a fire engine?

He honestly didn't care. All he knew was he was tired, cold and hungry, and his sore feet were killing him.

As he approached the next bend in the road, the sirens grew

louder and he recognised the sweeping beam of headlights on the road ahead. Too tired to walk any further, Billy waited, waving his arms in the air so they would know to stop.

As the police car flew round the corner, he smiled for the first time in what was probably hours. He was being rescued, at last.

The beam of the lights dazzled him and for a split second he understood his mistake, his smile frozen in place as he realised the car was going too fast, that it wasn't going to stop in time.

FUUUUCK!

35

AMELIA

They stuck to a similar story to what they had given to McCool, the three of them letting Griffin and Billy take the fall. Much of it was the truth. Billy had been driving and had hit Dougie, taking him to the house, but then it had been Griffin alone who had helped Billy dispose of the body. Later, when the others had discovered what had happened, Griffin had taken away their phones, leaving them unable to call for help.

That was when Kenny McCool had entered the picture.

Okay, so perhaps they shouldn't have lied at all, but was it really going to help, admitting what had really happened?

Amelia might have been the only truly blameless one, but Ross had been through enough, while Jonah had rescued both of them from the fire. They didn't deserve to pay for Billy's crime, or for the way Griffin had ruthlessly tried to cover it up.

He had been a master of manipulation and a cruel bully, and while Amelia would never have actually wished him dead, knowing he could no longer control her life with his mind games brought more relief than sorrow.

His body had been recovered from the loch, along with Dougie McCool's, and Dougie's brother, Kenny, along with his thug friend, Nigel, had been found stranded in the boat. Amelia had been amused at the irony that like Griffin, McCool couldn't swim and had refused to let Nigel go for help, scared of being left alone on the loch.

Along with Nigel and Greg, McCool had been arrested and faced a number of charges. McCool had been both devastated and furious to learn the truth about the money he had been searching for, and that it had been right under his nose the whole time. Had he not been wearing cuffs he probably would have taken Greg's head off.

Billy's death and the way he met his end had been more of a shock. The first responding police car crashing into him on the way to the house. Amelia had been torn over her emotions with him. On the one hand the pair of them had always got along well, but as Jonah later pointed out, it had been Billy's selfishness and intent to sacrifice the rest of them to save his own skin, that had led to the whole mess. She decided she would not feel sorry for him, especially as Nancy would likely have still been alive if they had been able to call for help.

Still, in that typically polite British way, Amelia, Jonah and Ross attended all three funerals. While it was out of genuine remorse for Nancy, it was more for closure where Griffin and Billy were concerned.

Griffin's funeral was the toughest of the three and although nothing had been said, Amelia had been aware of Griffin's parents staring at the three of them both before and after the service. She knew they didn't believe the official version of events, unwilling to accept that their son had been guilty of the things he was accused of.

The three of them were at the graveside as the casket was

lowered into the ground, but they didn't stay around to pay their respect to the Kings, suspecting they wouldn't be welcomed. As they walked out of the church grounds, Jonah slipped his hand into Amelia's.

They had spent much of the last few weeks together, conscious that they had to make up for lost time, both of them helping each other recover from the trauma. Ross had also been a firm fixture in their lives and Amelia regretted that it had taken such a catastrophic event to make her actually pay attention to him and realise there was so much more to him than being Griffin King's stooge.

She had resolved to become less shallow going forward, focusing more on the important things in life and less on the materialistic. She was even trying to embrace her new pixie cut.

At first she had been devastated, but as Jonah later pointed out, he had fallen in love with her, not her hair. It would eventually grow back.

'Fancy a drink?' Ross asked, as they headed into the car park. He still had a few scars on his face from where McCool had slashed him with his knife, but they were starting to heal.

Amelia's eyes widened. Was that a good idea? 'I don't want to go to the wake.'

'We don't have to. There's another pub on the other side of the village.'

'That sounds good,' Jonah agreed. 'You up for that?' he asked, looking at Amelia and letting her decide. It was still a novel feeling, being with someone who actually consulted her and didn't tell her what to do.

She squeezed his hand. 'Sure, okay. Let's go raise a glass to new beginnings.'

Ross nodded. 'I could go for that.'

Amelia slipped her arm through his, her other hand still

firmly in Jonah's, and together the three of them walked out of the car park onto the high street.

To a fresh start and new beginnings. With friends like these, it was going to be okay.

THE END

ACKNOWLEDGEMENTS

This is sadly my last novel for Bloodhound Books before moving on to pastures new and I am just a little bit emotional. Betsy Reavley and Fred Freeman are superstars and I will never forget that they took a chance on me. Thanks to them I have achieved success beyond my wildest dreams and leaving the kennels was one of the hardest decisions I have ever had to make. Thank you to both of you for everything you have done. That goes to the rest of the team too. Lovely Tara, who as well as being a top Production Manager is also the most welcoming person, always there to make the road to publication that little bit easier. Hannah, our brilliant publicity manager, who is a dream to work with, and of course Clare, my fab editor who takes my books and helps to make them so much better. Thank you also to the rest of the team, Abbie, Morgen, Ian and Heather. You have all been so supportive and kind over the last three years. Bloodhound Books are a family and one I will sorely miss, though I plan on staying in touch with all of you. Thank you so much for everything you have done for me.

To the Beevis family, Mum, Holly, Paul, Nicki, doggy nephews Bruce and Bodhi, my gorgeous pusses, Ellie and Lola, plus the rest of the feline crew, Lily, Frankie and Steve. My Lola puss was so ill while I was writing this book and I honestly thought I was going to lose her. Somehow she pulled through, but I will never forget that it was touch and go for several weeks. I pledge that a portion of the royalties from this book will be spent on Dreamies for my gorgeous girl.

Last year I broke my wrist and during the worst wave of Covid I had to spend several hours in A&E and then return to hospital for an operation. Karen and Charlie were my nurses in A&E and they made everything more bearable, while Jason looked after me during my op. To the three of you, plus Dr Yeoh and his team of surgeons, thank you so much. Our NHS staff are heroes.

I have dedicated this book to my lovely best mate, Shell, but given the title I should really mention some of the other brilliant friends in my life. Andrea, Ness, Jerv & Deano, Jo, Hannah, Caroline, Gem and Christine, plus my online pals, Daniella Curry, Stuart & Dee Beharrie, Mark Fearn, Allison Valentine, Bev Hopper, Aileen Davis, to name just a few.

And of course how could I forget my writer crew, Heather Fitt (yes, she has been mentioned twice), Nathan Moss and Patricia Dixon. We talk every single day, sometimes about rubbish, other times about our writing, and I love getting to share my journey with you three. Extra special shout-out to Trish though, who is my writing buddy. We read each other's stories as we go, are harshly and sometimes amusingly critical, but I honestly believe we pull the best out of each other. Here is to three years of critiquing, of plot-bouncing, of laughing until the tears are running down our legs, of fiercely supporting one another, and of always staying true to ourselves. I honestly couldn't wish for anyone better to be my wingman.

A NOTE FROM THE PUBLISHER

Thank you for reading this book. If you enjoyed it please do consider leaving a review on Amazon to help others find it too.

We hate typos. All of our books have been rigorously edited and proofread, but sometimes mistakes do slip through. If you have spotted a typo, please do let us know and we can get it amended within hours.

info@bloodhoundbooks.com

Made in the USA
Las Vegas, NV
07 June 2022

49945046R00173